MW00914095

Three fire teams moved off into the night to conceal our numbers. One fire team remained to organize the women and bury the dead enemy troops. Our hands and faces were covered with white camouflage paint. The women thought we were the spirits of the dead villagers. That, combined with the swift and silent way we dispatched the enemy troops, convinced them we were supernatural beings of some kind, an idea we did not discourage. The women had no problem helping us dispose of the dead bodies. Six holes were dug six feet deep . The women cut the dead bodies apart and threw the pieces into the holes along with the enemy troops weapons. The heavy rains washed away any signs of the massacre. The women were escorted back to their village. They proceeded to mourn, and burn the bodies of the dead, as was their custom. We left the women unmolested, disappearing as mysteriously as we had appeared. So began the legend of the "Ghost Shadows".

A Choice Of Arms

by

Montana G. Spillman

Commonwealth
Publications

A Commonwealth Publications Paperback
A CHOICE OF ARMS
Montana G. Spillman

This edition published 1995
by Commonwealth Publications
9764 - 45th Avenue,
Edmonton, AB, CANADA T6E 5C5
All rights reserved
Copyright © 1994

ISBN: 1-896329-66-7

No part of this book may be reproduced or utilized in any form or by any means, electronic or mechanical, including photocopying, recording, or by any information storage and retrieval system, without permission in writing from the publisher.

This work is a novel and any similarity to actual persons or events is purely coincidental.

Printed in Canada
Designed by: Danielle Monlezun
Cover Illustration by: Pat Bidwell

To my wife, Estelle
my daughter, Star
and my son, Jason

BOOK I

Introduction:

This story is in regard to the Four Horsemen of the Apocalypse: War, Famine, Pestilence, and Death, and how this Biblical Revelation affected the world order and the lives of an American Dynasty, held together by the strong female character of Ny Li Tu and her ambition for infinite wealth and world power. It is told and depicted in detail through the eyes of another one of the story's characters, Dakota Moon. An American Indian, he has the ability to recognize and relate all truth as he sees it, directly or indirectly. A direct truth is something you see first-hand, with your own eyes. An indirect truth is a shadow of the truth. For example, pick an object within your sight. Fix your eyes on it. Put your hand in front of your face into the line of sight of the object. Move your hand parallel to the object until it is almost out of sight, without moving your eyes and using your peripheral vision. The hand becomes almost indistinguishable, like a shadow, thus the term shadow of a truth.

Dakota Moon will lead you through the portal of time. Time past, time present, time future and time itself—the fourth dimension. Listen as he describes the mentality of a world at war, the elimination of organized hatred, the re-shaping of American Politics, the justification for murder. Listen as he describes the American Presidency turning into a dynasty.

Synthetic Germ Warfare accidentally unleashed on an unsuspecting world, epidemics wiping out world populations, the destruction of the Ozone layer and the effect the sun has on the earth unprotected by it, the conquest of the world by interracial marriages, and the homogenization of the races are blended with humor, romance, eternal love and explicit sex. The planet Earth is used as a stage to create the background for this epic tale of intrigue and adventure, laced with heroic bravado that can be limited only by the reader's imagination. I present to you for your reading pleasure, from the uncensored imagination of the author, A Choice of Arms, the Trilogy.

Preface

In 1920, the forces of evil gave birth to a plan to gain control of the planet. Famine, revolution and unemployment were the masters of the day. The forces of evil used Nationalism to unite the peoples of Post World War I Europe. This ideology led to the birth of ethnocentrism (the blind belief in the superiority of the Aryan Race). Germany, led by Adolph Hitler and the Nazi party from 1932 until 1945, is a prime example of ethnocentrism. The philosophy of the master race spread to every corner of the Aryan World. America, the shining example of Democracy, allowed itself to be influenced by the forces of evil and reshaped the documents upon which it was founded. In 1945, the Allied Armies invaded Germany. Among the spoils of war they found the plans for Chemical, Biological and Radiological Warfare—Hitler's final solution for world domination.

The discovery was kept top secret, and the only country that knew about it was America. The Secret Documents and the Germs were turned over to the Central Intelligence Agency. They were given orders directly from the President to test the Germs. The only problem was, the War had ended. In 1958, a decision was made to test the Germs on the unsuspecting Southeast Asian Countries in a covert operation, without the knowledge of the newly elected President of the United States. The C.I.A. was ordered not to risk the lives of anymore white soldiers. A Special Force of troops consisting of Negro and a few white volunteers were trained and used to conduct the operation. These were the best officers and non-commissioned officers ever recruited from the Negro Regiments. They volunteered in the hope of gaining recognition and acceptability as equals in the United States Armed Forces. Nine of these men would change the course of history for America and the World. They would gain immortality.

"Wide is the gate and broad is the way, that leadeth to destruction."
Matthew 7:13

Chapter One

Ghost Shadows, Disciples of Death

We walked the earth as gods among men. We possessed the power of life and death over mankind. We learned to kill painlessly, silently, swiftly and without conscience. We loved the war. We were young. We were never going to die. We were immortal. We lived in a turbulent time, in a mythical world, the planet earth had returned to the dark ages. Civilization had ceased. The world was on the verge of war, but then, there were many wars and rumors of war. This war would be used to test the weapons and the men of the day. The average age of a soldier was nineteen.

Boys, if you will. No offense to the Negroes who served. The year was 1958, the country was America. It is here that my story begins. The world around me was insane. Weapons of war were available, hatred and violence were acceptable, love and peace were in a parallel dimension. I knew they were there. I could hear people singing "We Shall Overcome", and "Give Peace a Chance". But that was not my destiny. I would follow the path of the Four Horsemen of the Apocalypse. I would lie prostrate before the altar of the Grim Reaper, and pray to the gods of War. We were issued automatic weapons. Equipped with silencers, crossbows and arrows, three feet of plastic fishing line, eighteen inch short swords, six inches of which was a crosscut saw, camouflage makeup, two pairs of camouflage fatigues, four cyanide capsules in a waterproof case, three flares, thirty germ grenades per squad. One radio per squad and twenty pounds of rattle snake venom. (This was used to poison the tips of sharpened bamboo shoots). The rattle snake is not native to Asia, thus, no antidote. In battle, we communicated in sign language so the enemy could not determine our nationality. We all spoke four Southeast Asian languages for reconnaissance. One thousand of the best trained troops in the world were committed to the field, specialized in death and destruction. Our twenty-four month mission was to seek out and destroy all armed forces covertly operating in Southeast Asia.

We were to leave nothing in our path alive that could testify to our existence. Those orders did not exclude the civilian populations. We lived exclusively off the land leaving no signs of our presence. A series of innoculations built up our immune systems to fight off diseases alien to our physiology. We hunted for food during the day and engaged the enemy at night; making the moonlight the enemy of our enemy. God, how I loved the war! I wanted nothing more of life than to be a professional soldier. There was no fear of death in our ranks. Capture meant suicide or assassination. Information was on a need to know basis. If it became necessary to die, suicide was the alternative to torture. The operation was divided into five companies, two hundred men each. The command post was located in the middle of four sectors. Each of the remaining four companies had a sector. Each sector stretched one hundred miles out, or two days march from the command post. Each company had ten squads. The command post was like an octopus. The companies acted as its tentacles; searching each sector for signs of life. Sending the information back to determine the fate of each sector's inhabitants. Anticipating each encounter with the enemy as if it were a feast, we fed upon each other's adrenaline. We were truly barbarians. Killing in the name of God and Country, without conscience or fear of retribution. After all, God was on our side. We lived for the day we would encounter a superior enemy force. Superior in manpower, not in firepower. It was in these encounters that we tested our training.

All else was senseless slaughter. In early March, 1959, The Monsoon had just begun. The rain was like being under a waterfall and there was no way to keep dry. You learn to live four months of the year submerged in water. Our squad was on reconnaissance in the southwest corner of our sector. Although we had come through this area several times in the past three months, the people in the village have never been aware of our presence. Today, something was different. There was no movement, no sound, only the smell of death and decay. The rain kept the odors adhered to the earth. A scout was sent to investigate the situation. This was a very delicate mission. The scout had to assess the situation without being detected by the people. If they discovered him, it would compromise our lives as well as theirs. The scout returned an hour later to report that everyone was dead. Their throats had been cut, and their sculls crushed with rifle butts. Not a shot had been fired. They were killed in their sleep. The elderly, the children, and the men. There were no young women to be found. We entered the village to make a full report to the command post. We found that a small force had killed the people and taken the women with them. This was not unusual for a force that had been in the field a long time. We estimated they were a day's march in front of us. The other nine squads were alerted. They may be a part of a larger force. If so, we would find them. We had the sector covered as tight as a drum. Nothing could slip through a net like that.

Twenty minutes later, the command post sent orders to seek out and destroy the enemy. We went to radio silence. Not a sound would be uttered until the encounter. The adrenaline was flowing, God, I loved the war! The enemy was one day's march ahead of us. We would have to march a day and a night to overtake them. The effort would require a short rest before the encounter. Standard operational procedure. Twenty three hours later we had them sighted. We continued to follow them until they stopped to rest. We rested for one hour before the encounter. The reconnaissance team estimated a force of sixty, armed with ten automatic weapons, hand grenades, and rifles. They had not used a rear guard, and were not aware of our presence. The element of surprise is a formidable weapon. The squad was split onto four man fire teams. The position of the women prisoners from the village was identified and two fire teams were positioned to block a retreat. The sound of a flare broke silence of the night. The light from the flare changed night into day. This was the signal. Simultaneous, muffled, automatic, rifle fire erupted into the midst of the enemy camp. When it stopped, nothing moved. The only sounds were the screams of the women prisoners. The fire teams moved into the camp to cut the throats of anyone remaining alive. The women prisoners could only see the outline of our shapes as we moved swiftly through the camp to complete the kill. The women calmed down when they realized they were in no immediate danger.

Three fire teams moved off into the night to conceal our numbers. one fire team remained to organize the women and bury the dead enemy troops. Our hands and faces were covered with white camouflage paint. The women thought we were the spirits of the dead villagers. That, combined with the swift and silent way we dispatched the enemy troops, convinced them we were supernatural beings of some kind, an idea we did not discourage. The women had no problem helping us dispose of the dead bodies. Six holes were dug six feet deep . The women cut the dead bodies apart and threw the pieces into the holes along with the enemy troops weapons. The heavy rains washed away any signs of the massacre. The women were escorted back to their village. They proceeded to mourn, and burn the bodies of the dead, as was their custom. We left the women unmolested, disappearing as mysteriously as we had appeared. So began the legend of the "Ghost Shadows".

The Monsoon ended in mid-June. Shortly after, the command post called in all the companies for a briefing. We had new orders. It was the first time we were all together in eighteen months. Twenty wild boars and other assorted meats which we had developed a taste for over the operation, were roasted for the occasion. During the next two days we spoke the language chosen for the briefing: English. Somehow, it seemed foreign. We were to be dropped into Vietnam by a troop transport aircraft. A ten thousand man force of Red Chinese, Vietcong, with Russian cadre, were traveling south on the Ho Chi Minh Trail. We were to intercept, massacre, and leave no trace of their existence. A job not unfamiliar to us.

From there we were to go to Saigon. For us, the war would be over and we would go home. The adrenaline began to flow. God, I loved the war! Two days later, under the cover of night, we were dropped into an open field on the edge of a jungle in Vietnam. We assembled into companies and marched to the Ho Chi Minh Trail thirty miles due west. The advance party had set up a base camp for the command post. We worked throughout the

night camouflaging the base camp. Points along
the trail were then picked for the ambush. The reconnaissance team reported that the enemy had
no gas masks, and we were outnumbered ten to
one. We would have to use the germs. It was decided to kill them in three stages. We would mine
the trail behind them to cut off a retreat, gas them
with the germ grenades, and kill the stragglers with
sniper fire. After the germ grenades they would be
too weak to put up much of a fight. It would be a
simple mop-up operation from that point on. The
only danger to us were the germs. There was always a chance of getting bitten by the gas. The
reconnaissance team estimated the operation
would take three to four days, including laying the
mine field. The enemy travelled the trail without
caution or care. They made no effort to conceal
their presence. You could hear them coming from
ten miles away. They marched double file. Their
numbers seemed infinite.

When they had passed the first checkpoint, two
squads laid the mine field. They would follow the
enemy, mining the trail for five miles. The two
squads would become the rear guard, delaying the
enemies retreat. The two squads were all volunteers. If caught in a retreat between the enemy and
the mine field, the two squads would be killed before support could arrive. Three hours later, the
enemy passed the second checkpoint. We fired the
germ grenades. The lines of enemy troops dived off
the road seeking cover in the bush, only to find
sharpened bamboo shoots with poisoned tips waiting to do its work. The enemy began firing ran-
domly at anything they thought they saw. We provided no targets. We discovered after the encounter that many of the enemy were killed by friendly
fire. We allowed the enemy trcops to regroup on
the trail before the sniper fire began. The enemy

troops started to break ranks, and run in all directions. The silencers on our weapons concealed the direction from which death was coming. The germs began to take a toll. The enemy troops dropped like flies from a squirt of insecticide. One day later, the sniper fire stopped. The mopping up began. We walked onto the trail cutting throats and taking a kill count. We had to account for ten thousand dead bodies. The whole operation took five days. Rest and recuperation in Saigon were a few days away. We deserved it. Three days later we arrived in Saigon. We were issued ten day passes. We were ordered to make reveille on the eleventh day.

The aircraft that would take us to Oakland, California was to land on the twelfth day and we would board them on the fourteenth day. The mission had been top secret. The events were never to be revealed. As far as I know, this is the only account of the operation ever recorded. After a complete medical examination, orders were cut for a thirty day leave of absence. Reassignment was Fort Bragg, North Carolina. Most of us were to become cadre in Special Forces Training Battalions. The rest were assigned to Reserve Units in their home states.

"Whosoever is angry with his brother without a cause shall be in danger of the Judgment."
Matthew 5:22

Chapter Two

The Home Coming

Since the rescue of the village women, our squad had become known as "Ghost Shadow," the name given to us by the survivors. Throughout the Southeast Asian jungles, villagers claim to have seen us. We were given credit for everything that could not be readily explained. Deep in the jungles of Cambodia, a child was born. It is said he speaks an unknown language in addition to his native tongue. His eyes are round, like the people of the West. His tribe claims to never have made contact with a Westerner. Many such stories are told all over southeast Asia.

The Legend of the Ghost Shadows will live for many generations in the remote jungles of Southeast Asia. Ghost Shadows! Ours was the only squad that had a name. In fact, none of us were identified for security reasons. The operation was called "Death". The five companies were listed A to E. The squads within were numbered one to ten. The men were numbered one to twenty. For example, I was in company A, 4th squad, number six. The lower your number, the higher your rank.

Let me introduce myself. I am Dakota Moon. My father was Ten Tall Bears, my mother was Mantila Two Moons. My father died when I was two years old. My mother married the Negro, Mason Knight. His people became our people.

We lived in a small town ten miles north of New York City. My father worked as a machinist in one of the factories along the Hudson River. My mother worked at home. She made Indian blankets, quilts and clothes. Retail stores bought them on consignment, paying her fifty-five percent of the selling price. These were my people and I was going home on leave for the first time in over two years. I dressed in the summer uniform, Khaki and Green Beret.

The flight home was pleasant. It was the first commercial flight I had ever been on. The plane landed at Idlewild Airport. I picked my duffel bag up at Baggage, hailed a cab and headed home. It was dusk when I arrived in town. It seemed as if the town was in a time warp. Nothing had changed in the last two years. It was as if I had never left— the epitome of boredom.

Suddenly, I remembered why I left. I knew that I could never be happy here. I could not spend my entire thirty day leave here.

My mother was happy for the week I spent at home with them. My father was proud of me. He had served in World War I₁. "I thought there would be change for the Negro after the War and there was!" he said with a chuckle as he had many times before, "It got worse.

"After watching us fight the Germans in France, and the way the French treated us with the same gratitude that they showed all Americans, I suppose they thought we would come back home and marry their sisters."

"The Black Panthers aren't far from wrong."

"What we need is a civil war."

"The only thing the white man respects is a good fight."

"Stand toe to toe with him and shed his blood for your self-respect."

"Then things would change in a hurry."

"Son, make the bastard bleed. It's the only thing he respects."

My parents died six months later in a car accident. I buried them in a cemetery in upstate New York along with my past. I will never forget my father's words, "Make the bastard bleed." And bleed they shall.

After visiting my parents, I spent the rest of my leave travelling through the South. I observed the pain and suffering of my father's people. I saw the work of the Ku Klux Klan first-hand. I identified a new enemy. I would seek him out and destroy him— a mission for which I was well-trained.

> *"I am a man under authority, hav-*
> *ing soldiers under me and I say to*
> *this man go, and he goeth and to*
> *another, come and he cometh."*
>
> Matthew 8:9

Chapter Three

A Few Good Men and a Woman

I spent the next three months recruiting. It would take at least ten, dedicated, well-trained men to carry out this mission. The best source to select from were the Ghost Shadows. I contacted number eleven, Everett Henry Jones, a Negro from Little Rock, Arkansas. Jones had lost an uncle to the Klan when he was nine years old. They cut off his head, his arms, his legs and delivered his torso to the front door. After listening to my plan, he simply replied, "We start here first". Arkansas was as good a place to start as any. Now there were two of us. The third, fourth and fifth men were picked by Jones. His old fire team, part of the rear guard on the last mission.

Number twelve was George Lee Brown from Greenville, Mississippi. Number thirteen, Calvin Coolidge Chipman from Macon, Georgia and number fourteen, James Edward Magee from St. Louis Missouri. Good Southern boys with a reason to join our cause. Now we were five. Next on the list was number eighteen, Moses Cribb. a White boy from Evansville, Illinois. Cribb had married an Asian girl from Laos. He developed some strong feelings about Civil Rights somewhere along the way. That was good enough for me. Besides, I really learned to trust him in Cambodia. Cribb was now a civilian. He volunteered to do the reconnaissance knowing he was the only man among us who could travel South incognito as a spy.

Two months after arriving in Little Rock, Arkansas, Cribb joined the local chapter of the Ku Klux Klan. We now had a man inside! Numbers nine, nineteen, and twenty were recruited shortly after. Number nine was an extremely light-complexioned Negro, with dirty blond hair, named Maxwell Mason Stone, from Saddle Brook, New Jersey, a man in his mid-twenties at the time, and a West Point Graduate. Stone would one day become one of the highest-ranking officers in the United States Army. Number nineteen, Alexandro Jorge Valdez, a Mexican-American from Los Angeles, California and number twenty, Samuel Nathaniel Turner, from Montgomery, Alabama, made us nine. Ny Li Tu Cribb, an ex-Laotian guerrilla fighter, and the beautiful wife of Moses Cribb, who had proven herself as good a soldier as any of us countless times in Laos, made us ten.

"Well done my good and faithful servant"

Matthew 25:21

Chapter Four

Cribb, Our Man Inside The Klan

Cribb found lodging in a boarding house in Little Rock. The landlady told him the house rules as she led him to his room. "No drinking, no smoking, no women visitors after 8 p.m.," she said with a thick southern drawl, "This here is a respectable place. Room and board. Can't be too careful about who you rent to these days. I heard about what goes on in some places and this ain't one of them. You hear me, Boy, I don't tolerate no foolishness. The Sheriff is a personal friend of mine. You mind that, Boy, personal friend."

"Yes ma'am," Cribb replied.

The room was clean, with a window facing the front street, just as he had requested. The toilet was in the hallway by the steps, and the door had a latch on the inside for privacy. A sign on the wall in the hallway informed you of meal times.

Cribb found work as an auto-mechanic at the garage in town. It wasn't long before Cribb fit right in with the local boys. When Cribb was invited on a coon hunt one evening, he knew it would not be long before he would be going to a Klan meeting. The Klansmen referred to the Negroes as 'coons'. The Negroes had a self-imposed curfew to protect them from perils of the night. The Klan only visited the homes of the so-called troublemakers. By and large, the Negroes were safe as long as they stayed home after dark, and were not considered troublemakers by the Klan. The Klan coon hunted three or four times a week. They seldom ever caught a

Negro out after dark, and when they did, they seldom murdered them. However, the unfortunate Negroes who were found were maimed to say the least. It sort of kept everyone in their place. The curfew worked well for the Klan and the Negroes. The night of Cribb's first coon hunt, an unfortunate Negro was found wandering drunk on the road. When he saw them, he seemed to accept his dilemma as fate.

"I smelled the fear and saw the terror in his face," Cribb would say in his report. The boys Cribb was with decided to castrate this one. The drunk Negro was tied to a tree, blindfolded and stripped naked. Cribb was given the honor of castrating him. When the Negro learned of his fate, his body went limp and he began to defecate involuntarily. As the boys laughed at the sight, Cribb spared the Negro the indignity.

One thrust of his hunting knife, drove the blade under the Negro's chin and into his brain, killing him instantly. This act of mercy was interpreted as unadulterated brutality by all who witnessed it. The murder had earned Cribb a place in the United Klans of America. Later. I would tell Cribb that in his place, I would have done the same. It was a good decision for all involved, especially the Negro. He was sacrificed to save the lives of many of his people in the near future.

Cribb's ability for public speaking earned him the right to represent Little Rock at the National Convention in Atlanta, Georgia that year. Cribb became a national hero among the Klan members and raised hundreds of thousands of dollars with his lectures throughout the South. Much of the success of the operation now depended upon Cribb. His celebrity status earned him the right to a bodyguard. He chose to hire a professional outside of the Klan. This caused no problem; Cribb's notoriety put him above suspicion, Cribb hired Maxwell Mason Stone. Now Cribb could secretly visit his wife, Ny Li Tu. He had not seen her in five months. That was the hardest part of his mission, being away from Ny Li Tu for such long periods of time. She was his only reason for living. The time they had spent in the jungle together in Southeast Asia were the happiest days of his life. One day Cribb and Ny Li Tu would be able to relive those times, even if Cribb had to bring the jungle of Southeast Asia to America.

Cribb had promised her that one day, he would buy her enough land to recreate her homeland. Cribb wasn't sure how, he only knew that he would. Cribb promised to buy her two white Laotian tiger cubs and populate the land with animals from Southeast Asia. Maybe, he would even build her a zoo. The land would have to have a river or a lake on it, and a waterfall, if he could find such a tract of land. What he was talking about would cost millions of dollars. Cribb promised, and she had the faith to believe him. Nothing in the world was too much for his love to ask. There was nothing that he would not do to get it. She was his only reason for living, and he, hers.

> *"What therefore God hath joined
> together, let no man put asunder"*
> Matthew 19:6

Chapter Five

Ny Li Tu

Ny Li Tu was born in April, 1944, to members of the Luang Prabang Dynasty, in Vientaine, Laos. Her parents were killed in a raid on the capital in 1945, by the Khmer troops from Cambodia. Family servants escaped with the child to the mountains which were still untouched by civilization. They joined a primitive tribe where they lived until Ny Li was sixteen years old. They came down from the mountains and joined a band of guerrillas fighting the Khmer Rouge, from just over the border in Cambodia. It was here that Moses Cribb first saw Ny Li Tu. The Ghost Shadows were well aware of the guerrilla band living in the sector. Their fight with the Khmer Rouge posed no threat to the operation. They were not viewed as the enemy by the command post. They had no idea they were under surveillance.

One day on reconnaissance, Cribb saw Ny Li Tu bathing under a waterfall. The drops of water sparkled in the sunlight as they rolled off her tan, lean body. Long black, wet hair hung down her back. Her little breasts looked like two scoops of coffee ice cream. The water trickled down her flat stomach sliding gently between her thighs, continuing down her legs, and terminated in a pool at her feet. He lay in the bush hypnotized by her exotic beauty.

Suddenly, she dived into the river and swam toward him. She emerged from the water and walked ashore to a pile of clothes. She began to dress without drying off. She seemed close enough for Cribb to reach out and touch her smooth, unblemished face. Ny Li Tu was undisturbed by the violence that raged around her. Cribb had observed Ny Li Tu in battle, but never thought of her as a woman. She was indeed a force to reckon with on the battlefield. Cribb was glad she was not considered the enemy. It was clear to him now. He was in love with this female warrior. He would have to meet her. He would court her, he would marry her, and he would take her back home with him or stay there by her side. Cribb did not see her again until we came back through this sector a month later. The squad came across a band of Khmer troops washing in the Mekong River. We did not consider them the enemy, but they were under surveillance. Suddenly, from out of nowhere, came the guerrilla fighters.

We were witnessing an ambush so well-concealed even we were not aware of the guerrillas' presence. The ambush was a commendable feat, to say the least. They fought for a half hour before the Khmers were able to turn the tide of battle in their favor. In the end, all of the guerrillas lay dead and dying. The Khmers retreated, unaware they had won the day. Fifteen minutes later, we examined the battle site. All of the guerrillas were dead, except one, Ny Li Tu. She lay there bleeding from gun shot wounds, unconscious, but alive. Cribb knelt at her side and began tending her wounds.

"What the hell you doing, Eighteen? We can't get involved here." The question was posed by number fourteen as he pointed his weapon at the unconscious Ny Li Tu, "I'll finish her off!"

Cribb threw his body across her saying, "I found her, she's mine. I am going to keep her."

Appealing to the rest of us, Fourteen, said, "this white boy is going to get us all a court martial. He finds a half-dead woman, and announces he's going to keep her. Have we all gone mad?"

Number six interceded, "Leave him alone! I will put your objections in the report tonight." I was senior officer on the patrol and nothing more was said about it. Cribb removed two bullets from her, one from her left shoulder. and another from the fleshy part of her buttocks. The head wound bled profusely, even though it was not life threatening, once the bleeding had stopped. Cribb cared for her day and night, not allowing anyone else to touch her.

When she finally regained consciousness, despite the frightening appearance that Cribb must have made all painted in white camouflage, she knew there was nothing to fear. Somehow, I knew then that Cribb was going to keep her. The command post ordered Cribb to bring her in. After much discussion with number one, who was never really trusted, because he was C.I.A., Ny Li Tu was allowed to remain at the command post for security reasons for the duration. However, she was allowed to go on patrol with us whenever we went into new territory. She new every inch of the jungle and in battle she fought like a wildcat, the equal of any man. Cribb and Ny Li Tu were married in Saigon while he was on rest and recuperation before returning to the States. And that is how Cribb got to keep her.

"A man after his own heart"
Judges 13:14

Chapter Six

Maxwell Mason Stone:
Life Across the Color Line

Maxwell Mason Stone was born to a wealthy, New Jersey family. He was well-educated, well-groomed, and well-spoken. It would be hard to dislike Stone. He had charisma and charm to the tenth power. Stone was extremely handsome—his chiseled features and streamlined body were envied by male and female alike. He made you feel like voting for him even if his name was not on the ballot. Whatever Stone was selling, without hesitation you said, "I'll take two." He was a Negro who passed for white. His father was Swiss and his mother was a Negress. This combination gave Stone a complexion of a white man with a slight tan, and blond hair. An all American Ivy League look.

Stone assumed his new position as Cribb's bodyguard in his usual suave manner. Silent and emotionless, his face showed no expression. Dark sun glasses hid his eyes. He played the role perfectly. One of the first things Cribb put on his agenda was to set up a rendezvous with Ny Li Tu. Stone's family influence helped him to secretly purchase some of the weapons, needed in large quantities, without questions from the local authorities. All purchases were made in New York, New Jersey, and Connecticut. The germs grenades would have to be requisitioned from Dugway Proving Grounds, Utah. After the operation in Southeast Asia, Stone's natural abilities as a soldier, and his family fortune had advanced him in the military to the rank of Colonel. A Special Force of men were formed, hand-picked by himself, of course. All of the old squad except Cribb. Stone then managed to get himself appointed to a high position in the Central Intelligence Agency. This gave us the ability to move freely through the country at his command, on top secret covert operations. Most people who out-ranked him, were afraid to inquire about these operations because of his C.I.A. status. The weapons that were secretly purchased were stored throughout the Southern states. The weapons waited for the day we would strike the Klans operating in those locales. Within six months, Stone was promoted to the rank of Major General. The United States Senate could not have a man with that much power be anything less than a general.

By now, Stone had become a personal friend of the President and some say, the President's wife. He had advanced far beyond his expectations and he was only twenty-six years old. He began looking for a wife with family influence in Washington, D.C. The future of America was directly linked to the future of Maxwell Mason Stone. He once made the analogy that the political arena was like a deck of cards. The winner would be the man who was able to stack the deck in his favor. Stone believed this to be true, and every move he made was to this end.

"It is not good that man should be alone"

Genesis 2:18

Chapter Seven

The Rendezvous

Stone rented a suite for Cribb at the luxurious Washington Hilton. Cribb was speaking at a fund raiser there for "The Sons of Southern Patriots", an organization formed by Cribb to make the Ku Klux Klan more acceptable to the educated, and wealthy Southern genteel. Without the financial support of these people, the Klan activities would come to a grinding halt. Cribb was a genius. He was also in charge of the distribution of the funds. Unknowingly, they financed the operation that destroyed the Klan. Cribb also used some of the money to set up a retirement fund for the Ghost Shadows.

After the fundraiser Cribb took the elevator to the suite that Stone had rented for him. He let himself in with the key he had just picked up from the front desk. He started taking his clothes off at the door, and left a trail of apparel behind him that led to the bathroom. The bathroom was decorated with black and white floor and wall tiles. Mirror tiles covered the ceiling. The bathtub was at least three feet deep, filled with hot, soapy water and sweet smelling bath salts.

Sitting in the water was his only reason for living. They did not speak out loud. Cribb made no effort to hide his intent; his penis stood straight and hard. He slid into the tub with his back to her. She started washing him, massaging the soapy water into his skin, using her body, instead of her hands. He felt her little nipples harden, rubbing against his back, as her desires aroused. She rubbed his chest with the bar of soap in her hand, moving it down his stomach and then between his legs. She stroked his penis ever so gently. He brought his knees up to his chest to allow his legs to receive the same attention as the rest of his body. With his penis fully erect and pulsating with every beat of his heart, he turned to kiss her. She wrapped her legs around his waist not allowing him to enter her. Her tongue probed his mouth as if in search of something she had lost.

He stood up with her still wrapped around him, their tongues still probing each others mouths. Cribb walked into the bedroom. She released his waist from her legs. He instinctively slid his arm under her legs and carried her to the bed. They moved as one body, seeking the middle. Her mouth moved gently from his lips and her tongue moved over his neck. She started licking and biting his chest, little love bites that stimulate the senses. She turned her body, as she licked his stomach on her way to his penis, putting it into her mouth as far as her throat would allow. Her fingers caressed the shaft of his penis and stroked the sensitive scrotum with her pinky. She stopped as she tasted the prelude of his sperm. She wanted to feel it inside of her. For the past five months, she had dreamed about this moment. As she opened her legs he slipped his tongue deep into her vagina, thrusting at first, as he would have done with his penis and licking the lips of her vagina in search of the sweet moisture she was discharging as she came in his mouth. She turned around in search of his lips. As she rolled over her legs parted, allowing his penis access to her vagina, his penis penetrated the moistened lips of her vagina, picking up her body rhythm, as if they had never been apart. She dug her nails into his back as she thrust her pelvis up to meet his penis. She screamed in ecstasy as he thrust his penis deeper and deeper inside of her. In and out, deeper and deeper, until they reached a climax.

The sperm covered his pubic hairs and ran down her legs. Still caught up in the heat of passion they gave each other access to the sperm, licking and sucking until all the sperm was gone. She turned around again, kissed him deeply, and fell asleep in his arms until daybreak. They made love again in the morning, this time with the tender passion of seasoned lovers. Before she left, he gave her a message for me. "October fifth, Little Rock, Arkansas, the woods on the south side of town. Germ Grenades. I'll wear my mask under my hood."

"For many are called, but few are chosen"

Matthew 22:14

Chapter Eight

Stones Commandos

General Stone had become a Washington socialite. He dined with heads of state and political power brokers. It was no secret that his ambition was the White House. He was engaged to the President's daughter. The wedding plans were arranged and a date set. Stone was promoted to the rank of Lieutenant General. When he helped to promote Dakota Moon to Lieutenant Colonel, the most powerful trio since the Roman Empire was led by Pompey, Julius Caesar and Augustus was formed; Maxwell Stone the power, Moses Cribb the financier, Dakota Moon the sword.

Dakota Moon was an American Indian who stood six feet seven inches tall. His muscular build was natural, he did not lift weights or exercise excessively. His weight was maintained by his diet. He reminded you of the comic book character Conan, and his only love was war. Now he led Stone's commandos. Second in command was Captain Everett Henry Jones. Jones stood six feet four inches and weighed one hundred and ninety pounds. He was a dark-complexioned man with a deep scar on his right cheek from a whip lash he had received when he was nine years old. Jones was a career soldier on his third enlistment. He seemed to enjoy Army life. The Commandos included the following people:

Second Lieutenant Alexandro Jorge Valdez was twenty one years old. He was short compared to the others, only standing six feet tall. A good-look-

ing young man with a quick smile, he was a man
without fear, living for the moment, one day at a
time.

Sergeant First Class George Lee Brown had
been in the Army all his life. His father was a soldier. Brown was raised wherever his father was
stationed. The Special Forces had been his dream
since he was a little boy. He stood six feet one inch
in height and weighed one hundred eighty pounds.
He specialized in explosives. One of his jobs was to
help the rest of us pass a proficiency test in explosives.

Sergeant First Class Calvin Coolidge Chipman
was a Southern boy from Georgia. He stood six
feet four inches and weighed one hundred ninety
seven pounds. A natural athlete, he could run the
mile in under four minutes and pole vault over fourteen feet. His ability to climb any tree, to any height,
made him the best point man I have ever served
with. Chipman could spot an enemy patrol in the
densest jungle; he had the eyesight of an eagle. He
was used as a scout during the operation in Southeast Asia. It was he who went into the village to
assess the situation in Cambodia, where we res-
cued the women villagers who gave us our name.

Staff Sergeant James Edward Magee was six
feet three inches tall. He had a thin wiry build.
Well-trained, lean and mean, Magee was a killing
machine. He especially liked the mop-up missions
in Southeast Asia. I have never seen anyone who
enjoyed killing more. Magee would have killed Ny
Li Tu back in Laos had Cribb not stopped him.
Magee, Cribb, and Ny Li Tu would become lifelong
friends. In fact, he was Best Man at their wedding
in Saigon.

Staff Sergeant Samuel Nathaniel Turner was a
Negro with a light tan complexion and green eyes.
He was six feet two inches tall, and weighed one

hundred ninety pounds. He spoke with a deep, Southern accent, when he spoke at all. He was strong, silent, and dependable. He was trained for Chemical, Biological, and Radiological Warfare at Dugway Proving Grounds in Utah. It was he who Stone sent to pick up the Germ grenades. The Ghost Shadows were finally together again.

"The way of the transgressors is hard"

Proverbs 13:15

Chapter Nine

Little Rock, Arkansas: The Epidemic Starts

Sergeant Turner arrived at the Dugway Proving Grounds with a three man detail. He had come for General Stone's germ grenades. The Officer in charge checked requisition papers and signed the release form. Sergeant Turner signed the receipt form and took his copy. The germ grenades were loaded carefully into the truck, then they started back to Fort Bragg immediately without first resting. General Stone wanted a full report on the trip within five days. They drove in four hour shifts, day and night, careful not to exceed the speed limit permitted for transporting dangerous chemicals. They arrived at Fort Bragg five days later.

Sergeant Turner reported to Colonel Moon upon arrival. Colonel Moon inspected the shipment and reported to General Stone, "All the weapons are ready!" For security reasons, General Stone outlined the plan twenty-four hours prior to implementation. He and Cribb would arrive and depart by helicopter. The germ grenades would be fired after the helicopter lifted off. General Stone wanted to be sure they had enough time to put on their gas masks and get out of harm's way. The gust from the helicopter, when lifting off, would dispense the gas through the unsuspecting crowd. The noise from the engine and the rotor would muffle the sound of the exploding grenades. The squad would then regroup, and return to Fort Bragg in a convoy.

The mission was executed, just that simply,

twenty-four hours later. The newspapers reported that a plague of some kind, in epidemic proportion, had swept through the town of Little Rock, Arkansas, killing people by the thousands. It seemed to have had a devastating effect on the people attending a local Klan rally in the woods at the edge of town.

"Many waters cannot quench love"
Song of Solomon 8:7

Chapter Ten

If Not Me, Then Who?
If Not Now, Then When?

The President appointed General Stone as Chairman of the Joint Chiefs of Staff just three weeks before the wedding of Stone to the President's daughter. Stone's appointment delayed our next strike against the Klan. The Vietnam War was escalating fast, and Stone was told to pay strict attention to this. The President was not in favor of escalation so Stone was told to do everything possible to end the war before the next election. This would require an on-site inspection of the troops in the war zone. The general would not go without the commandos as his personal bodyguard.

Stone ordered Moon and the Ghost Shadows to Saigon to ensure his safe arrival and provide a warm welcome. Moon was told to identify and annihilate the elusive and evasive Vietcong. Upon arrival in Saigon, the Ghost Shadows took the field against the Vietcong. They found the task of identifying the enemy almost impossible; however, by the time Stone arrived, the mission had been completed as ordered.

General Stone's wedding to the President's daughter was a gala affair. Almost every dignitary alive was invited. The President's daughter, Tara, wore her long blond hair pinned up. Terminating in a bun, Tara's hair was held together by a series of diamond studded combs, that graced her head like a crown. The wedding gown was white on white, with a diamond sequence pattern running down the front. Her white, patent leather shoes glittered like glass slippers from a fairy tale. Her blue eyes sparkled in the sunlight. General Maxwell Mason Stone wore his dress blues, with a saber hanging at his side. It looked more like a coronation than a wedding ceremony. The whole thing was like a page out of a story book. Before the reception had ended, the couple slipped away and boarded a plane bound for Tahiti. They spent two weeks there, hidden away from the outside world. Civilization, as they knew it, was left behind. Alone, in a world of sea and sand, they simply loved, and made love.

They returned to Washington D. C. two weeks later, to find the world and all of its problems had not gone away. He was still the Highest Ranking Military Man in the United States of America and the war still raged on. He took his beautiful new wife and the promise of their future life together, put it on hold, packed his bags and followed his men to War.

> *"The words of his mouth were smoother than butter, but war was in his heart; his words were softer than oil, yet were they drawn swords."*
>
> Psalm 5:21

Chapter Eleven

Saigon: General Maxwell Mason Stone, Child of God?

On his return to Vietnam, the Ghost Shadows met their General's plane at the airport in Saigon. The military gave him an eighteen gun salute. All of Saigon came out to meet the general. Colonel Moon and his men provided security as the General walked to the limousine that would take him to his hotel suite. Stone had been told, prior to his arrival in Saigon, of the terrible epidemic that had wiped out whole villages within a hundred mile radius of Saigon. Stone knew how Moon had carried out his mission. Without waiting for Moon to bring him up to speed, the General turned on him.

"Have you gone mad? Your orders were specific. Identify the Vietcong, I repeat, identify the Vietcong, and annihilate him. Those were your orders."

Moon replied simply, "The sun shines equally, on the just and the unjust." Stone was a soldier; he knew what Moon meant.

During the next two months, General Stone inspected the troops. He inspected the war zone and threatened the South Vietnamese Government with the loss of Foreign Aid and a U. S. troop withdrawal unless peace talks with the North Vietnamese Government were initiated immediately. His words carried weight as he announced that his was a message from the President of the United States. He was simply the messenger. Within the week, a truce was negotiated and both sides were talking. The United States was represented by General Stone. The General, under the impression that the result would be another unconditional truce like Korea, made arrangements for himself and his men to go home. They returned as heroes. General Stone had ended the war before it got out of control. He was a soldier, a statesman, and a peacemaker.

"Blessed are the peacemakers: for they shall be called the children of God," thought Maxwell Mason Stone. "'Child of God?' Possibly, the end will justify the means".

"Vengeance is mine; I will repay, saith the Lord"

Romans 12:19

Chapter Twelve

Selma, Alabama: The Epidemic Strikes

Cribb set up the next attack for Alabama. The United Klans of Alabama would hold their annual membership rally in Selma. The Klan had enjoyed a sixty percent increase in membership for the year. The white people of Alabama were not particularly violent, as long as the Negroes knew their place. This year, the Negroes had gone too far.

Negroes had boycotted the bus company in Birmingham, staged sit-ins throughout the state, and marched to Selma to protest for the right to vote. Negroes wanted to integrate the Public School Systems. As a result, they were jailed, beaten, and sometimes killed. Nothing, however, seemed to stop them. They were led by an out of state trouble-maker, Dr. Martin Luther King Jr., a Baptist Minister from Atlanta, Georgia. He stirred them up with fiery speeches about civil rights, non-violent protest, and integration. All of these events contributed to the rise in Klan membership and their violent activities in Alabama.

The turnout was exceptionally large that night, an estimated twelve thousand people. The plan remained the same. Cribb arrived and departed by helicopter. This time Stone was not with him. General Maxwell Mason Stone was too well-known to chance his career by going on missions anymore. Cribb's speech was expected to raise seven hundred thousand dollars in Alabama. This evening, at the end of his speech, Cribb boarded the helicopter. As the engine started and the rotor blades turned, the germ grenades were fired. The sound of the grenades was drowned out by the noise of the helicopter. The gas dispensed into the crowd.

Many would die that night. Others would linger through the next day. But one thing was for sure, die they would and die they did. Like Little Rock, the epidemic had hit Selma, as coincidence would have it, during a Klan rally.

> *"A good name is rather to be chosen than great riches"*
>
> Proverbs 22:1

Chapter Thirteen

Tara Stone:
The President's Beautiful Daughter

Tara spent much of the day before Maxwell left for Saigon crying. She insisted that he did not have to go personally. He could send someone in his place. She would ask her father to insist that he stay. After all, they had just been married. Secretly, she called her mother who explained to her the importance of Maxwell's mission to world peace. Even more important was what this would do for Maxwell's career, if he was successful.

Tara stayed close to Maxwell, not letting him out of her sight. She even accompanied him to the White House for his last meeting with the President before departing for Saigon. She made up some weak excuse about having to see her mother. Maxwell did not mind, in fact, he would have asked her to come along anyway. Tara was a spoiled brat, a daddy's girl. She was used to getting her own way. Maxwell did not intend to change her. Tara was his love, and his love was his love.

The President had sensed this in their relationship from the beginning. He knew Maxwell was the right man for Tara. He also knew that Maxwell met with his wife's approval. His father-in-law had helped him get to the White House. The President would do the same for Tara. She, like her mother before her, would someday become the First Lady of the Land. She had been groomed for it from birth.

Oral sex was Maxwell's true love, and his love was his love. Tara's tongue moved into Maxwell's mouth, taking his breath away. Releasing him to breathe, she moved down his stomach in pursuit of his penis. She did not stop until he came in her mouth. She made love to Maxwell up to the last minute before he had to leave. Tara was the only woman who had ever met and matched his sexual desires. Sex was one of Maxwell's weaknesses. He lived for sex. He thrived on sex. It had been suggested by many of his former lovers that he was a sex machine. Until making love to Tara, he believed that it might be true. His love was truly his love.

> *"For the love of money is the root
> of all evil"*
>
> I Timothy 6:10

Chapter Fourteen

The Root of all Evil

Cribb was by now a very wealthy man. The moneys he raised for the Klan went into Swiss bank accounts. Even though he distributed most of it back to the local Klans throughout the South, he kept a considerable amount to finance the operations against the Klan. He paid the Ghost Shadows generous salaries. In fact, he paid key people in the Klan generously. Moses Cribb purchased the loyalty of everyone he touched. He was known to every Klansmen in the nation, as Mr. Cribb.

Mr. Cribb was invited to speak at the National Convention in Atlanta, Georgia. This was to be the largest audience ever assembled at a Klan rally. Whole families gathered to hear top Klansmen from around the nation speak. They were in for a special treat that night. The surprise guest speaker was the Grand Dragon of the United Klans of America. The excitement was at the point of hysteria. It was like going to the County Fair. There were rides for the children, venders selling food, game booths and a live band playing Dixie. The fireworks were as beautiful as the fourth of July. Along with all of those beautiful fireworks were the germ grenades exploding under the cover of a multitude of sounds at the feast of hatred.

Many families would not return home and many children would never grow up. Many people were at their first Klan rally. All of them were at their last. A gentle breeze blew that night, relieving the heat of the day. It left them all holding their throats and gasping for air, choking on the gas. It went through the crowd, extracting the life sustaining oxygen from the air and leaving piles of bodies lying where they had dropped.

First Little Rock, then Selma, and now Atlanta. The Southern Plague, as it was referred to by the press, had struck again. Mister Cribb walked off the dais that night wearing a gas mask and looking like the Angel of Death. In his hand he carried a suitcase. The suitcase was filled with money, the Root of all Evil.

"A virtuous woman is a crown to her husband"

Proverbs 12:4

Chapter Fifteen

The Truce Ended, the War Escalated, the Profits Rolled In.

Dakota Moon was promoted to the rank of Major General upon his return from Vietnam. The operation against the Ku Klux Klan was going well. The Ghost Shadows added the Mississippi, Louisiana, Missouri, and Virginia Klans to their list of executions. After the Tennessee, and Kentucky Klans were exterminated, Mr. Cribb ordered the splinter groups to disband or go underground. For the first time in five years, Moses Cribb could begin to lead a normal life. Cribb and Ny Li Tu moved to Dover, Delaware, where forces were in motion to assure Moses Cribb a newly vacated Senate seat.

Stone wanted Cribb in the United States Senate. There he would lobby friends and identify their political enemies. Cribb won the election easily. His political opponent took ill and died unexpectedly of some unknown disease. Moses Cribb went to Washington as the newly elected Senator from Delaware.

Cribb purchased an old mansion in Dover. Ny Li Tu spent the next year making it home. The compound was enclosed with wrought iron fences with a gigantic gate and a gate house from which the security system for the grounds and the house operated. The house was built of stone, brick and mortar. It resembled a castle, but not quite that dark and gloomy. The foyer opened into a great hall which at one time must have been used to host hundreds of guests. A huge, spiral staircase

led to the upper rooms. To the left was a library
with oak walls and floor. The cathedral ceiling was
twenty feet high with a glass skylight. To the right
was a dining hall, the size of which was in proportion to the other rooms. The main floor of the house
had a maze of corridors that led into the four wings
of the mansion. Upstairs, there were twenty-three
more rooms on the second floor, and ten more on
the third floor. The basement consisted of three
enormous rooms that were left dry and empty.
There were a total of fifty-eight rooms, each heated
by a fireplace. There was also a carriage house with
a three bedroom apartment for the chauffeur's family. Ny Li Tu would need a staff of servants.

She started by renovating the carriage house
as temporary living quarters for herself and two
female servants from Hong Kong. The carriage
house only required plaster and paint, floor tiles,
carpeting, and a new bathroom. Ny Li Tu had fallen
in love with American hotel bathrooms. A gas heat-
ing system was installed to replace the oil burner.
This took all of two weeks. They lived at a motel
close by until it was completed. The compound was
ninety-nine acres with a small man-made lake fed
by a mountain stream. Ny Li Tu had the stream
dammed to create a waterfall. Ten acres were made
into a park, with a gazebo in the center. On the
edge of the park was a maze of hedges and flowers.
There was a marble birdbath in the center with a
cupid spitting water from his mouth. The compound already had a swimming pool and a tennis
court. She had the zoo for her pet tiger cubs, that
Moses had promised her when they left Saigon,
installed. The rest of the land remained untouched
to encourage the local wildlife to stay. Although Ny
Li Tu enjoyed the luxuries and comforts America
offered, she was getting homesick for the jungles
of Southeast Asia. Ny Li Tu had three of the bed-

rooms on the main floor renovated first so she and the two Oriental servants could move into the main house. She immediately began to search for a bodyguard chauffeur. She interviewed thirty people over a two week period, but none met the requirements.

Finally, she called Moses. Ny Li Tu had a special person in mind for the job. She asked her husband to arrange for Staff Sgt. James Edward Magee to take it. Magee reported for his special assignment three weeks later. He was picked up at the airport by Mai Lee Qwuan, one of the Oriental servants. Mai Lee was a beautiful young woman of nineteen years. Ny Li Tu had purchased Mai Lee and her twin sister, Lin Lee Qwuan, from their family in Hong Kong a year before. The Qwuan sisters were to be Ny Li Tu's indentured servants for ten years. This was an arrangement Moses was never comfortable with, but he accepted it because Ny Li Tu treated them as if they were her sisters.

Mai Lee took Magee to the newly renovated carriage house. She helped him unpack and ran his bath water. She informed him that she would attend to his needs until Ny Li Tu was ready to see him. Ny Li Tu was busy with the contractors working in the mansion. They had completed the main floor and were ready to start upstairs. Ny Li Tu would see Magee at supper that night in the dining hall at the mansion. Magee was anxious to see Ny Li Tu. She greeted him warmly. They spoke in her native tongue and it was like old times.

"This assignment was a blessing," he confessed to her. He did not want to go back to Vietnam with the unit, not just yet. He said, "I understand they will be fighting a conventional war. We can't win a war like that. It is the enemy's game in his own ball park."

Ny Li Tu agreed saying, "Moses told me Stone wanted to win the war using the germs and bring the troops home. He said 'The politicians won't allow that to happen. Too much money is being made to end it so soon.'"

"I don't want to go unless it is to cover a retreat. The only way out of a mass evacuation is if the Ghost Shadows cover the retreat with Germ Warfare," Magee commented.

"I hope it never comes to that," replied Ny Li Tu. "America would lose face with the rest of the world."

They talked far into the night, partly on the subject of Mai Lee Qwuan. Magee thought she was the most beautiful creature on God's earth. He asked Ny Li Tu, if he could have her.

Ny Li Tu replied, "She is like a sister, my old friend. How do you mean, have her? Are you asking for her hand in marriage, or for the use of her body? I want you to know up front, she is not for sale!"

"My very dear friend," said Magee, "I would never insult you, or Moses, with a less than an honorable proposal."

"I will speak to Mai Lee, in the morning." replied Ny Li Tu, "If she is agreeable. I will make all the necessary arrangements."

Magee kissed her hand and said, "Until tomorrow."

The renovations to the mansion took six months to complete. Three of the rooms on the second floor were converted into a suite. The walls were painted green and brown, with murals of trees native to Southeast Asia. Pictures were hung on the wall, of animals native to Ny Li Tu's country. The bathroom shower was made to resemble a waterfall terminating into a pool. These rooms were her only link to the past.

When she visited the jungle suite she would

disrobe and walk naked from room to room. A stereo soundsystem mimicked the sounds of the Asian jungle. She would stay in the suite days at a time, visiting her homeland by using the vivid imagination that had created the phenomenon.

A room was dedicated to Moses. It had a mural of his face on the ceiling, looking down on all who entered. There were pictures of Moses hung on the walls wherever you looked. A nude picture of Moses and Ny Li Tu hung on a lone wall. They sat on a bed with his arms around her. This room summed up all the love Ny Li Tu had ever had for Moses throughout their sensuous and romantic love life. The door to this room was kept closed, and locked, to seal her most intimate thoughts of Moses inside. The master bedroom was a six room suite. The sleeping chamber had a circular bed in the middle of the floor, surrounded by mirrored walls, and a skylight ceiling for sleeping under the stars. The floor was covered with wall to wall, white plush carpet. Otherwise the room was bare.

The bathroom was another one of Ny Li Tu's works of art. The walls were tinted black, and made of glass. You could see out, but nothing inside was visible from the outside. It had two toilets and a bidet. There was a sauna room, a hot tub, a four foot deep bathing pool, and a shower. The suite also offered a dressing room and a sitting room for reading and entertaining guests.

The other two rooms in the suite were reserved for a nursery. Children, from infancy to five years old, should live in close quarters with their mother. These were the living arrangements that Ny Li Tu remembered from her youth before the raid on the palace in Laos. Ny Li Tu renovated the mansion as if she were going to house the royal family of an Asian Monarch.

In the days that followed, Magee and Mai Lee

Qwuan fell in love. Ny Li Tu made all the arrangements for the wedding. The guest list included Magee's family from St. Louis, Missouri and all of the Ghost Shadows and their families. Mai Lee's family was flown in from Hong Kong as a wedding present from the Stones. Moses was Best Man and Ny Li Tu was Maid of Honor. They were married at the mansion and the reception was held on the grounds. They honeymooned aboard an ocean liner in the Bahamas. When they returned, they lived in the carriage house in the compound. It never crossed Mai Lee's mind that she was now free. She had never been treated as a slave. She went back to her duties and her sisters Lin Lee and Ny Li Tu.

The truce lasted exactly a year. The war demanded that General Moon and the Ghost Shadows go back to Vietnam. All except Staff Sgt. James Edward Magee. He would continue his special assignment.

General Moon and the Ghost Shadows were stationed in Saigon. They were not ordered to take the field. General Stone would use them to win the war, when and if Congress would allow, or he would use them to cover a mass evacuation should they decide to retreat. General Stone lobbied in the Senate for the invasion of North Vietnam. If he were allowed to launch such an invasion, he knew he could win the war. The invasion was denied. Instead, the Senate ordered the bombing to be escalated, a decision that would inevitably cost America the war.

The President was in favor of winning the war quickly or bringing the troops home. He had made deadly enemies over the years and his life was in danger. Stone could do little to save him. He ordered the Ghost Shadows home from Vietnam, reasoning that if General Moon could act in time he could take out the President's enemies before an assassination attempt could be made. General Moon and the Ghost Shadows arrived three days after the President was assassinated. The country was in mourning.

Stone would have to keep the Ghost Shadows close at hand. There was work to be done at home. General Moon waited silently and patiently for his orders. He gave the Ghost Shadows a thirty day leave of absence. There was no need to keep his men from seeing there families. They were always on twenty-four hour alert. They would come, when he called, without hesitation or question. They were professional soldiers.

The call came and answer they did. The C.I.A. was the enemy and Moon smiled as he read the orders. He hated the Central Intelligence Agency and its pompous director, his old Field Commander in Southeast Asia, number one, Charles Lassey.

"A soft answer turneth away wrath, but grievous words stir up anger."

Proverbs 15:1

Chapter Sixteen

On Leave in El Barrio

Alexandro Jorge Valdez, newly promoted Captain, went home on his thirty day leave to El Barrio in Los Angeles, California. As a youth, Valdez had escaped the life of a gang member. Valdez's father owned a little bodega in the Barrio. The older Valdez was once a gang member himself. After a short prison term, and no chance for an honest job, the gang he was with put the money up to buy the bodega in order to wash their illegal money. The bodega made an honest profit every year, and Alexandro's father paid the loan back with interest. Because of his old gang affiliations, the Valdez bodega was on neutral turf. None of the gangs bothered the Valdez family business.

This was the only reason Alexandro escaped gang life in El Barrio. He went to school every day and his marks were excellent. He worked in the bodega seven days a week, and never had time to associate with the gang members after school. He went into the Army upon graduation, then to Officers Candidate School. His family and friends were very proud of him. He looked good in his uniform as he walked down the street that day. He had just left his parents' apartment over the bodega and was on his way to see his girlfriend Carmella.

Carmella lived on the other side of town, but still in the Barrio. She was a pretty girl with long, jet black hair. She wore it in a single pony tail. To Valdez, she was an angel. They were to be married soon, although no date had been set. Carmella was in her last year of high school. Valdez wanted her to graduate before he took her away from her family. She only had two months to go before graduation and the gang members were making it very difficult for her to continue school. She wanted to quit and leave with Alexandro immediately. Rafael Lopez, one of the gang members, wanted her to be his girl. He claimed her refusal was disrespect. He had slapped her in the face, leaving a hand print on her cheek, two days before. She had not gone back to school since. Today, Valdez would take her to school and deal with Lopez.

When they arrived, Lopez was waiting. He was accompanied by six of his gang members. Valdez was ready for this. He had already decided to make Lopez pay for the hand print on Carmella's face.

Lopez blocked the path leading to the steps of the school and the other five gang members encircled them. They had circled wide enough to allow Valdez to use karate. He moved Carmella an arm's length to the left, in back of him and then swept Lopez off his feet using his own right foot, as he turned to ward off a blow from one of Lopez's gang. He caught the attacker's arm and swept him off balance. The bone could be heard breaking as he fell. He then turned, kicking Lopez in the ribs as Lopez tried to get up off the ground. He knew he had broken Lopez's ribs with this move. Two of the other gang members moved in, one armed with a knife. Valdez caught the fist of one, twisted the attacker's arm in back of him, and maneuvered him into the path of the knife. Using his foe as a human shield, Valdez moved close enough to hit the other in the face with his elbow, breaking his nose. The blood covered the walkway, causing the gang member fear as well as pain.

Lopez staggered to his feet. Valdez kicked him

once in the groin and Lopez grabbed his testicles with both hands. Then Valdez kicked him in the face, shattering his jawbone in several places. The other two ran to their car to get a gun from under the seat. In one swift motion, the soldier pulled his hunting knife out of his boot, and threw it at the slowest runner. The hunting knife caught him in the shoulder blade and he screamed with pain. Valdez caught the other one as he opened the car door. Slamming the door on his arm, he then took him by the hair and beat his face into a bloody pulp, pounding it into the car door. He then retrieved his hunting knife from the back of the other gang member. He wiped the blood on the victim's shirt, and broke the gang member's arm by stomping on it to discourage any further aggression. He told Carmella to go to class and that he would see her that night.

Valdez walked away from the scene as police cars arrived, sirens blaring and tires screeching. In the Barrio, you can never find a witness. The cops came just in time to take the gang to the hospital. The victims could never hold their heads up again if they revealed the truth. The story would be that they were attacked by a rival gang. The more it was told the truer it became; things like that happened there all the time. Alexandro Jorge Valdez married Carmella De Jesus that June after she graduated from high school. Shortly after, Valdez bought a house in San Bernardino, away from the City and the danger it breeds.

> *"For where your treasure is, there*
> *will your heart be also"*
> Matthew 6:19

Chapter Seventeen

Everett Henry Jones: Little Rock Revisited

Captain Everett Henry Jones was promoted to Colonel upon his return from a second tour of duty in Vietnam. General Moon had recommended the promotion a year before, after they had returned home for the first time. The paper work had been held up by a glitch in the computer system so he was paid retroactive from the original date. Jones was married to Betty May Johnson, a local girl with whom he had grown up. Betty May had only been out of Arkansas once in her life, when she attended the wedding of Magee and Mai Lee. She was a real country girl. She wore very little, if any, makeup. She dressed in the simplest style, and she was pretty.

They had two children; Everett Henry Jr. was six, and Elizabeth Susan, whom they called Ellie Sue, was four. The Jones owned a farm on sixty acres of land. They raised chickens, a few cows and four horses, and Betty May ran a dog kennel for a living. Since Jones was away so much of the time, she had started doing it for a hobby. She became one of the top breeders of collies in the country. Between the farm, the children, and the kennel, Betty May was always busy. She and Jones had a private joke; they conducted their marriage by mail. She wrote Jones a letter every day, detailing every minute that they were apart. It was easy to see that they were in love.

Jones spoke of Betty May, and the children, to anyone who would listen, especially anyone he out-

ranked. Now he was on his way home for at least
thirty days, "The good Lord willing, and if the river
don't rise." He did not tell Betty May he was back
in the country. He had gone shopping in San Francisco and bought presents for them all, and this
was to be a surprise. He arrived at dinner time.
The dogs raised such a commotion, that Betty May
came out armed with a double-barreled shot gun.
When she saw him, she dropped the gun, called
the children, and ran into his arms. They kissed
for what seemed to be a long time to the children,
who wanted to be picked up, thrown into the air,
and caught in his arms.

Ellie Sue had so much to tell her daddy, she
could not finish eating. Her mother kept telling her
not to talk with a full mouth at the dinner table.
Everett Jr. could not wait for the presents to be
opened after dinner. He asked his father why they
were eating so slow. Jones pushed his plate aside
and started for the living room where the packages were waiting to be opened. He handed the
children their packages first. While the children
were ripping them open, he gave Betty May one of
her gifts to open. The moment had all the excitement of Christmas.

The children did not want to go to bed that
night. While they were talking to their father, Betty
May washed the dishes and put away the lefto-
vers. When she came back she announced it was
bedtime. The children went to bed reluctantly, but
Betty May went eagerly. She put on the black nighty
her husband had bought her in San Francisco. She
had it on a second before she took it off. They made
love all night. They would have made love the next
morning if it were not for the children. The children were up at the crack of dawn, pulling their
father out of bed and resuming the stories they left
off telling the night before. They talked to him all

day and half the night. They had saved things to tell him for six months. If he had not had to return from leave they would probably would be talking to him still.

General Moon called him at home, personally. They had new orders. The time had come to avenge the President's death. Jones had been especially fond of this President. He had met him in 1950 when he reviewed the troops at Fort Benning, Georgia. He was a senator then, and Jones had been a Second Lieutenant at the time. He had told Jones about his days as a naval officer during W.W.II, and that he understood the problems of segregated units in the Armed Forces. He had promised that things would be different for the Negro soldier in the future. He told Jones how proud he was of the Negro officers in the Military, and that the country needed more men like Jones in the service. Jones had voted for him in the last Presidential Election. For Jones, the chance to avenge the President's death was an honor. He took it seriously.

"I was a stranger and ye took me in"

Matthew 25:35

Chapter Eighteen

Turner and Brown On Leave in Alabama: Love Made Turner Brown

Sergeant First Class George Lee Brown was promoted to Sergeant Major and his best friend Staff Sergeant Samuel Nathaniel Turner was promoted to Sergeant First Class. Brown looked forward to this leave. He was going home with Turner to Montgomery, Alabama. He had never had a home off of a military installation. After his father retired from the service, his parents had gone to live in the West Indies, and Brown never had a chance to see their new home.

Brown had met Turner's sister, Lula Ann, at Magee's wedding. It had been love at first sight and they went on to develop a serious relationship by mail. She was in her last year of teachers college. Brown had quite a bit of money saved, and he wanted to settle down and buy a house somewhere in the South. Lula Ann wanted to live in Alabama, near her family. And now Brown was going home with Turner to make all the final arrangements with Lula Ann. The Turner family was very pleased with her choice of husband, especially since he was a friend of Samuel's. Turner was excited about going home to see his mother and father. They had not gone to Magee's wedding with Lula Ann, so they would be meeting Brown for the first time. Turner also had a girlfriend, Janie Smith, one of Lula Ann's friends from college. She was going to be there too.

Lula Ann and Janie met them at the bus depot in Montgomery. After fifteen minutes of introductions, hugs, and kisses, they went home to the Turners' house. The Turners were waiting with a surprise, welcome home party. Brown and Lula Ann decided on a fourth of July wedding, three weeks after her graduation. Samuel was to be the Best Man, and Janie, the Maid of Honor. Samuel and Janie also announced their engagement. They were to be married the following year.

Then Brown and Turner got a call from Colonel Jones. All that he said to Brown was, "It's time to go back to work, son. Bring Turner with you."

Brown replied, in jest, "Don't start the war without us." When the Colonel didn't laugh, he said, "On the way, sir." The silence on the other end was deafening. Then he heard the dial tone.

"Why," asked Turner, as they were on their way back, "would you joke with the Colonel? I just got my stripes. You mind if I keep them?"

Brown replied, "Man, you know how dry the Colonel is. Unless he is talking about Betty May."

"Yeah, Betty May, and the children," they said at the same time, laughing.

> *"A wise son maketh a glad father"*
> Proverbs 10:1

Chapter Nineteen

Calvin Coolidge Chipman:
On Leave in Georgia

Sergeant First Class Calvin Coolidge Chipman received a long-awaited commission to Second Lieutenant. He was awarded a Battlefield Commission for his part in the rescue of the village women that gave the Ghost Shadows their name. He went home on leave to Macon, Georgia. Chipman had been married five years before to Hanna Pearl Henderson, his childhood sweetheart. She had died in childbirth a year later. The baby, Marion Matilda, was being raised by his parents while Chipman was away in the service. He drove home in a car he had rented at the airport. He went, as he always did, to see Hanna, and place flowers at her gravesite. She was the only woman he had ever made love to.

They had just been children. Their marriage, right out of high school, seemed a natural thing to do; they had been going steady since the seventh grade. They never had a place of their own. The day after they were married they had moved in with his family. Hanna got pregnant immediately and she was sick the whole nine months. The mid-wife had said there was nothing she could do for Hanna. She needed to be in a hospital, but there were no hospitals for Negroes. The baby was to be born at home, just like all Negro children. Chipman did not complain. That was the way most people in the South had babies. But Hanna was just not strong enough to survive childbirth, and Chipman swore on Hanna's grave that he would never marry again.

He reaffirmed the oath every time he came to visit.

Chipman was determined to give Marion all the advantages of life, just as if Hanna had never died. His parents did not know how he did it, but there was always more than enough money in the bank to cover their needs. When Chipman bought the ranch style house, he told them it was the GI Loan Program that enabled them to have such a fine place. Chipman insisted that his father stop working as a field hand, saying his mother needed him more around the house. Besides, he had told them, it did not pay enough money to warrant the time away from home. Chipman wanted him to be a full-time grandfather to Marion. And he was.

After his visit with Hanna at the grave, Chipman drove home. Marion ran out to meet him, as he pulled into the driveway.

"Daddy," she asked, forgetting the manners her grandma had taught her, "what did you bring for me?"

Her grandmother followed her outside saying, "Child, say hello to your father before you start asking for things. A body would think you was raising yourself." She turned to her son. "Cal, I don't want you to think we ain't teaching her no manners," she said, giving him a big hug.

"It's all right Ma. I know she loves me. She just doesn't see me that often, and I did bring her something. I brought something for all of you."

"See Grandma, I knew he did. Daddy always brings me something," the child said as she jumped into his arms.

"Well I'm sure glad he did. Looks like he wasn't getting a hug until you found out, good as your daddy's been to us."

Chipman hugged his father and shook his hand. He had come out behind his wife when he heard the car roll in the driveway. Chipman opened the trunk of the car and distributed the gifts, starting with Marion. Although they had as much or more than some white folks, the older Chipmans did not believe in wasting money on things they considered luxuries. They were determined not to throw away Cal's hard-earned money, but they always appreciated his gifts. Chipman's father had once told a friend, "I know Crackers that don't have half the things my son gives us."

The next day they all went to visit Hanna at the gravesite. Chipman placed a picture of Hanna, that he had enlarged for the occasion, on the grave. He told Marion, as he always did, the story of how he and Hanna had been friends from the seventh grade. They had married upon graduation, and given birth to the most beautiful little girl in the whole world. The family prayed together, thanking God for all the blessings he had bestowed on them and for the happiness they had shared with Hanna.

Chipman's leave was almost up when Colonel Jones called him. The Colonel really liked Chipman. Of all the officers he had ever served with, Chipman was the most like himself—dedicated to his family and the United States Army.

*"Whatsoever a man soweth, that
shall he also reap"*

Galatians 6:7

Chapter Twenty

The Hit

Stone got up early that morning. Unable to sleep,
he had formulated a plan to assassinate the director and all the agents of the C.I.A. who were connected to his father-in-law's death. He had gone
over the plan a thousand times, tossing, and turning most of the night. Although Tara knew nothing
of his plan, she sensed her husband was troubled.
She had tried to relax him with sex, which had
always worked in the past, but he had performed
mechanically, though not unsatisfactorily. His body
was there, but his mind was some place else. She
did not get much sleep either, but worried about
him all night.

Tara decided to call her mother after Maxwell
had left for work. "Mother will know how to handle
the problem," she concluded. "Mother knows everything about men of destiny. After all, with the
help of Grandmama she groomed a President,"
thought Tara, "and so will I."

The Ghost Shadows reported for duty that
morning. The anticipation of battle always kept the
adrenaline flowing. They were ready. They were
always ready. They would follow General Moon
anywhere on the planet.

"Attention!" Colonel Jones called as Generals
Stone and Moon marched to the dais. Then, "At
ease. Be seated," before General Stone stepped forward to start the briefing. They all knew immediately that General Moon himself was hearing the
plan of attack for the first time, or he would have

briefed them himself. They listened carefully as General Stone painted a mental picture of the assassinations, exactly as they were to be carried out.

They would all wear civilian clothes because, as the General explained, it would make them almost invisible. The enemy was some of the best trained men in the service of the country. The only weapons to be used were hollow bamboo shoots— the same weapons used by the mountain tribesmen of Laos. Loaded with a plastic ball, the size of a pea, with a tiny dart in the middle, such a weapon would not be detected by a security system. The dart would be treated with a new poison that would cause death within two seconds. After the hit, the ball would disintegrate, leaving no trace behind. The poison would be almost undetectable. It would take an autopsy, and a damn good coroner, to find the cause of death. The weapon had been designed to be used like a pea shooter; it's target, the jugular vein. The assassin would get only one shot. If the jugular vein was missed, the victim would take a few seconds longer to expire. After the assassin had hit his target a diversion would be created in another area to allow the assassin to leave the scene unnoticed.

The assassins would work in teams of two, one the shooter and the other the diversion. Smiles crossed the faces of every man in the room, including General Moon. The simplicity of the plan was the basis of its brilliance. At that very moment, the Ghost Shadows saw their commander-in-chief in a new light. General Maxwell Mason Stone had just earned the respect and admiration of men who previously held only one man in that regard: General Dakota Moon. The plan renewed General Moon's faith in his decision to follow General Stone.

Three days later, Captain Valdez and Staff Sergeant Magee hit Operative Mitchell McLean, one of the shooters in the Presidential assassination team. McLean was at home, washing his car in the driveway. He slapped his neck to kill what he thought was an insect. This drove the poison dart deep into his flesh. He expired three minutes later. That same day they drove to a little town thirty miles away, and dispatched his partner, Operative James Mac Ellis in the same fashion.

On the same day, four hundred miles away, Sergeant Major Brown and Sergeant First Class Turner hit Operatives Carlton Pierce and Fletcher Hill at two different locations in the Mid West. Colonel Jones and Second Lieutenant Chipman took simultaneous and similar actions against Operatives Hyman Horner and Sandar Wellerman. Horner was in a movie theater with his wife when he suddenly slumped in his seat. His wife was not alarmed. She thought he had fallen asleep, as he often did at the movies. Wellerman was taken out as he returned home with his girlfriend from a party. Chipman hit the target perfectly, piercing the jugular vein. Wellerman was so drunk he never felt the sting of the dart. He expired two seconds after being hit.

C.I.A. Director Charles Lassey ate lunch at the Washington Hilton Arms from twelve o'clock noon to one thirty every day. That day was no exception. The only difference was that he was to meet General Maxwell Mason Stone for lunch. Lassey and Stone chatted casually for ten minutes, then Stone told him of the evidence linking him to the President's assassination. After twenty minutes of denial and threats by Lassey, the C.I.A. Director asked General Stone what the alternatives were for him.

In reply Stone said, "A lengthy trail that would cause your family embarrassment and pain, or you could mix the liquid from this vial in my hand with your drink." He promised it would kill Lassey instantly and spare his family the pain of a trial. History would not record Lassey's treacherous deed.

The director mixed the potion in his drink, stirred it twice and said, "I will see you in hell." He sat there awhile, glaring at Stone, and then drank. His eyes watered and he lost control of his body functions as he keeled over, dead.

"Is there a doctor in the house?" Stone called out in his best pitch of distress. The prearranged drama ended there, when the doctor pronounced him dead. Stone arranged for the death certificate to read heart attack. He allowed Lassey a Military Funeral, like any other fallen statesman. Charles Lassey, ex-Colonel, Special Forces, ex-State Senator, Director of the Central Intelligence Agency, after forty years of service to his country, died an honorable man.

Within the next four months, sixteen Congressmen, twelve Senators, and a Supreme Court Justice all died honorable men. This was a dark time in American history. Treachery and treason had reached and penetrated the highest offices and officials in the land. A war ravaged Southeast Asia for the sake of profit. Foreign Governments were toppled, and their leaders assassinated or exiled. Illegal drugs became a large part of American Commerce and Trade. Like the Roman Empire, America was beginning to crumble. Corruption was eating away at the democratic way of life like a cancer from within.

On the bright side, the first Negro was appointed to the United States Supreme Court. A Civil Rights Bill was passed. Sixteen new Congressmen and thirteen new Senators went to Washington representing twenty-two States. Oh yes, I almost forgot, Moses Cribb was appointed as the new Director of the Central Intelligence Agency. They were all honorable men.

*"Who so sheddeth man's blood, by
man shall his blood be shed"*
Genesis 9:6

Chapter Twenty-one

Life On The Compound

Staff Sergeant James Edward Magee was promoted
to Master Sergeant before being reassigned as Ny
Li Tu's bodyguard. Magee was anxious to get back
to his new wife. The eight days he was away from
her seemed more like eight weeks. Her English was
improving faster than he had anticipated. He told
her how proud he was of her, when he called to
have her pick him up at the airport. He loved her
accent, it was one of the things that turned him on
about her.

Magee had bought a collie from Betty May,
Colonel Jones's wife. She was going to ship the
dog to him at the compound. It was to be a surprise for Mai Lee. She had wanted one ever since
she and Betty May talked about the kennel business at the wedding. She had said, "Magee, I will
have a miniature collie dog?" She threw in "please"
as a second thought. He had told her, the first
chance he got he would arrange with Betty May for
a dog to be shipped. Mai Lee was expecting the
collie, although she did not know when it was coming. The one thing she knew for sure, Magee would
not forget.

The flight arrived on schedule. Mai Lee spotted
Magee immediately. He towered over most of the
other passengers. She shouted, "Magee, Magee."
Of course, he had seen her long before she saw
him. As she ran to him, he leaned over to allow her
to leap into his arms, and wrap her arms around
his neck. When he stood upright again, she was

three feet off the ground. The reunion of the tall
Negro and the tiny little Asian was the center of
attention at the airport that day. People speculated
that he was a basketball player, returning home
from a road trip. They did not quite understand
the relationship of two so obviously different people. However, there was no accounting for what
you might see at J.F.K. Airport in 1970. Magee
drove the car home. Mai Lee massaged his neck
with one hand as he drove. She turned her body
toward him, placing her other hand in his lap and
stroking his penis through his pants.

"You miss me, Magee?" She asked, unzipping
his pants.

He replied with a smile, "Does a hobby horse
have a wooden dick?"

She said, "I don't know what is, how you say
hobby horse? But, if his dick is as hard as yours, I
already know the answer." She lay prone on the
seat, putting his penis in her mouth.

"Mai Lee, your going to cause me to wreck the
car," he protested.

She applied pressure on his penis with her
teeth. "If you wreck the car, you loose your penis,"
she said, jokingly.

"Don't stop now, don't, don't stop," he gasped,
in pleasure.

"Then you will drive carefully, won't you'?" she
replied. She didn't stop until they were almost to
the front gate. She zipped up his pants, saying, "I
will finish this later."

He hit the electronic eye and the big gates slowly
swung open. Magee waved to the camera, he knew
Ny Li Tu was watching the arrival. They drove to
the carriage house, laughing at the humor in their
conversation. Magee opened the trunk of the car
to get his luggage, laughingly saying, "Later, huh?
Promises, promises."

She patted his behind as they entered the door, saying, "That's a promise."

They all ate dinner in the dining hall of the mansion. Moses and Ny Li Tu, Magee and Mai Lee, and their sister, Lin Lee Qwuan, sat at the long table. The Negro cook, Mavis, and her husband Thomas, the butler, served dinner. Lin Lee had been corresponding with a young man from her country. They had been betrothed from birth. Lin Lee asked Ny Li Tu, at the dinner table, for permission to marry him. She also said that he would need a sponsor and a job to obtain a visa to get into the country.

Ny Li Tu listened carefully to what her adopted sister was saying. Ny Li Tu wanted Lin Lee to be happy, but truthfully she wanted Lin Lee to marry an American, just as Mai Lee had done. Both Ny Li Tu and Mai Lee saw the pain on their sister's face when she did not get an immediate approval.

Ny Li Tu said, "First we will bring him into the country and then we will talk of marriage."

Lin Lee knew this was a compromise, but it would have to do for now. Once he was in the country, Lin Lee would do whatever she had to do to persuade Ny Li Tu to let her marry the man she loved. Magee knew this was an Asian dilemma. They wanted to be Americans, and still hold on to old customs. He dared not offend his wife and speak his mind. Moses felt, as he always had about Ny Li Tu's arrangement with the girls, that it was one step away from slavery. However, he did not want a confrontation with his wife over the matter. Ny Li Tu stared at Moses, waiting for him to say what she knew him to believe. Moses stared back until she smiled. She knew then he would not interfere. In fact, it was his way of saying he knew she would make the humane decision. Deep down inside, he knew his wife would allow Lin Lee to marry. After all, she was not losing a sister, but gaining a servant. Ny Li Tu got up, walked over to Lin Lee, and kissed her cheek.

"You know I love you. Trust my judgment in this as you would your own parents," she said.

Lin Lee smiled as Ny Li Tu held her hand, but she knew she had not yet heard her say yes. She would ask Mai Lee to help her persuade Ny Li Tu. She was determined to marry the man she loved, Soo Sing Wong.

The arrangements for Soo Sing Wong to come to America from Hong Kong were made by Moses. He arrived shortly thereafter, and just as Ny Li Tu had suspected, he arrived penniless. At first he was put to work in the kitchen. And then, Magee discovered that he was proficient in the Martial Arts. He was trained by Magee for security duty. He learned the security system exceptionally quickly and well, and Magee knew that one day he would have to return to the service of his country. Soo Sing Wong was the best choice to protect the compound that he had come across to date. Besides, he would have a vested interest when he married Lin Lee. Ny Li Tu saw the wisdom of the advice given her by her old friend. The wedding date was set and all the arrangements were made. Lin Lee waited for the appropriate time, and then thanked her sister and Magee for their help.

Magee was happy now. He knew that when he went away, Mai Lee and the baby she was carrying would be safe under the watchful eye of his new brother-in-law, Soo Sing Wong, Master of the Martial Arts. Moses was able to spend quite a bit of time at home, now that he lived so close to Washington, D. C. He was at home at least four or five days a week . He wanted to spend as much time with Ny Li Tu as possible.

He was insatiable. He made love to her every

free moment she had. There were times when you did not see them for days. They lived in the woods on the compound, several days at a time. They swam nude in the lake, and showered under the waterfall. They stalked the wild animals in the compound with cameras, taking pictures of them without being seen. They pretended that they were in the jungles of Southeast Asia again. Those were the happiest days of Ny Li Tu's life. Actually, they were the happiest days of Moses's life too. Moses knew Ny Li Tu missed the life they had had in the jungles of Southeast Asia, and he wanted her to be happy again the way they were during the operation, with the camaraderie of soldiers. He loved her more than life, a love she returned by the happiness she brought to him. The renovation of the compound had made a new life for them and they relived the days when they fell in love.

Moses became obsessed with Ny Li Tu's nude body. He wanted to have another nude portrait painted in oil. He had several artists paint her, but he was never satisfied. Finally, he met a young Italian artist named Yugo Santini. Santini painted her sitting on a rock by the waterfall, and he captured the essence of her beauty on canvass. It was the female warrior that Moses had fallen in love with. Moses hung the portrait in the room Ny Li Tu had remodelled for him. He spent hours staring at it in silence. Nothing made him happier. Two months later, Ny Li Tu announced she was pregnant.

Lin Lee and Soo Sing Wong were married that same week. They had an Asian ceremony, just as Lin Lee had wanted. Ny Li Tu and Moses gave them a hundred thousand dollars for a wedding present. Now Ny Li Tu was happy since Soo Sing Wong was not penniless anymore.

Magee and Mai Lee had twins that summer. Mai Lee was glowing all over. She had presented her Magee with identical male children. Among her people, she could not have done better. They had her jet black hair and a light tan skin tone. Their eyes were slightly slanted with black pupils and irises. They named them Roman Micheal and Mica Mark Magee.

Six months later, Moses and Ny Li Tu gave birth to a male child. He weighed fifteen pounds and was twenty-three inches long. His hair was jet black like his mother's, his skin tone was milk-white, and his eyes were those of an oriental. The pupils were black on black. They named him Rameses Ryan Cribb.

The following year, Soo Sing and Lin Lee also gave birth to a male child. They named him Ali Khan Wong. All of these children were raised together as cousins in the compound of Moses Cribb.

That same year, Maxwell and Tara Stone gave birth to a son. His hair was blond like his mother's. His eyes were steel blue, his complexion was dark, or perhaps a tan, non-white color. Tara thought he looked like one of her great-great-uncles, the one who was born to a slave. Even back then, no one commented on a white baby's complexion. Maxwell was relieved to hear the story. When he first saw the baby, he felt the Presidency slip away. They named him Canyon Mesa Stone.

Three more children were born to Ghost Shadows that year. Alexandro and Carmella Valdez gave birth to a son whom they named Juan Pablo Valdez. George and Lula Brown gave birth to a son. They named him George Lee Brown Jr. Samuel and Janie Turner gave birth to a son. They named him Tyler Samuel Turner, after Samuel's great-grandfather.

The second generation of the Ghost Shadows numbered eleven, counting the son and daughter of Everett and Betty May Jones, and the daughter of Calvin Coolidge Chipman. Their story is a legacy yet to be told.

"For they have sown the wind and they shall reap the whirlwind."

Hosea 8:7

Chapter Twenty-two

The Evacuation

The war in Vietnam was lost. The strongest nation on the face of the earth chose not to use its best weapon against the enemy. Its leaders, under the pressure of the pacifists and anti-war demonstrators, decided to evacuate and bring the troops home. General Maxwell Mason Stone was ordered to retreat. He had already devised a plan for that six years before: he had started to withdraw troops six months before, and he had not sent replacements in over a year. The Ghost Shadows were ordered to return to Vietnam and provide the firepower needed to cover the largest mass evacuation since Napoleon's retreat from Russia in 1812.

Master Sergeant James Edward Magee received his orders to report for reassignment to Vietnam along with his unit, the Ghost Shadows. He had known this day was coming for four years. He had been preparing Mai Lee for it since their marriage. The discussion had come up many times, and Mai Lee would always change the subject. Now they would have to face the reality of he being gone for a year. Mai Lee cried for hours, but finally she accepted the fact that she had married a professional soldier. The day he left, she did not shed a tear. He kissed her and the babies, got into the limousine, and was driven to the Airport by Soo Sing Wong.

Soo Sing told him not to worry about his family or the security of the compound. He was more than capable of the duties entrusted to him. Magee hugged him and said, "See you soon, my brother."

Soo Sing Wong had tears in his eyes as he watched the plane fly away. He had promised Mai Lee he would stay until the plane took off. The tears Mai Lee did not shed were saved for privacy. Magee would never know she cried, and she would never know that her Magee cried as well.

The aircraft landed in Saigon two days later. The Ghost Shadows immediately took the field. General Moon did not want his men to get used to the comforts of living on a military installation. All of them had been living at home for the last year. They had been training for this mission on the weekends. They knew exactly what had to be done. They went to work straight from the airport. Troops were pulled in from every outpost, and the enemy followed close behind. The Ghost Shadows used their germ grenades to stop the hordes of Vietcong from entering Saigon before the planes could evacuate the people. The American Embassy was to be evacuated last, and the civilian population was evacuated first. This took three months. They were taken to South Korea, Japan, the Philippines, and Hawaii.

The Military fought off the thousands of Vietcong who somehow survived the barrier of deadly germs laid down by the Ghost Shadows. Unknown to General Stone, a new virus was being tested in the grenades, one far more deadly, but having no immediate effect. It was designed to attack the immune system and it had no cure. The wind took this disease in all directions, indiscriminately infecting all who came in contact with it. The new grenades ran out and were replaced by the original germ grenades. This allowed the time needed for the military to evacuate the troops from the Embassy. When this information was discovered a year after the evacuation, they realized the disease could remain dormant for as long as ten years. The Ghost Shadows replayed the chain of events in their heads every day, trying to pinpoint the time they took off their gas masks.

Now, Magee lay on the floor of a troop transport aircraft, reliving the events of the last twenty-four hours. The Ghost Shadows had laid down the last barrage of germ grenades. Evidently they were the last of the new supply since they had had no immediate effect on the charging Vietcong. The Ghost Shadows had returned the fire of the enemy with their automatic weapons. The enemy had fallen in heaps before them, but they came wave after wave. Magee had reloaded, and was beginning to fire again when suddenly, out of nowhere, an enemy soldier was right in front of him with his rifle and bayonet leveled at Magee's face. He deflected the bayonet downward as he thrust his short sword deep into the chest of the soldier. At the same time, the enemy's bayonet penetrated Magee's shoulder blade. He remembered screaming out in pain, "Mai Lee," as he pulled the bayonet, still attached to the rifle, from his shoulder. "I am immortal, I cannot die." Using the rifle as a spear, he had hurled it into the chest of an attacker, managing to pick up his weapon and fire it until he lost consciousness.

While he was out, Turner came to his aid. He picked Magee up and carried him over his shoulder as he ran full speed to the aircraft where he immediately began to administer first aid. Turner had stopped the bleeding and saved Magee's life. The others had hop-scotched their way to the aircraft under the cover fire of a machine gun manned by the copilot of the plane.

Valdez had filled Magee in on the missing pieces twenty minutes before. They were now underway, headed for Seoul, South Korea. For the first time in his military career, Magee realized he was not immortal. He could die. When Magee was wounded, all of the Ghost Shadows realized their own mortality. And when Turner saved Magee's life, he had symbolically saved the lives of all of the Ghost Shadows. Now it was over and they were going home.

"Home," thought Magee. "Mai Lee and the children." The war was over. He would relish the peace. The sedative Turner had given him was just starting to work and he soon drifted into a deep sleep. He slept through the pain and soon he was in a hospital in Seoul. News of Magee's wounding reached Mai Lee back at the compound.

"Magee cannot die, he is immortal," she said to her sisters, "I heard him call out to me, 'Mai Lee, I am immortal, I cannot die.' Magee will live. Magee will come home." Her sisters hugged and kissed her, and then they left her alone. Ny Li Tu knew she was right. Her old friend Magee was immortal. He would live to return home to the compound and Moses, Lin Lee, Soo Sing, Mai Lee, and the children. They were family and they would live here forever. For them, forever was promised.

*"He that maketh haste to be rich
shall not be innocent"*

Proverbs 28:20

Chapter Twenty-three

Enemies

Moses Cribb had made many friends in his short career, but he, like all successful men, had also made enemies. One such group in particular had more reason to hate him than most. It was a right wing organization named "The Sons of Southern Patriots". They blamed Cribb for the demise of the Ku Klux Klans in America, and they blamed his commie chink wife, the name commonly used by them in reference to Ny Li Tu. They claimed Cribb had used millions of dollars in donations to the Klans for his own personal use. They had vowed to make him pay for his treachery against the Aryan race.

A bounty of one million dollars was placed on the heads of Moses and Ny Li Tu. Now that he was the Director of the C.I.A., it was almost impossible to get to them. However, their best chance would be at the Dover compound. The Compound had a state-of-the-art security system, but it was not impenetrable to professionals. A small group led by two ex-C.I.A. operatives, financed by "The Sons of Southern Patriots", would take on the perilous mission. They had reason to believe that Moses Cribb's relationship to General Stone and General Moon was in some way linked to the deaths of former C.I.A. Director Lassey and several agents loyal to him. They were among the twenty-one agents who were asked to retire, or resign, when Cribb was appointed the New Director.

Money was not the only motivation for this

mission. Six months had passed since the evacuation of the troops from Vietnam. The mission had been hailed as a success and General Maxwell Mason Stone was awarded a fifth star. Sergeant First Class Samuel Nathaniel Turner was awarded the Congressional Medal of Honor. Master Sergeant James Edward Magee was awarded a Purple Heart.

Magee was met at the airport by Mai Lee and the twins. Soo Sing Wong drove them out to meet him. Magee looked as if he had just came back from vacation. He showed no signs of the wear and tear. He greeted Mai Lee with a long kiss. Then he took the children from her arms and carried them to the car.

Soo Sing could not shake his hand while Magee held the twins in his arms, so he patted him on the back and said, "Welcome home, my brother."

The twins had grown in the last eight months and Mai Lee spoke perfect English. He was home again and all was well on the compound. What more could he ask for? Moses, Ny Li Tu, Lin Lee, and the children were waiting in the mansion dining hall for him. They hugged, kissed, shook hands, and spoke in three different languages for hours. Mai Lee held on to him every minute of the time.

After dinner, Mai Lee and Magee excused themselves and took the children to the carriage house where they bathed them and put them to bed. Then they took a bath together, as they always did, before they went to bed.

"Magee, you are immortal," said Mai Lee. They made love and went to sleep. It seemed as if they had been together forever and that forever was promised them.

The security system allowed the gate guard to observe the entire compound on closed circuit T.V. screens. Four armed guards, with attack dogs, patrolled the grounds inside. A patrol car with two guards patrolled the perimeters. Soo Sing Wong checked the security system and the guards hourly, just as Magee had trained him to do, without the slightest deviation from his instructions. The compound was as secure as it possibly could be under ordinary circumstances.

Everyone that lived on the compound slept without fear of danger that night. Except, of course, Soo Sing Wong. He patrolled the compound hourly, all through the night. Something seemed wrong, the east side of the compound was without light. He immediately switched on the generators and then went to the gate house to check the closed circuit TV screens. He found the gate guard with his throat cut. He knew immediately that they had an internal security problem when he found the lock on the door of the gate house had not been broken. He scanned the closed circuit TV. screens, looking for signs of the intruders. He knew it would have taken several people with high-tech equipment to penetrate the security system, and even then, they would have needed inside assistance. Monitor screen six showed a dead guard dog lying on the ground outside of a window at the east wing of the mansion. That was where Moses and Ny Li Tu were sleeping that night. He pushed the automatic over-ride button on the security system to alert the mansion. The intruders must have overlooked that feature on the security system for it was not jammed. He raced to the carriage house to awaken Magee. Soo Sing did not stand a chance against the intruders alone. He had to assume the other guards were either in on the attack, dead, or both. These people were professionals, they would not leave witnesses to testify against them.

Ny Li Tu had neglected to install the security system in the carriage house. She had already moved into the mansion when the system was being installed, so the carriage house was not included in the contract. Soo Sing Wong felt a hand cover his mouth as he let himself in the door of the carriage house using the master key. A hushed voice, spoke in his native tongue, "They are in the house." Soo Sing motioned with his hand that he would search to the left; Magee searched to the right. Magee knew he had come upon the intruder when he felt the gentle breeze from an open window. He located the intruder's position from the smell of an unfamiliar bath soap with a lye base. He knew the intruder was armed with an automatic weapon and he would not take the chance of missing anyone with a weapon that had to be aimed. Magee knew the only chance he had of taking him out was the fact the intruder did not know he was only armed with a hunting knife. They both stood perfectly still. Magee needed a diversion. He could see a man in the darkness, staring at the bed. The intruder's eyes were locked on Mai Lee who lay there sleeping with the moonlight shining down on her through the open window. The intruder seemed to be in suspended animation, which was exactly the distraction Magee needed to make his move. He moved silently, swiftly and deadly, like a cat in the dark, and then drove his knife into the intruder's throat.

Magee caught the lifeless body in his arms and laid it out gently on the floor, not making a sound. He looked over at Mai Lee, still asleep in bed with the moonlight covering her nude body like a blanket. Her beauty had saved his life. As he stood there looking at her, he understood the intruder's dilemma. Her hypnotic beauty had incapacitated his brain. Magee had only put him out of his misery.

He stopped Soo Sing at the bedroom door, before he could walk in, and arranged to meet him at the mansion. They arrived in time to see an intruder with an arrow stuck through his head and Ny Li Tu holding a crossbow. Moses was bleeding from a wound to his leg, but it was not serious enough to warrant immediate attention. Ny Li Tu, speaking in her native tongue, ordered them to help her search the compound for the rest of the attackers. She went to the zoo and released the tigers who were full grown by now. Dead bodies were all over the compound; the guards and dogs must have been taken by surprise. Then a scream of terror came from the direction of the tigers. The big cats had found the last intruder. Ny Li Tu ordered the families to sleep in the mansion for the remainder of the night with the doors and windows locked. Outside, the tigers roamed the compound in search of human prey.

The next day, Cribb ordered C.I.A. agents to secretly dispose of the intruders' bodies, find out who they were, and by whom they were sent. The investigation revealed the source of the attack and the names of the attackers. Moses Cribb never let his enemies know the result of his investigation. He simply kept them under surveillance. He owed them a surprise visit.

Three of the executive officers of "The Sons of Southern Patriots" died in their sleep that year. Oh yes, along with their wives. A flag with an emblem in the center was found draped over their bodies. The emblem depicted an arm with a sword clutched in its hand. Wrapped around the arm and the sword was a snake with its tongue flickering out. The words embroidered around the emblem read: "Don't tread on me".

*"Track an animal by his foot
prints, track a man by his habits."*
The Spirit of Mantila Two Moons

Chapter Twenty-four

Dakota Moon:
In Search of His Mother's People

General Dakota Moon went on a long-needed leave
of absence. The war was over, and the future was
uncertain. Stone's commandos were demobilized.
The Ghost Shadows were now a part of the C.I.A.,
under the command of Moses Cribb. That suited
Dakota Moon fine. He had been in uniform for over
twenty years. His new job was Assistant Director
of the C.I.A. This was another of General Stone's
strategic appointments on his road to the White
House. The duty of protecting the President was
transferred to the C.I.A. under the Direction of
Moses Cribb. The Ghost Shadows were assigned
the task of protecting the President and the Presidential Candidates.

This last move put everything in place for
Maxwell Mason Stone to run for the Presidency of
the United States without fear of a plot from within
the government to assassinate him. Moon was instrumental in setting up the twenty-four hour,
seven day a week security schedule. The Ghost
Shadows were the only people in the world Maxwell
Mason Stone trusted with his life. They had protected him during the war, and now they would
continue to do so in civilian life. Dakota Moon went
first to the gravesite of his parents in Putnam
County, New York. This was the place where he
had buried his past and he went there to speak to
the spirit of his dead mother. Dakota lay prostrate
on the ground in front of the grave for an hour

before his mother's spirit appeared to him.

"My son," the spirit of his mother said, speaking to him in the language of the Seminole, "you are a War Chief like your father before you. You must travel the same path. His spirit dwells within you. Trust the spirit of your father. At the end of the path there is a light. The light shines on an empty seat. The seat is your place in the Council of Chiefs. There your spirit will join the greatest chiefs of our nation. That is to be your destiny. That was the destiny of your father, and his father before him, just as it is to be the destiny of your son, and the sons of your son." The vision of the spirit of his mother went away as mysteriously as it had appeared.

Dakota lay on the ground in a trance. When it passed and he regained consciousness again, he found the feather of an eagle by his right hand. He knew this to be the sign his father would leave. He would pass the feather to his son before he went to join the Council of Chiefs. When he was able to stand on his feet again, he knew without being told, he must go to the Seminole Reservation in Florida, on Lake Okeechobee. The mother of his son was waiting.

Cheyenne Sunset was a beautiful, young woman. She had a degree in Primary Education from Florida State and she taught Elementary School on the reservation. She was twenty-seven and still unmarried, which was unusual for an Indian girl. She had received many offers of marriage from the men on the reservation, but she had no intention of being a squaw, even though she wanted to marry a Seminole brave. She was looking for that special man.

Cheyenne was educated in the ways of the white man, but despite her education she was an old-fashioned Indian girl. She was not interested in marrying a white man, or leaving the reservation. Being an Indian and living on the reservation was what she wanted, but on her own terms, with an Indian man of her equal. Until then, she would be, as she was called by her people, "She who awaits a stranger."

Dakota Moon arrived at the house of his mother's cousin, Walking Crow. Walking Crow never left the sanctuary of the reservation. He had never trusted the white man, and it was not likely that he ever would. Walking Crow knew Dakota Moon immediately. He was the spitting image of his father, Ten Tall Bears, who had been Walking Crow's closest friend. They had grown up together. As children, they had hunted and fished all over the Everglades. They had both been members of the secret warrior society, "The Order Of The Eagle".

Walking Crow knew the destiny of Dakota Moon and was eager to help him fulfill it. He was not fortunate enough to have a son. When he died, he would be the last of his line to join the Council and sit with the spirit of the great Seminole War Chief, Osceola. Walking Crow knew the father of "She who awaits a stranger". He would introduce Dakota Moon to her father the following day.

Dakota Moon did not sleep that night. Instead, he walked the land of his father's birthright. He listened to the sounds of the night. He heard the insects crawl, he watched the swamp birds fly, and he talked with the spirit of his father until the moon and stars went to hide from the sun. After sleeping until noon, he returned to the house of Walking Crow where he was to meet the father, of the mother, of his son. Ten Shades of Tan was another member of the Council who had no son, but he was destined to have a daughter who would give birth to a warrior equal to Osceola .

Dakota and Cheyenne saw each other for the

first time, and yet they knew it was not the first time they had met. They had always been together, living in a time warp that was repeating their life cycle, time after time, for eternity. They met again once every century and relived the romance that spawned their love child. Their love was infinite. They married as they had many times before. They honeymooned in the wilderness of the Everglades, living off the land as their ancestors had in centuries past. When Dakota left Cheyenne to return to Washington, she was carrying their son. The spirit of his dead mother would watch over his family as she had been doing since the beginning of time, and would continue until the end of time.

"Your destiny is not the end of your life, it is the beginning."
                                    Dakota Moon

Chapter Twenty-five

The Campaign:
Maxwell Mason Stone for President

Maxwell Mason Stone, the youngest general ever to attain the rank of Chairman of the Joint Chiefs of Staff, retired at the age of forty-two. He would campaign for the Candidacy of President of the United States of America, turning forty-three a few days prior to the Election. The American peoples' overwhelming approval of Stone's candidacy had both major political parties wooing him to run as their candidate. Stone appealed to the American people, as no candidate in American history ever did before. He was young and handsome. He was an American hero.

He was married to the daughter of one of America's most popular Presidents, and his campaign chairwoman was the most popular ex-First Lady in American history. Tara's mother had insisted she be his Campaign Chairwoman. Stone saw the wisdom of the move since there were members of the House, on both sides of the aisle, who owed their political careers to her. How else could her husband have been so successful in office? She planned for Stone to run virtually unopposed by orchestrating a fusion of the two major political parties in America. Stone would run against a weak third party candidate, who was running only for the sake of a democratic election. Stone was allowed to choose anyone he wanted as a running mate. After many discussions with his mother-in-law, and with her full approval, he chose Moses

Cribb. Maxwell, Tara, Moses, Ny Li Tu, and the children campaigned together that year. All of America got the opportunity to see and shake hands with the candidates. They campaigned on a platform of peace, prosperity, humanity, and full employment (insured through fourteen years of mandatory public school education), federal health and life insurance, a revised Social Security system based on lifetime individual deposits, and a revised tax system.

In his speech at a voter registration drive in Harlem, Presidential Candidate Maxwell Mason Stone made the following comments:

"If you believe that you are all that you deserve to be, then you are lost, mired in the lack of your own self-esteem. If you believe that you are all that you are going to be, then you are lost, mired in the lack of your own self-confidence. If you believe that you are all that you want to be, then you are lost, mired in the lack of your own ambition. Whatever you believe, believe this; you are more than you were. You are no longer a pagan, you have found the only living God. You are no longer a slave, the white man freed you to assure freedom to the free. The ballot is stronger than the bullet. The right to vote has been paid for with the blood of your fellow countrymen. Cast your ballot for me in November, and I promise you will not need the bullet to enjoy your Constitutional Rights as Americans."

The Stone and Cribb Presidential ticket won a landslide that November. Dakota Moon was appointed the new Director of the Central Intelligence Agency. He appointed Everett Henry Jones as assistant director. Maxwell Mason Stone and Moses Cribb served the country as Presidents and Vice Presidents for forty years. Every eight years, they changed office. According to the law, no President could serve more than two consecutive terms. During their terms in office, the world was without a war or rumor of war. All American people enjoyed peace and prosperity, just as Stone and Cribb had promised in their campaigns. The families that lived in the compound of Moses Cribb, Magee, Mai Lee, Soo Sing Wong, and Lin Lee, set up a factory to manufacture computer chips in Tokyo, Japan, and another in Taiwan, China, where they manufactured a new product—a light-weight, plastic body armor that would make a man invulnerable. Magee dressed in this body armor every day to please Mai Lee. She thought, "This will truly make him immortal."

Ny Li Tu Cribb was voted the Chairwoman of the Board. Under her direction, the businesses made billions of dollars annually. Ny Li Tu enriched the people who protected Moses from harm. She said, "This will truly make him immortal."

Maxwell Mason Stone died at the age of eighty-three after developing a strain of the virus with which the Ghost Shadows had killed so many people over the years. He said on his death bed, "The end will justify the means."

Dakota Moon retired after the third election of Stone and Cribb to the White House. He went to live on the Seminole Indian Reservation with Cheyenne. He lived to be one hundred and three years old, before taking his seat on the Council of Chiefs with his father and the Great Chief Osceola.

BOOK II

Preface

It is the year 2003. Moses Cribb has just been elected President of the United States. Ex-President Maxwell Mason Stone is now the Vice President. They will maintain control over the office of President by alternating terms every eight years. They have eliminated the traditional two party political system in America. It has been replaced by a fusion party consisting of the two major political parties. Make no mistake, there are other political parties. After all, this is still a democracy, but none with the financial resources of the new Fusion Party. As President of the Strongest Nation on Earth, Maxwell Mason Stone has disarmed the planet and brought about world peace. It is enforced by the threat of the dreaded Germs, held exclusively in the hands of America, under his control. The Germs were first unleashed during the last fifty years of the twentieth century in Southeast Asia, leaving the people dissipated by disease and hunger. It was here that the world was introduced to the dreaded Disease Without a Name as America retreated from a war it chose not to win.

Eight years ago, Maxwell Mason Stone took the Office of President of the United States of America. He chose to strengthen the economy of the country while the rest of the world waged war. He stood by and watched silently as the Europeans slaughtered each other after Communism failed. He imposed his idea of peace on the victors and disarmed them. Peace was forced on the oil-rich nations of the Near East that waged war on their neighbors as well as each other. He stepped in, giving them a choice of peace or death, disarmed them and set himself up as the keeper of the peace.

Now, this self-appointed peacemaker is Vice President of the United States. The children born to the Ghost Shadows are of school age. They spent the first part of their lives training in the Martial Arts under the tutelage of Master Soo Sing Wong. They have learned from him the long forgotten ancient art of Self-Healing. The business ventures of Ny Li Tu, Magee, Mai Lee, Soo Sing Wong and Lin Lee have grown far beyond their wildest dreams. The Body Armor is worn by sixty percent of the world's population. The new computer chip has revolutionized the computer world.

Ny Li Tu spends much of her time looking for new business ventures in order to expand their influence and wealth. She has graciously allowed Tara Stone to continue in her natural role, saying that "Tara Stone is irreplaceable as the First Lady." The truth is, Tara is as American as apple pie. Tara remaining as the First Lady takes the rough edges off the changing of the guard that never really happens.

The Armed Forces of the United States is reduced to five thousand men because the need for armed men on the battlefield was eliminated by Germ Warfare. The Special Force of men are under the command of Dakota Moon and the Central Intelligence Agency. They move swiftly around the world, eliminating the discontented with the deadly Germs of war. There is peace on the planet for the first time since the Creation. It is an uneasy peace, but it is, nevertheless, a peace. This peace that Maxwell Mason Stone inflicted on the world and maintained by Dakota Moon and the Special Force of Five Thousand created many new enemies for Stone and Cribb. Dakota Moon constantly investigates plots to assassinate them and gain control of the Germs.

The real and more immediate danger is the dreaded Disease Without a Name. Millions of people die annually and there is no known cure. Scientists the world over are working day and night seeking the cure to save us.

The following chapters will place you in a world dictated by the demons of man's own creation. A place where man holds the fate of the planet in his hands. A place where he has the opportunity to choose a new beginning or embrace his predicted end. Welcome to the Present!

"Give a wise man instructions and he will be yet wiser."

Proverbs 9:9

Chapter Twenty-six

The Children

On the last day of August, in the year 2003, the temperature was 117 degrees Fahrenheit in the shade. Scientists said that the extreme heat was a result of the hole in the Ozone Layer. Scientists had been saying that for decades and people never listened to them, so what would make them listen now?

Soo Sing Wong had just completed the final class of the children's Martial Arts instruction, and this was their graduation day. On Monday of the next week, they would go off to the Military Academy to complete the next phase of their basic education. They had all picked their major subjects of study, but first, they must become soldiers. Discipline is the mother of education.

Their parents made this day a very special occasion. This was the first of many graduations, a fact of life that the children had been made aware from the cradle onwards. Friends and relatives from around the country were invited to the compound of Moses Cribb. Despite the extreme heat, the ceremony was held outside, using the gazebo as a dais. The children spoke briefly about their chosen majors and their expectations of the future. Soo Sing Wong presided over the ceremony. Each child was awarded a Black Belt, and each gave their speech, in turn, according to their age. The older children spoke first. Although none of them had ever spoken publicly before, they spoke without hesitation or fear of failure. There was no question that they would be, one day, the best the country had to offer in their fields of expertise. The twins of James and Mai Lee Magee spoke first.

"We will major in Business, with the expectation that one day we will return to run the family business and find new markets for the products," Roman Micheal and Mica Mark announced. They indicated that their aunt, Ny Li Tu, had given them her approval and blessings.

"I will study Law," said Rameses Ryan Cribb, the son of Ny Li Tu and Moses Cribb, speaking second. "I hope to go into politics and follow in my father's footsteps," he announced proudly, "I will one day become President of the United States of America."

The son of Soo Sing and Lin Lee Wong spoke third. Ali Khan told the audience that he would study Computer Science, saying, "The computer chip is being improved every day, and I will have to develop new technology to help the business keep abreast with the industry. I have also spoken to my aunt about my choice. I will work in the Research Department of the factory in Tokyo." He looked over at his mother, and added, "To begin with."

"I will be a scientist. I will major in Biochemistry," proclaimed the son of Vice President Maxwell and Tara Stone, Canyon Mesa, "I intend to discover the cure for the Disease Without a Name, and I will do it before the age of twenty-five." He concluded with "thank you" and then sat down.

The son of Alexandro and Carmella Valdez spoke fifth. Juan Pablo said, "I will study Medicine. I will be a surgeon."

George Lee Brown Jr., the son of George and Lula Brown, spoke sixth. He announced, "I will go into Banking and Finance. I want to manage the enormous wealth that is being acquired by the family. Aunt Ny Li Tu has said that is a job in itself."

Samuel and Janie Turner's son spoke next. Tyler Samuel said, "I will also study Law. Rameses Ryan will need a Vice President. I discussed it with Aunt Ny Li Tu, who said I would be a natural."

The son of Dakota, and Cheyenne Moon spoke last. The seven year old was the youngest, but was very tall for his age. He walked to the microphone with the self-assurance of a child much older. Cheyenne's Dakota Moon said, "I will be what my father is, a warrior. I will command the Special Forces for President Rameses Ryan, and when the time comes, I will take my place alongside my father in the council of Chiefs. I will go to West Point and study the Art of War. That is my destiny. I have known this from birth." He walked over to Rameses Ryan and Tyler Samuel and hugged them. His destiny and theirs were linked to the future of American Politics.

After the crowd had given them a standing ovation, the children left the gazebo to seek out their parents and bask in the glow of approval and pride. Ny Li Tu, Moses, and Rameses Ryan walked through the garden searching for the families of Everett Jones and Calvin Chipman. Seven years earlier, Everett Jr., Elizabeth Susan, and Marion Matilda had earned their Black Belts at a commencement ceremony at the compound. They were older than this group, but no less enthusiastic about continuing their education. Everett Jr., now sixteen, was majoring in Astronomy and Oceanography. Elizabeth Susan, fifteen, was in her first year of college studying Physics. Marion Matilda at fourteen, was studying Meteorology. After earning their Doctorates, they would serve in the Special Forces before going into the family business with Ny Li Tu.

Ny Li Tu took a special interest in the children

of the Ghost Shadows. She made herself instrumental in shaping their individual futures, for the future of the family business. The business was the family's future, and as Chairwoman of the Board of Directors, it was her duty to recruit and train the best minds available. This was now her life's work; Moses, the growth of the family business, and the education of the Ghost Shadows' Children, in that order. Over the years, Ny Li Tu had became the head of the families. Although self-appointed, she was unchallenged. It was silently and unanimously agreed upon that her strength was the bond that held them together.

Everett Jr. and Marion Matilda were still at the Academy—Everett a junior, and Marion Matilda a sophomore. They had become best friends, and they saw much of each other. The relationship was encouraged and blessed by Ny Li Tu. With the Disease Without a Name running rampant, they were not allowed to see other children socially. Ny Li Tu refused to take chances with the lives of the children. She believed that they would develop a bloodline immune to the disease. They had been betrothed to each other at the commencement ceremony that ended their training with Soo Sing Wong seven years before. Ny Li Tu noticed signs of the friendship turning to love when she spoke to them at Rameses' Commencement Ceremony, and she began to have them chaperoned, in order to prevent premarital sex. She wanted Marion Matilda to be at least eighteen before there was any chance of pregnancy. They were scheduled to be married upon her graduation from the Academy, and then complete their undergraduate work together.

Elizabeth Susan was another matter. There was not a male child in the family close enough in age to betroth her. She had graduated the Academy, and entered college, at the age of fourteen. Her beauty equalled her brains. This fifteen year old Amazon stood six feet three inches in her stocking feet. She feared nothing—man nor beast. Surely the intimidation felt by boys her own age could be understood and appreciated. Ny Li Tu knew that attending college while young would expose the girl to boys much older, although not necessarily more mature. Elizabeth Susan was her pride and she planned to mold her in her own image.

"What a pity that Rameses is so much younger," she thought aloud, "but time will equalize the circumstances."

The chaperone that she assigned to Elizabeth Susan had orders to discourage any suitors brave enough to approach her. This would solve the problem temporarily. Time was the solution. Time would allow the children to mature. Time would allow the children to fulfill their destinies. Time would allow the children to save the planet. Time was definitely the solution.

"If a thing can be created, it can also be destroyed. all life is vulnerable".

Canyon Mesa Stone

Chapter Twenty-seven

The Disease Without a Name

The world population decreases each day by the millions. A plague threatens to bring on Armageddon. If it cannot be delayed or halted, the end of the world is now. There is panic and fear. For no more than the suspicion of infection, men are killed and cremated. The fortunate ones are killed first. Parents kill their children. Children report their parents to The Board of Infectious Diseases, an organization of world renown doctors and scientists set up by the President to control the spread of infectious diseases. The common cold is suspect enough to cost a life. Fear, and suspicion are almost as deadly as the disease itself.

Once again, the Dark Ages have returned. Witch hunts for the infected are common place. The world's scientists work day and night, seeking the cure for the Disease Without a Name. The disease is caused by a synthetic bacterial parasite, which is carried by the wind from country to country, or perhaps even from planet to planet throughout the galaxies. This, of course, is only scientific speculation based on the speed by which the disease is travelling on the planet Earth. The exact origin of the disease is a top secret, guarded jealously by the Central Intelligence Agency and its Director, Dakota Moon. It was a Nazi secret weapon, intended to ensure world domination. The Nazi scientists developed the deadly Germs prior to the Allied Invasion of Germany in 1945. Had Germany been able to use them, the outcome of the War would have been much different. So now, the keepers of the peace hold the ultimate weapon of war. President Cribb's concern about the maintenance of peace keeps him awake nights. In a letter to his son at the Academy, he wrote:

My dear Rameses,

You have learned to hunt without a weapon, to fish without a rod, to see without eyes, to listen without ears, to feel without fingers, to move without motion. The hardest lesson to learn is to live in solitude. You may, one day, be the last man on earth. This is a responsibility for which you must be prepared. The planet is in peril. Grow strong, and grow quickly, my son. Time is not in our favor. Only you can save us from our selves. Your loving father, and President of the United States, Moses Cribb.

P.S.I understand from your teachers that you are an excellent student. Although I know it is true, I often wonder what else they could tell their President. Study incessantly, Rameses my son, your father loves you.

It is the year 2013. Vietnam, Laos and Cambodia have fallen to the common enemy, The Disease Without a Name. Not a soul survives. The only life remaining in that part of the world is the vegetation of the jungle. Grow strong and grow quickly my children, the world awaits you. Come and save us from ourselves.

> *"I know they will have the answers; hopefully there will be someone left to ask the questions."*
> Moses Cribb

Chapter Twenty-eight

The Stage is Set

In the year 2015 Maxwell Mason Stone was the President of the United States, re-elected four years before. The ex-President, Moses Cribb, had been elected Vice President again. Elizabeth Susan, Everett Jr., and Marion Matilda received their Doctorate degrees, and were serving in the Special Forces under Dakota Moon. Everett Jr., and Marion Matilda married as planned.

Elizabeth Susan was still single. Rameses had graduated from the Academy, and was in his second year of college. He and Elizabeth Susan had become close friends despite the age difference. His mother, Ny Li Tu, was extremely happy with the relationship. She made sure they spent much of their time unchaperoned. She always believed that time would equalize the circumstances. Elizabeth Susan helped him to make the Deans List on a regular basis. Ny Li Tu had assigned her to him as a bodyguard and tutor. This move eliminated the need for a chaperone. Now, Rameses spent all of his time with her, unchaperoned. He was eighteen and madly in love with this Nubian Amazon Warrior. Elizabeth Susan showed no emotion to indicate that she felt the same. However, there was no doubt that he was her favorite person. To Rameses, that was as good as love. He graduated from college and started on his Masters immediately. He was twenty years old now, and very mature. As of late, Elizabeth Susan began to see him as a man.

He was seven feet tall with shoulder length, jet black hair. His skin was milk white and his eyes were slanted, like his mother's, with the deep black on black irises that gave him the appearance of having no pupils. Other than his skin tone, he looked Asian. His body had been well-developed through the extensive exercise program he had been following for the last five years. He trained along with Elizabeth Susan. She was in the Special Force of Five Thousand, and his mother insisted that wherever she went, he went also.

When they were alone, she allowed him to lean against her and touch her without objection. The smell of his after-shave lotion gave her a rush. The six year difference in their ages began to dwindle. They began to hold hands all the time. Now when they kissed, she found herself kissing back. She wanted him as he had always wanted her. But it was happening much too fast for her. She would have to speak to his mother.

"Speak to his mother?" she thought to herself, "I am twenty-six years old and I still a virgin." Part of the reason was his mother.

That evening, she asked Rameses to marry her. He accepted the proposal with a big grin. He said, like a little boy, "Really Elizabeth Susan? Love, sex and everything?" "Yes," she replied, "that is what happens in these matters, you know."

He said, "I love you, Elizabeth Susan, I really love you."

"I know that," replied Elizabeth Susan, as if she were talking to a child, "I have always known that."

"Shall I call mother to make the arrangements?" he asked her.

She would have responded with sarcasm, but another look at his body was all she needed to convince her that she could make it work.

"Yes, call mother," she said, thinking to herself that the arrangements had probably been made years before. 'Mother' made them at birth. Time had equalized the circumstances.

Mother, as Elizabeth Susan now called Ny Li Tu, arranged a wedding that was equal to the wedding of Maxwell and Tara Stone. They did not go away on a honeymoon; the world was far too dangerous for that. Besides, Elizabeth Susan was not interested in going anywhere before Rameses finished his graduate work. Frankly, her only interest right now was sex. She wanted to try it. She wanted to do all the things she had read about. They had slipped away during the wedding reception to go to Rameses' room in the mansion. The only one who noticed that they were missing was Ny Li Tu. When they returned, an hour and a half later, the expression of self-satisfaction on Rameses' face told her that this had been the first time he penetrated his wife. The glow on Elizabeth Susan's face told her it would not be the last.

Over the next three years, Rameses Ryan, Roman Micheal, Mica Mark, Ali Khan, Canyon Mesa, Juan Pablo, George Lee Jr., Tyler Samuel and Cheyenne's Dakota Moon all earned degrees in the fields of their choice and entered the Special Force of Five Thousand, under the command of Dakota Moon. The stage was set, the children had come of age, and the world awaited them, ready to be saved.

"The Ghost Shadows slew tens of thousands, their children slew hundreds of thousands."

Soo Sing Wong

Chapter Twenty-nine

The Hate Groups Must Die

In 2020, Moses Cribb had been in the Oval Office for a year, working closely with his vice-president, Maxwell Mason Stone. There was some discontentment among the voters and the opposition party was growing larger each year. The opposition was controlled by the hate groups who managed to survive the Exterminations of the late 1960's and early 1970's. They had gone to Europe and revived the Nazi Party, then returned to America in the 1980's. Moses Cribb had not felt threatened by their presence until now. Yet, although his election was not a landslide, it was far from being called close.

Moses knew the danger of allowing these people to live. The faces had changed, but the ideology was the same. He would have Dakota Moon start the Exterminations again, this time in Germany, the point of origin. The Neo-Nazis were fighting the German police openly in the streets, and it was time to support the German government in their fight against the insanity of racism before it spread any further. History would not be allowed to repeat itself. Moses was sure that the problem of racism would one day eliminate itself. Each year, the races of the world grew darker. There was much interracial marriage and cohabitation all over the planet; the races seemed to be going through a homogenizing process. Moses felt that if this were true, racism would die out on its own. However, until then, he would continue to exterminate the hate groups as he had in his youth.

Seven months had passed since the order to exterminate the hate groups was sent to Dakota Moon. He was told to plan the operations around their rallies, as they had done in the old days. He was told to hit them in Germany and America at the same time, on the same day. He had been waiting for the opportunity to strike for months. Elizabeth Susan and Rameses would lead the strike force in Germany and Cheyenne's Dakota Moon and Tyler Samuel would lead the strike force in America. The others were allowed to rally to the leaders of their choice. Roman Micheal, Mica Mark, Ali Khan, and Canyon Mesa would follow Elizabeth Susan and Rameses. Everett Jr., Marion Matilda, Juan Pablo, and George Lee Jr. would follow Cheyenne's Dakota Moon and Tyler Samuel. Each squad would have an additional fourteen men.

Under the command of Dakota Moon, they trained day and night. They climbed mountains, swam rivers, lived in the desert, the Arctic, and the jungles and practiced urban warfare house to house, and street by street. The likelihood of hand to hand combat was remote, but Dakota Moon wanted them ready for anything and everything. They wore uniforms made of the new Body Armor, fitted with a helmet designed to filter the air and protect them from the Germs. It was also equipped with an anti-gravity device that allowed them to leap great distances in any direction. It gave the appearance of flight. The uniform made them look like the Storm Troopers led by Darth Vader in "Star Wars," the science fiction movie made back in the 1970's. The plastic could not be penetrated, nor burned, and the helmet could filter the environment of all the known planets in the universe. The uniform made them virtually invincible—the closest thing to immortality. Their father's had only created the illusion of immortality.

Meanwhile, across the Atlantic Ocean in Berlin, Germany, Franz Stolz, said to be the reincarnation of Adolph Hitler by his followers in the European Neo-Nazi Party, was busy planning a worldwide televised rally of the Aryan Peoples Party. He had invited the White Supremacist groups, the Ku Klux Klans, the American Nazi Party, and what remained of the Sons of Southern Patriots and its splinter groups from around the world to participate. Stolz and his party estimated the rally would raise one billion dollars which would be shared among the groups, according to the amount invested by each. They marketed the affair as "The Day Their God Would Come and Destroy All Who Bore the Mark of Cain".

Word of the rally spread like wild fire throughout the Aryan world. It caused riots in many of the major cities of the world where the hate groups attacked Non-whites and Jews openly, killing them in the streets because they bore the 'Mark of Cain'. Militant Non-whites and Jews united to meet the hate groups in battle and defend their families against the roving bands of murderous marauders. Dakota Moon made no effort to stop the bloodshed since the hate groups seemed to be getting the worst of the encounters. Franz Stolz made a televised speech in which he told them to wait for the day their God would come. He announced the date of the rally and told them to prepare for battle because on that day, the Holy War would begin. The bloodshed ended and the people prepared for the Holy War impatiently, but obediently. On January 1, 2021, at the end of the last speech from the televised rallies in Berlin, Germany and Chicago, Illinois (the home of the American Nazi Party), the Holy War would begin. This was the announcement

Dakota Moon had been waiting for: the date of the Rally, the day their God was Coming, the day the Holy War would begin, and ironically the day their world would end, the first day of the year 2021.

It was 0:500 hours on the thirty-first day of December in the year 2020. Many years ago they had called this day the Eve of the New Year. It had been a time for much celebration in those days. There had been many holidays and days of celebration in the past. Now people were happy just to see the new sun.

The strike force headed by Elizabeth Susan and Rameses had arrived in Berlin, and they were now at the American Embassy with their cousins Roman Micheal, Mica Mark, Ali Khan, Canyon Mesa, and the team of fourteen chosen from the Special Force of Five Thousand. There was an identical strike force in Chicago, Illinois, headed by Cheyenne's Dakota Moon and Tyler Samuel, along with Everett Jr., Marion Matilda, Juan Pablo, George Lee Jr., and the other fourteen soldiers chosen from the Special Force of Five Thousand. They were in the old building on Union Square that was once used as C.I.A. Headquarters ready to strike at twenty-two hundred hours the next day. They would spend today checking their equipment. They would put the uniforms on an hour before the strike. Two of them stood guard while the others rested in private quarters.

In Germany, resting in their room at the American Embassy, Rameses stroked Elizabeth Susan's cheek with the back of his hand and asked if she was nervous about the mission.

"Nervous," she replied, "Why? It is not we who are about to die."

"She is as cold as she is beautiful," Rameses thought as he twirled the ends of her hair around his finger tips and slipped his arm around her neck. He drew her face to his, rubbing his cheek against her lips.

"I love the fragrance your body emits," he whispered in her ear, "I can locate you in a crowded room."

She wrapped her arms around his waist, and replied, kissing his lips, "I bet you say that to all your wives before a battle."

"Only to my favorite," he answered, kissing her deeply, probing her mouth with his tongue.

"That fragrance is the oil we all use to identify one of the group in total darkness. How would you know me from one of them?" she asked, pushing him back gently.

He put his hand down into her pants and she parted her legs to allow him access. He gently inserted his index finger into her moist vagina. He pulled his hand out and waived his finger under her nose.

"It smells like my vaginal douche," she said.

"Exactly my point, Darling. The two fragrances combine and form an aphrodisiac that drives me insane," he quipped as he put his finger in his mouth.

"Well, don't tell your mother. She would probably try to market it," laughed Elizabeth Susan.

Rameses laughed with her, but part of him did not find this funny. The subject of his mother was not a source of jest. "If she did, I'm sure that it would make millions," he replied in defense of his mother.

Elizabeth Susan started stroking his penis without removing it from his pants. She knew this would not only change the subject, but resume the mood he was in before his mother came into the conversation. She felt his penis harden to her touch before unzipping his pants. She pushed him down on the bed and his movements helped her to take off his pants as she tugged at the legs. Rameses quickly removed his shirt as she took off his underwear along with his shoes and socks. He lay there anticipating the foreplay of oral sex as she removed her clothing. Elizabeth Susan was naked in seconds, although it seemed an eternity to him. She inserted two fingers into her vagina, then put them in his mouth. She knelt beside him on the bed, digging her nails into his chest, applying enough pressure to send sensations to his brain, promising the best was yet to come. She kissed him long and hard, taking his breath away as she moved her tongue down his chest and across his nipples, gently biting them to increase the pace of his sensations. Her tongue moved slowly over his chest and down his stomach until she reached her objective.

She took the shaft of his penis in her hand and began to stroke him slowly and intensely as if his pleasure was her only mission in life. He lay there gasping as if he were going to have a heart attack as she relentlessly sucked on his penis, letting up only to use her tongue to try to tantalize and seduce his sperm into her mouth. He did not come. And she knew he would not from the countless love encounters of the past. With his penis still in her mouth, Elizabeth Susan turned around to allow him access to her vagina. She came immediately with the first thrust of his tongue. She continued to come as he sucked the sweet moisture that he loved so much from her, leaving her weaker and weaker. Feeling her body go limp, he spun her around and rolled on top of her, thrusting his penis inside of her deliciously wet, awaiting vagina with a force that caused her to scream in ecstasy as he spent what seemed to be a cup of sperm inside of her.

They lay there in each other's arms, too tired to move. Her eyes closed, and her face had a glow that lit the room. In her hand, she held Ramses' penis, still stiff as if rigor mortise had set in. They lay there as still as death. They lay there in the arms of Morpheus, sleeping the sleep of the innocent. Tomorrow they would slay hundreds of thousands.

Meanwhile, in Chicago, Cheyenne's Dakota Moon went over the attack again, for the fifth time, with Tyler Samuel. They drilled the strike force on every detail before finally allowing them to rest before the battle. Cheyenne's Dakota Moon got very little sleep that night. He paced the floor in his room, thinking about the battle, if you could call it that. His father had told him of the Exterminations of the Ku Klux Klans in the 1960's and 1970's. He described the effect of the Germs that they used back then on all who came in contact with them. He told him how the gas cut off the air supply and slowly suffocated the women and children. Some of them, he was sure, were innocently there out of curiosity.

He remembered his father saying, "I wish there was a humane, effective, efficient alternative to the Gas." As much as his father hated these people, he would have rather killed them in hand to hand combat, the way warriors were supposed to kill, and be killed. But he was a soldier like his father before him, and they had their orders. The hate groups must die.

It was twenty-one hundred hours on the first day of January in the year 2021. At the American Embassy in Berlin, Elizabeth Susan was awakened from her sleep by a knock on the door. ,

"The call to arms is in a half hour, ma'am," the sentry said through the door.

"Wake the strike force. The Call to Arms is in twenty minutes, soldier," she answered him.

"Yes ma'am," was his reply.

Rameses was awakened by the sound of the voices. He got up and walked into the shower. Elizabeth Susan followed him. They always bathed together. They dressed in fifteen minutes, and then waited for the Call to Arms. After roll call, they put on the uniforms and checked each other's helmets for air leaks. The procedure was followed on both sides of the Atlantic simultaneously. Both strike forces were in place before the last speech ended and the Holy War began.

At twenty-three hundred hours on the first day of January, the year 2021, in an open field outside Berlin, the Neo-Nazi's rallied behind their leader. An estimated seven hundred and fifty thousand people gathered to witness the coming of their God, and the massacre of the Jews and Non-white people who bore the 'Mark of Cain'. Franz Stolz was the last to speak and the crowd cheered wildly as he walked to the microphone. They hailed him with cries of "Heil Hitler." At the base of the dais stood fifty of his personal bodyguards, in the uniform of Nazi Storm Troopers. He was dressed in the brown uniform worn often by his predecessor Adolph Hitler. He was six feet tall with yellow blond hair and deep blue eyes. He was the picture-perfect model of how the Aryan race saw itself.

"What a beautiful man," thought Elizabeth Susan to herself, "Surely, he must be their God." But she remembered the Christian teachings that told how Satan was once the most beautiful angel in heaven before he was cast out to the earth. "Could this be Satan?" she wondered aloud.

Franz Stolz spoke in a thunderous voice that brought the crowd to silence. They were hypnotized by his presence as he spoke to them of the end of the world as they knew it. He ended his speech by telling them, "Tonight we will take control of the world. Go out and kill all who bare the 'Mark of Cain'."

The crowd roared in one voice, "Heil Hitler, Heil Hitler, Heil Hitler, Heil Hitler," with right arms outstretched in the massive salute. Then, in a frenzy, they went out to obey the mandate of their God.

The strike force, on both sides of the Atlantic Ocean, shot the first of a series of gas grenades into the crowd. The crowds stood motionless as they watched the strike force fly above their heads, shooting the gas grenades. It was not until they saw the Storm Troopers firing at these strange beings that they realized it was not a part of the program. The bullets from the Storm Troopers hit their targets without any effect, giving them the appearance of immortals. The fact they could fly added to the confusion. If they were the Angels of God, then why were they killing the faithful? The questions would never be answered; the gas was beginning to take effect. People started to drop to the ground, holding their throats, choking on the air they were trying to breathe and calling on their God to save them, only to find he did not hear.

In Chicago, Cheyenne's Dakota Moon watched them die as his father had done, and a prophecy came to his mind: "Every knee shall bend, every tongue shall call his name." He was not sure where he had heard it, but he knew it was true. In Berlin, Canyon Mesa waded through the bodies of the dead and dying, listening to their moans and cries. Sometimes, he took pity and crushed the skull of a dying enemy, dispatching him to hell sooner than the gas would have allowed him to go. In the midst of the lifeless masses, he noticed the severed arm of a woman holding a baby. The arm seem to hold the baby out to him as an offering. The tears streaming from her eyes, touched his very soul. In his head, Canyon Mesa heard the voice of its mother saying "Take her, save her, and you will save us all."

He blinked several times to be sure his eyes were not deceiving him, but the child was really there. A female with golden blond hair and blue eyes, she was crying, but not choking. She was breathing the gas without dying. "Impossible," he thought aloud as he walked over to her, freeing her from her mother's arm. He picked her up and carried her with him, looking like a giant carrying the child in his arms. The others watched him, but did not question his motives. Rameses knew immediately when he saw the child was still alive. It was not Canyon Mesa the soldier who carried the child, it was Canyon Mesa the scientist fulfilling his destiny.

"I have come back to the exterminations, where it all began, among the unrighteous, and found you hiding in an Innocent."
                    Canyon Mesa Stone

Chapter Thirty

The Cure

In March, 2021, Canyon Mesa was working full time on the cure for the Disease Without a Name. The child he found during the Exterminations, two months before, was immune to the Germs. He had exposed her to the deadliest Germs on the face of the earth, and yet she remained uncontaminated. The child was about four months old, and even though she was being used as a guinea pig, she needed care. Every day that passed, Canyon Mesa's devotion to the child grew stronger. Against his better judgment he had given her a name. He called her Tomorrow.

He was both father and mother to Tomorrow. She had won his heart and he truly loved and cared for the child as if she were his own daughter. She was the perfect child to care for. She had not cried since he took her from the severed arm of her mother on the battlefield. They lived on the compound of Moses Cribb, where Ny Li Tu had set up a laboratory for him to work in. Canyon Mesa and Tomorrow spent most of their days in the laboratory. They left only to take their meals and to sleep. He had a baby crib set up in a corner of the lab, and she slept most of the time. That was fine since Canyon Mesa only needed blood, hair, and skin samples to run his tests. Test after test, after test, day after day, after day, he ran tests in search of the cure and immunization for the Disease Without a Name.

Dakota Moon sent Everett Jr. and Marion Matilda to Germany in search of information on Tomorrow. Canyon Mesa had requested the information three weeks before. Dakota Moon decided on the persons responsible for the assignment just a few days prior to their departure. Everett Jr. and Marion Matilda were still excited about the assignment as they boarded the plane. They would use this time alone together for a honeymoon. When they were married, no time had been scheduled for such a luxury because they were in college. When their graduate work was completed, they enlisted in the Special Force of Five Thousand, as expected. This was really the first chance they had to travel alone together.

Marion Matilda had every right to be excited. She had heard about the honeymoons of Tara Stone and Mai Lee Magee from her grandmother. Marion Matilda and Everett Jr. had originally planned to honeymoon after their tour of duty was over, and she felt this assignment was a blessing. When she told her father, he had simply said, "You kids enjoy the trip, and don't forget why your going." Ny Li Tu made reservations for them at the Berlin Hyatt Hotel, in the Honeymoon Suite. She and Moses had stayed there many years ago, before he went into politics, and she knew the kids would enjoy their stay as much as she and Moses had.

Marion Matilda did a back flip onto the bed as soon as Everett closed the door behind the bellhop.

"Georgia girls," he said in jest. "You can't take them anywhere. Don't you know enough not to jump on a bed without first taking off your shoes?" He kicked off his shoes and belly flopped onto the king-size bed beside her. Then he rolled over on top of her, kissing her and using his tongue to explore her mouth.

She shoved him off, using both hands and saying in her best Southern accent, "Us Georgia girls don't do that. At least not until we remove our shoes." She rolled off the bed, onto her feet. Kicking off her shoes, she ran into the bathroom.

Everett began taking off his clothes when he heard her running the bath water. He walked into the bathroom as she flushed the toilet. She rinsed her hands in the bath water and dried them on his naked chest. She had removed all of her clothes while sitting on the toilet, and they lay neatly in a pile by the sink. He savored her beautiful body with his eyes as she stepped into the tub, first testing the water temperature with her toe.

Marion Matilda stood there waiting for him to join her with the same innocent look she had when they had first experimented with sex on their wedding night. His eyes slowly devoured her naked body, from the pointed tips of the nipples on her firm breasts to the coarse black pubic hair between her legs. His long, hard, circumcised penis stood erect as he stepped into the bath water beside her. Her eyelids closed as he rubbed the bar of soap between her legs. He continued up her stomach, over her breasts, around her neck, and down her back to her buttocks.

Taking the soap from him, she lathered his chest. She knelt in the water taking his penis in her hand and rubbing the soapy lather between his legs, stroking him as she worked the soap into his skin. She rinsed the soap off the lower part of his body with a washcloth and put his penis in her mouth. She began sucking hard and fast while squeezing his testicles with just enough force to cause pleasure without pain. He held her head in his hands, moving it in the rhythm she had created. She pulled his body to her as she relentlessly sucked the life-giving semen from his penis.

Exhausted, Everett leaned against the cold, tiled shower wall as the fluid from his body burst into her mouth, leaving him too weak for his legs to support his weight. As she released his penis from her grip, he slid down the shower wall and knelt in the water. She pulled his head between her legs and rested one foot on the soap dish handle while he instinctively used his tongue. She kept his head between her legs, unwilling to release him until the climax met her expectations. Satisfied, she let his head go and eased her body down into the water beside him, completely exhausted from the encounter.

They finished bathing and retired early, that first night of the trip, without going out to dinner. Everett watched his wife as she slept so soundly, and he thought of how much he loved her. He leaned over and kissed her on the lips. He wondered how their Aunt Ny Li Tu could have possibly known how right they were for each other without being able to see into the future.

At noontime in Delaware, at the compound of Moses Cribb, Canyon Mesa looked up from his work in the laboratory at the child he had named Tomorrow. Her blond hair was reflecting the sunlight from the window, giving the appearance of a halo around her head. That, coupled with her pale skin, made her look like an angel incarnate. She sat in her playpen, amusing herself by playing with her toes and making the sounds that babies make when they are content. He walked over to her and picked her up. She smiled at him with a broad grin that covered her whole face, and he kissed her before putting her back in the playpen. Her eyes followed him back to his lab table, her stare penetrating his being. He would have to work faster to find the cure. His daughter, as he now referred to her, needed a mother. Unlike his cousins, Canyon Mesa did not feel the need for a lover; his love had always been his work. But Tomorrow needed a mother, and he needed a mother for Tomorrow. He would discuss it with his aunt Ny Li Tu. "Yes," he thought to himself, "I will put the matter in her capable hands." He looked over at Tomorrow and said to her, "We are going to get a woman to be your mother and my wife."

Tomorrow said something in baby talk, as if in response.

He said to her, as if she could understand, "Don't worry, you will like her. Aunt Ny Li Tu will pick the best one available for us. She will know her as soon as she sees her. She always does."

Berlin, Germany, two days later. The sun had just begun to set. Everett Jr., and Marion Matilda had been searching the town, door to door, with the help of the local authorities. They hoped to find a living relative of the baby, Tomorrow, and they had a lead which they were checking on before calling it a day. Greta Fraun was a twenty-one year old German girl whose parents had been lost during the Extermination Campaign. She was living in a shelter for the homeless in a suburban area of Berlin, and she attended the Free University in Berlin. That was one of the conditions for receiving food and shelter from the State. She was summoned to meet with them before dinner.

Marion Matilda and Everett Jr. watched as the tall, thin girl with long, golden hair wrapped in two braids around her head walk into the room. Dressed in a plain skirt and blouse of faded blue and brown, she had the palest skin Marion Matilda had ever seen. The melancholy expression on Greta's face told Marion Matilda just how alone

Greta was in the world. She told Greta that she was to be their guest for dinner that evening. The child did not question the order, mainly because of the authoritative tone in Marion Matilda's voice. She assumed the visit was important.

"I have nothing other than the clothes on my back," she responded, "Will we be dining out in public?"

"Yes," answered Marion Matilda, "but I have the proper attire for you to wear."

Greta stared at the darker-complexioned woman for a few seconds and then said, "I am ready when you are."

Everett pulled his wife aside and asked, "Why are we taking her with us?"

"Everett, I have a strange feeling she is why we are here," Marion Matilda replied. He accepted the answer without further discussion.

Greta spoke English without a German accent and Marion Matilda was impressed with her vocabulary. She had Everett request a single room for Greta to stay in, and it adjoined their suite in the hotel. Marion Matilda laid out the clothing Greta would wear while Greta bathed before dinner. When they returned to collect her, it was as if she had gone through a metamorphosis. Greta looked absolutely beautiful in the evening attire. Everett could not take his eyes off of her. He kept stammering, and stumbling over his words.

"Everett, take our arms and escort us to the dining room, please," Marion Matilda finally said. She questioned Greta extensively during and after the meal while Everett stared at her all evening and refilled her water glass each time she took a sip, much to his wife's annoyance. Greta, who hadn't acquired the attention of a man in quite awhile, was pleased. But she did not want to upset Marion Matilda by acknowledging her husband's fascination. Marion Matilda informed Greta that arrangements were being made for her to return with them to the United States in a few days.

"Am I your prisoner?" she asked Marion Matilda.

"While it is true that you don't have a choice about going," Marion Matilda replied with a disarming smile, "I can assure you that you are not a prisoner." Greta was pleased with the answer. She explained that she had no reason to stay in Germany, and that she would be happy to have them as her friends.

The next day they went shopping for Greta's wardrobe to wear in the States. Greta was not sure of what the future held for her, but she was not afraid to face it with her newfound friends by her side. Everett reported the chain of events to Dakota Moon, by videophone, and received their new assignment from him. They were to become the bodyguards of Greta Fraun, and live with her in the compound of Moses Cribb.

Everett, Marion Matilda, and Greta Fraun were met at the airport by Canyon Mesa and Tomorrow. They were driven back to compound in one of the limousines by a chauffeur bodyguard from the security team. Canyon Mesa greeted his cousins with hugs and kisses as he always had done from childhood. Marion Matilda took Tomorrow from him, and kissing her, explaining that they had just come back from the country of her birth. Tomorrow responded in the sounds that all babies make. It was as if she understood what was being said. The three cousins laughed, and joked about the possibility that she did. Greta stood there staring at the child in amazement. The child resembled her baby sister who was lost, along with their parents, during the Extermination Campaign.

Canyon Mesa looked at Greta for the first time.

He stood motionless as their eyes met, waiting for one of his cousins to introduce them formally. Marion Matilda took Canyon Mesa by the hand and walked him over to Greta, introducing him as her cousin, and the child, Tomorrow, as his adopted daughter from Germany.

Greta fumbled for the right words, and finally said, "pleased to meet you, Canyon." She left off his middle name as if she had always called him, simply, Canyon.

He responded by kissing her hand and saying, with as much familiarity as she had shown, "Greta, you are as beautiful as I anticipated."

She blushed, bringing more color to her face than any of them had ever seen. Marion Matilda could see the mutual physical attraction instantly. Greta tore her eyes away from Canyon Mesa, for fear of seeming too bold, and asked Marion Matilda if she could hold the baby. The movement broke Canyon Mesa's trance-like state, bringing him back from the world of infatuation created by his desire to sweep Greta off her feet and tell her that he wanted to marry her with or without Aunt Ny Li Tu's blessing.

Greta held Tomorrow with the same love and care that she had used while holding her baby sister. Canyon Mesa noticed the tenderness and loved her even more. She held the baby in her lap during the ride home to the compound. Ny Li Tu watched the limousine from her bedroom window as it moved up to the driveway that led to the front door. She observed the love that Everett displayed for Marion Matilda, taking her hand as she got out of the car after the chauffeur had opened the door. She watched Canyon Mesa as he assisted Greta from the car as she carried Tomorrow in her arms. He appeared to be far more at ease with Greta holding the baby than he was with anyone else.

The servants went out to greet them, and took their luggage from the limousine to the guest rooms in the house. Ny Li Tu had announced the week before which rooms the guests were to stay in. The servants then, had their instructions long before their arrival. They were directed to the library by the butler, there they awaited Ny Li Tu. She always met her houseguests in the library before allowing them to go to their rooms. It was almost like a ritual.

Greta was fascinated by the size of the compound and the mansion. It seemed as large as the University she had attended in Berlin. She looked at the ostentatious display of wealth that the compound and mansion represented, and wondered how she fit into the scheme of things. She had revealed everything about herself, but she knew virtually nothing about her benefactors. Instinctively, she knew they meant her no harm. She was sitting there, with the baby in her arms, when Ny Li Tu appeared. A little Oriental woman, whose aura radiated self-confidence and competence, entered the room. Greta had seen pictures of her in magazines, but had never dreamed of being in her presence. She rose to her feet, along with the others, not knowing if she should bow, or even how to address her, if she were spoken to.

Ny Li Tu smiled and the others seemed relieved. It was as if a burden of anticipation had been lifted from their shoulders. She walked over and acknowledged each of them with a kiss and a few words of encouragement about how they were conducting their careers. She stopped in front of Greta and Tomorrow.

"The child has grown since I last saw her," she said without looking at Canyon Mesa, but staring directly into Greta's eyes.

Canyon Mesa answered, "Yes, Aunt Ny Li Tu."

Then, understanding what was meant by the statement, he added, "We work all day and most of the night in the laboratory. We don't get to see many people."

"Am I now considered just one of the many people around here, my nephew?" She turned to see his face as she spoke.

"Heavens no, Aunt Ny Li Tu. I never meant it like that," he replied.

She let him off the hook by returning her attention to Greta, saying, "Greta Fraun, I presume?"

"Yes, Frau Ny Li Tu," Greta answered, not really knowing how to address her properly. She held the baby closer, as if to shield herself from a verbal assault.

Ny Li Tu looked her in the eyes, this time with less intimidation, and said, "You will be a welcome addition to this family. There are not enough women." Ny Li Tu winked at Greta, as if they had shared a private quip that no one else in the room understood. She turned and walked toward the door. Stopping, she turned and said to the women, "I expect you all to join me for dinner every evening at six. We dress for dinner." She left the room with the same grace and eloquence that she had entered it.

Canyon Mesa was so pleased that he could hardly contain himself. Aunt Ny Li Tu had just approved of Greta. Everett and Marion Matilda were ecstatic. Greta was the only one who did not understand the implication of what had happened between them and the old matriarch. When Ny Li Tu was home all the family members at the compound dined with her at the mansion, in the great dining hall. They were expected every evening at six o'clock sharp, dressed in formal attire. Tonight was special because Moses was home for the first time in months.

As usual, Moses sat at one end of the long table, and Ny Li Tu at the other. Magee and Mai Lee, Soo Sing and Lin Lee, Everett and Marion Matilda, Canyon Mesa, Tomorrow and Greta Fraun filled the other spaces. Moses had not seen Tomorrow since the last time he was home. He noted, in general conversation, how beautiful she was, and how fast she was growing. The others agreed, commenting on how nice it was to have a child in the compound again after so many years. He then turned his attention toward Greta. Moses asked if she enjoyed her trip to the States and her stay at the compound, and if she and Canyon Mesa had started working together in the laboratory, all in the same breath.

She replied "yes," to all three questions collectively.

He then looked at Canyon Mesa, and said, "I understand from the Chairman of the Board of Infectious Diseases that you brought Greta into the country without their stamp of approval, as you did Tomorrow."

"I spoke to those bureaucratic imbeciles by videophone six times in twenty-four hours. If I had left it up to them, neither of my wards would be here until next year," replied Canyon Mesa.

Moses's voice remained even toned, as he spoke to his nephew, "Doctor Helmsmitz is one of the world's leading scientists. I would not have appointed him to that position if he was not. I realize that you don't always agree with the theories of his team, but he is still in charge of finding a cure for the Disease Without a Name. I expect you to treat his authority with more respect. I expect it, despite the fact you are the President's son."

"I have never used that fact as a weapon, Uncle Moses. You know that my training prevents that. I am my own man. I have my own opinions and theories. One of them is that the Doctor is a pompous ass," said Canyon Mesa. Moses smiled, not the least upset by his nephew's choice of words. None of the other children would have dared speak to him in this tone of voice. It was obvious that Canyon Mesa was a favorite.

Sensing the tension of the other family members, the smile faded from Moses's face as he looked around the table. "Your father and I want you to accept a position on the Board of Infectious Diseases. Your father wants you to think it over. In a year or two, who knows, maybe you will be Chairman."

Canyon Mesa looked at him squarely, "I thought that was an appointment for life."

"Yes, it is," Moses responded, without the slightest display of emotion. It was apparent to everyone at the table that Canyon Mesa's acceptance of this offer would sign Helmsmitz's death warrant; everyone except Greta, who did not yet understand the barbarous, ruthless, political practices of her American benefactors.

The next morning, in the laboratory, Canyon Mesa became aware of Greta's suspicions that Tomorrow was her baby sister, Helga. She showed him pictures of the child who was presumed to have died, eight months before, in the Extermination Campaign. The blood work that Canyon Mesa did on Greta proved that she, like Tomorrow, was immune to the Germs. Canyon Mesa was sure the blood of his two wards was the key to the cure. He would run two more tests in order to be sure.

Greta loved working with Canyon and Tomorrow. She felt like she had regained her family. They spent all of their time together, just the three of them. Canyon, as she called Canyon Mesa, treated her like she was the only woman on the face of the earth. He made it easy for her to fall in love with him; he truly understood how to treat a woman. He made Greta feel special and no man had ever made her feel that way before. She had several courtships prior to the loss of her family, but those relationships were nothing like the one she shared with Canyon. He was a romantic. He loved the feeling of being in love, and Greta loved being loved by him.

Canyon ran the last two tests, using blood samples from Greta and Tomorrow. He injected the blood samples into a tube containing the isolated Germs and the Germs died. He had the vaccination. He tested the vaccination on an infected ape. The ape died. He tried again, this time vaccinating another ape first, then infected him with the disease. The ape was immune. He had found the cure. He, Greta and Tomorrow. He could not have done it without them.

Canyon Mesa was the first human subject. After vaccination, he exposed himself to the Germs. He was immune. He named the cure I.W.A.N., the Innoculation Without a Name. During the next thirty days, orders were sent for the Ghost Shadows and their families to report to the compound of Moses Cribb. They came for the innoculation, the adoption of Tomorrow, and the Wedding Ceremony of Canyon Mesa and Greta Fraun. It was one day before Canyon Mesa's twenty-fifth birthday.

"Marriages are the pacts that form alliances and secure the World's Peace."

Ny Li Tu

Chapter Thirty-one

Alliances

In the year 2022, the dreaded Disease Without a Name was under control. The cure, I.W.A.N., was carefully administered to the world's population by the Board of Infectious Diseases, led by Dr. Helmsmitz. His power had increased immensely since the cure was discovered. He used his position as Chairman of the Board of Infectious Diseases to provide the cure to nations who could pay the price. The third-world nations then, continued to die at the same rate as they did prior to the discovery of the cure. Helmsmitz had successfully carried on his enterprise without the knowledge of the government, and the data and reports had been altered to keep his secret.

The powerful Board of Infectious Diseases was now completely under his unscrupulous control. Dr. Helmsmitz fought the appointment of Canyon Mesa Stone to the Board on the basis of his youth and lack of administrative experience. President Maxwell Mason Stone was furious about the Board's opposition to his son and wanted to eliminate Dr. Helmsmitz. The only thing that prevented him from doing so was the prudent advice of the Vice President, Moses Cribb. Cribb believed that such a move would hurt them at the polls in the next election. The people were not sure that there wasn't something un-American about the way they had maintained control of the Oval Office. Dr. Helmsmitz could not be disposed of in the usual manner, but he would be disposed of.

Secret orders were dispatched to the office of Dakota Moon, but he was away on vacation in Florida, visiting his wife Cheyenne on the reservation. Unhappy about the amount of time that he spent away from home, Cheyenne claimed she did not see enough of her husband, or her son, since they had become indispensable to the government. She claimed this, even though it was her choice not to leave the reservation to live in Washington, D.C. at her husband's side.

Dakota Moon had gone to the reservation to reconcile with her. He explained to the President that he would not allow his work to interfere with his marriage. It was agreed that his son, Cheyenne's, Dakota Moon, would temporarily fill his position, while he was away. They agreed that the experience for the heir apparent would be of consequential significance to his career. Cheyenne's Dakota Moon would dispose of Doctor Helmsmitz, discreetly and expediently.

Cheyenne's Dakota Moon contacted his father, by a secret coded message, at the reservation in Florida to seek his advice on the mission. His father sent the messenger back with an answer in code. It said simply, "Incapacitated is as good as dead." The younger Moon smiled as he read the coded message from his father. Dakota Moon had been essential in the series of assassinations that brought Stone and Cribb to power in the late 1970s. His advice, short and explicit, would be followed.

Two weeks before, following a lead from an informant inside the Bureau of Infectious Diseases, Cheyenne's Dakota Moon sent his cousin, Ali Khan, to audit the information put out by the Bureau's computers. As suspected, it had been altered. The information about Doctor Helmsmitz selling the I.W.A.N. serum was confirmed by the twins, Roman Micheal and Mica Mark, upon their return from South America. They had found that people were still dying from the dreaded disease because they could not afford to buy the cure.

Cheyenne's Dakota Moon had made his case against the doctor. He would now save the taxpayers the expense of a prolonged trial. He had Canyon Mesa mix a concoction of undetectable poisons that would leave the man in a coma. The Doctor would die, but not immediately. He did not want to expose the Doctor publicly—that would give the C.I.A. a motive. The Doctor's death would have to appear to be of natural causes, a direct result of the coma. He would then be given a State Funeral and buried as a National Hero. Six months later, Doctor Helmsmitz fell into a deep sleep, a coma from which he never returned. Canyon Mesa was appointed to the Board of Infectious Diseases. After his appointment, several other members fell sick and died, or resigned. It seemed that whatever Doctor Helmsmitz had died of, was contagious and had infected his closest friends on the Board.

Roman Micheal and Mica Mark Magee, while on their mission in South America, had stayed in Brazil with friends of Ny Li Tu and Moses Cribb. They were joined in Brazil by Tyler Samuel, and together, they recruited and trained several operatives for the C.I.A.. One of the operatives was Pedro Salvestia—a medical student in his last year at University. He was from a prominent Brazilian family of fourteen children, thirteen of which were female.

"The most beautiful girls on the face of the earth," Roman Micheal had said. Three of the dark-haired beauties were triplets. Ny Li Tu had chosen them as possible mates for Roman Micheal, Mica Mark and Tyler Samuel when they were twelve years old. Now they had completed college and were working for the Brazilian government as interpreters.

The Salvestia triplets were going to meet the boys, for the first time, at dinner that night, chaperoned by their family. Ny Li Tu had arranged the dinner party, at the Rio De Janeiro Hilton, four months before, making reservations to stay for the week. She came specifically to work out the details of the marriage arrangements. The dining room was arranged like a wedding reception hall. The Salvestia girls, Brillante, Brillantez and Brillosa, sat on the dais with Roman Micheal, Mica Mark, and Tyler Samuel. Since the girls were identical, each boy took the first vacant seat next to a girl on the dais. Tyler Samuel was a little nervous as he introduced himself to Brillosa. He was the only one on the dais who did not look like someone else. But the smile on Brillosa's face told him that she was pleased with the seating arrangement. Roman Micheal sat next to Brillante, and Mica Mark sat next to Brillantez. The boys danced with the girls while dinner was served.

Ny Li Tu talked to the girls' parents, who were seated at her table, about how soon the girls could come to the United States and wed the boys. The Salvestias wanted the girls to be wed in Brazil, in a church ceremony, so all of their family and friends could attend. The girls would be moving so far from home, the likelihood of seeing them frequently was remote. But this posed a security risk for Ny Li Tu. The entire family would be together, under one roof, on foreign soil, and at the mercy of the Brazilian government's security. Ny Li Tu glanced over at her nephews and the triplets. They seemed to be getting along splendidly. She accepted the conditions, knowing that Cheyenne's Dakota Moon would not go along with the plan unless he took charge of the security measures. The date was set.

Since the children would not see each other again until then, they got acquainted, and dined and danced until dawn. Before the month's end, they had trained their future brother-in-law and two other operatives as moles.

Cheyenne's Dakota Moon did not need a large number of agents; he only needed them to be well-trained, faithful, and family. He sent Juan Pablo and George Lee Jr. to Oman. They would stay with the Sultan and his family, a long time friend of Ny Li Tu and Moses Cribb. The Sultan had seven daughters, and he wanted the two youngest married into the family in order to solidify his alliance with the United States. The Sultan was one of the wealthiest men on earth, but he did not have an army strong enough to protect him and his small country. In the past, he had used mercenaries, but in these times there were none to be trusted. He hoped to use the beauty of his daughters to attract the strength of Ny Li Tu's family through an alliance of marriage. He offered to make her nephews kings. Recognizing the window of opportunity, she moved quickly to unite the families. The ceremonies were to be in Brazil. All five boys would be married at the same time.

The Sultan insisted on bearing the entire cost of the weddings. However, he wanted Juan Pablo and George Lee Jr. to marry his daughters in an Islamic ceremony first, and then marry them again in a Christian ceremony in Brazil. Ny Li Tu did not think this was too much to ask, and she agreed without hesitation. Juan Pablo married the nineteen year old beauty, Arabesque, and George Lee married Jasmine, the twenty year old beauty. The marriages would not be consummated until the second ceremony in Brazil. The boys returned home to await the second ceremony. Ny Li Tu had again made excellent choices. Cheyenne's Dakota Moon dispatched ten soldiers of the Special Force of Five Thousand to train the Sultan's army and await the arrival of their new commanders.

Fifty percent of the Rio De Janeiro Hilton Hotel was reserved for the Wedding Party, their guests and the security teams. Regular service to their floors was cut off by the management. The Sultan supplied the servants and the service. Dakota Moon brought in one hundred soldiers of the Special Force of Five Thousand, despite the objection of the Brazilian government, to provide security. The Diplomatic Corps would smooth the ruffled feathers after the wedding. All the security teams, the Wedding Party, and the wedding guests arrived on Friday morning and occupied the reserved floors. The wedding took place on Saturday at noon. The reception took place Saturday evening, and went on until Sunday morning. Everyone was checked out of the hotel by six p.m. Sunday evening, and were on their way back to wherever they came from. It worked like a well-planned attack. The brides and grooms went on a four week honeymoon cruise, to secret locations, without the benefit of a security team. The Sultan gave an undisclosed amount of money to the Brazilian government. And the Brazilian government, in response, denied that any diplomatic problems had arisen during the invasion of their country by Cheyenne's Dakota Moon and the Special Force of Five Thousand.

"All of Islam mourned his death"
Juan Pablo

Chapter Thirty-two

The Kings of Oman

In the year 2025, the oil rich Eastern nations had formed an alliance called United Oriental Petroleum, and they had used the profits from their enterprise to raise large armies. They were held in check by the strongest member of their Alliance, the Sultan of Oman. The Sultan has gained a tremendous amount of power among the Eastern Nations since his daughters had married into the family of Ny Li Tu. People feared his sons-in-law, and they did nothing to provoke their anger. The Sultan's army was small, but he had the support of the Two Moons, as Dakota and his son were referred to in the Near East. The Two Moons had provided the Sultan's Army with ten soldiers from the Special Force of Five Thousand. This alone could devastate the combined forces of United Oriental Petroleum.

The Eastern nations knew this, but they did not admit it willingly. Their armies were hyped on religious fervor, and were told they could not lose if the Jihad were to begin. They had secretly agreed not to start the Jihad until the Sultan died, and his infidel sons-in-law came to power. Juan Pablo and George Lee Jr. had already made plans to use the Germs to wipe the United Oriental Petroleum Armies from the face of the earth on the day their father-in-law, the Sultan, died.

Ali Khan had been dating an American girl of Greek descent for the past year. The girl's name was Maria Theopopulous, and he had met her during the Extermination Campaign. She was a member of the Special Force of Five Thousand, chosen by Elizabeth Susan, to go to Europe. They had become friends, and now they were lovers. They had violated the family code of no premarital sex, and Ny Li Tu was not pleased with them. She searched Maria's medical records and found that she was four months pregnant. Ny Li Tu called the couple to the compound and confronted them with this knowledge. They claimed that they were in love, and that one thing had led to another. They had no intention of bringing shame to their families. Ny Li Tu told them their secret was safe with her, and that she would arrange a wedding for them, in two weeks time. The baby would be passed off as a premature delivery.

Cheyenne's Dakota Moon had signed the orders for Maria's leave of absence from the Special Force of Five Thousand as soon as he read the medical report. It was he who had advised Ny Li Tu of Ali Khan's situation. He did not think it was the worst thing that could have happened. Maria Theopopulous was a damn good soldier and comrade-in-arms. As for a baby, the family had accepted Canyon Mesa's baby, Tomorrow, so why not Ali Khan's? He already knew the answer. They would, but they wanted him married. It was their way of life. They did not condone premarital sex. However, Ali Khan was one of them, and they would forgive him, or any of their children, because they loved them.

Ali Khan and Maria Theopopulous were married in a military ceremony in the chapel at the Academy. The entire family witnessed the ceremony, and the reception was held at the compound of Moses Cribb. Afterwards, the newlyweds honeymooned in Greece, and they did not return until the birth of their baby, a boy they named

Millennium.

On the seventh day of February, 2026, at 9:53 a.m., the Sultan of Oman died. All of Islam mourned his death. At twelve noon, the armies of the United Oriental Petroleum began the Jihad. They stormed across the borders of Oman like the desert wind, in tanks, by air, and on foot. They came by the hundreds of thousands to slay the new kings and queens of Oman. Juan Pablo, George Lee Jr., and the ten soldiers of the Special Force of Five Thousand met them on the desert flats at the Oasis of Allah. Flying over the heads of the United Oriental Petroleum Armies, they fired their germ grenades into the midst of the attacking troops. The enemy fled in fear of the Germs, stampeding, and trampling each other into the sand. Many dropped their weapons and tried to surrender, as their comrades lay dying in the desert sand. The Germs spread and killed everyone in their path.

The bodies of the dead enemy lay strewn across the Desert of Oman. All who had dared to come to battle were devastated by the Germs and the heat of the Sun. All of Islam mourned their death. In the year 2027, Ny Li Tu expanded the interest of the family businesses into oil, founding Oman Petroleum Enterprises Unlimited. The President of Oman Petroleum Enterprises Unlimited was George Lee Jr., one of the Kings of Oman.

*"Unity is the solution when fight-
ing a common enemy."*
George Lee Jr.

Chapter Thirty-three

The Common Enemy

By the year 2028, the Ozone Layer no longer protected the earth. People had to wear jumpsuits
made of a plastic to reflect the harmful rays of the
sun. The jumpsuit, complete with hood, gloves, and
sun glasses, covered the identity of the wearer. It
was manufactured by one of Ny Li Tu's companies. Racial discrimination was a thing of the past,
since interracial marriages had homogenized the
races. This, and the jumpsuit, made it impossible
to distinguish a man by his ethnic origin. The sun
was now the common enemy. Third World peoples
had retreated back to caves to hide from the deadly
rays of the sun. They walked the earth by night,
like vampires foraging for food in the dark. In some
places, cannibalism and self-preservation were
synonymous.

The civilized world united to find a way to protect itself from the rays of the sun. The jumpsuit
was a temporary solution, like the sun domes being constructed over every major city in the world.
The families of the Ghost Shadows had come to
live in the compound of Moses Cribb, and a dome
was constructed over it. It was like living in a bubble. Food was scarce. The country had returned to
the use of ration cards, and the Ration Card System had created a nationwide black market. Organized crime returned, but the government did
not fight it. All government resources were put to-
wards fighting the sun.

Everett Jr., Marion Matilda, Ali Khan, Elizabeth Susan, and Canyon Mesa were collaborating in an effort to save the earth. The climate-controlled environment under the bubble was like Camelot for the families of the Ghost Shadows. Although they were well aware of the harsh conditions of the world outside of the dome, they did not feel guilty about the comfort they had created in the compound. Their family had taken advantage of the opportunities the war had presented. To the victor go the spoils. All they had acquired was at the risk of their own lives. They had earned it and would defend the right to keep it for the generations of offspring that would follow. It was imperative that the family survive in these times of peril. The fate of the world depended on them.

Canyon Mesa, Greta and Tomorrow were in their suite of rooms on the second floor of the third wing in the mansion. Tomorrow had just gone to sleep. Greta had read her a few pages out of an old story book Ny Li Tu had used to read to Rameses when he was a little boy.

"She is asleep," said Greta, in a voice just above a whisper. Canyon lay naked on the bed, waiting for her to return from Tomorrow's room. Greta slipped out of her negligee and sat down on the bed next to him. They always slept in the nude. Canyon loved the feel of Greta's naked body against his at night. She slept in an 'S' shape with her back to him, as if she was sitting in his lap.

Greta picked up a bottle of body lotion from the night stand beside the bed. Canyon rolled onto his stomach so she could massage the lotion into his back. Greta's hands and fingers worked wonders on Canyon's tight muscles. First, she worked the muscles of his neck and shoulders, then she massaged his back, running her fingers along the vertebrae. She kneaded the muscles of his buttocks, and then moved down to the back of his thighs, and on to his calves. He rolled onto his back. She gently rubbed the lotion over his chest, and down the front of his body. She massaged the soles of his feet, using a method unfamiliar to Canyon. It left his entire body feeling weightless, like he was floating in space.

She straddled his legs, taking his penis in her hand, and stroking him until it began to pulsate to the rhythm of his heart beat. She then put his long, thick penis into her mouth, moving her tongue along the shaft as she drew it deeper down her throat. She sucked on him, easing off each time she thought he would ejaculate. Finally, she moved her body up and slipped his penis into her vagina, which was lubricated in the anticipation of his erect penis inside of her. She flipped her long, blond hair over the top of his head and stuck her tongue deep into his mouth as she moved her hips in an up and down motion until he came in a heated rush that left him spent and exhausted. He was asleep by the time she returned from the bathroom with a wet washcloth to clean him up. She kissed him as he slept and then settled her body into their favorite sleeping position. There, in the serene moonlit darkness of the bedroom, wearing only a smile, she closed her eyes and enjoyed the prospect of finding Canyon in her dreams.

It was seven months into the year 2028. On the fifth day of the month, Ali Khan returned from Greece with his family, Maria and Millennium. They occupied a three bedroom suite on the second floor of the third wing in the mansion, next to Canyon Mesa, Greta, and Tomorrow. Ny Li Tu wanted all of the third generation of children to be in the same wing of the mansion. The third wing had a nursery room on the first floor, with a nanny living in a room just off of it. The remaining rooms in the third wing would remain vacant until the other girls started their families.

Ali Khan and Canyon Mesa returned from the laboratory to the mansion in order to dress for dinner. They had two hours before they were expected in the dining room. Ali Khan had designed a software program to determine the components of the Ozone Layer and their exact proportions. With the help of this new program, he hoped to make a replacement layer. Each member of the family worked in their area of expertise and discussed their theories at the end of each week.

Maria had run Ali's bath water, and was waiting in the room for him. The baby, Millennium, was with the nanny. She stepped into the tub just as Ali Khan came through the door. He heard her in the bathroom, soaking in the water, and decided to sneak up on her quietly. He covered her mouth with his hand, and grabbed her around the waist, but she managed to get her arm around his neck, and flip him into the bathtub fully clothed. She held his head under the water for thirty seconds before letting him go. Then in one swift motion she heaved him over the side of the bathtub. Finally looking down on him, she said, "Ali, I didn't know it was you! I thought you were a rapist."

Ali lay there dripping wet with a smile across his face, and said, "I was just testing your reflexes. You were several seconds late countering, so you are lucky it was me. There is no telling what would have happened if I had been the enemy."

"Sweetheart, if you were the enemy, there is only one thing that would be certain; you would not be able to tell anyone what happened," she said, laughing between each syllable. She was offering him her hand to help him up when they heard a knock on the door.

"Mister Ali, Misses Maria, is everything all right in there? I heard a loud noise, and there is water leaking from your bathroom to the room down-stairs." Ali Khan answered the door with his clothes still wet.

"The bathtub ran over. My wife is mopping up the water as we speak," he said. The servant looked at him, craning his neck to see past him, and asked if he could be of any help. Seeing the mop and pail in the servant's hand, Ali Khan, under protest by the servant, took the mop and pail and closed the door in his face.

"Really Mister Ali, this is not a job that you or your wife should be doing," protested the servant.

"Thank you," Ali Khan said through the closed door. His voice trailing off as he went into the bath-room. "We will be all right."

Ali Khan removed his wet clothes while Maria mopped the bathroom floor and washed the bath-tub so he could shower. Maria was in the nude, and bent over washing the bathtub when Ali Khan came back into the bathroom. She heard him, but did not turn around to acknowledge his presence. He kissed her shoulders and down her back. He kissed the cheeks of her buttocks while inserting two of his fingers into her vagina. Then he pulled back her long, black hair until her neck arched, and gently bit her neck. And at the same time, Ali Khan rubbed her breast in a circular motion with his free hand. Maria leaned forward to give him the position he needed to enter her from behind. He slid his penis into her vagina, using short strokes to allow the vagina to lubricate. They sel-dom used this position in their lovemaking because Maria's excitement caused her to climax faster than usual. He thrust his penis into her vagina, as far as it would allow, and came along with her. They remained in that position until his penis went limp. She turned her head to meet his lips, kissed him briefly, and whispered in his ear.

"We are going to be late. Let's get moving, sweetheart."

He turned the shower on to rinse off. They dressed quickly, and went downstairs to the dining room. The nanny had already brought Millennium to the table and he was sitting in his high chair. His grandmother, Lin Lee, was talking to Millennium about the front tooth he was cutting when Maria and Ali entered the room. Lin Lee greeted her son with a kiss. She gave Maria a dry smile, and said, "I understand you let the bathtub run over?". Lin Lee could not understand how Maria always caused her son to be late for dinner. She intended to have a heart to heart talk with her in private one day. Maria did not respond. She sat in the chair that her husband had just pulled out for her, smoothed down Millennium's bib, and smiled at Ali who had said nothing in her defense.

"Thank you for not blowing up at my mother," he said to Maria later that evening.

"Don't worry, Sweetheart," she responded, "someday she is going to forgive me for taking your virginity."

"Touché, my love," Ali Khan answered, kissing her tenderly on the side of her mouth.

The work of replenishing the components of the Ozone Layer proved to be a difficult undertaking. The last areas of rain forest had been gone since the late 1990's; all were lost to fire and progress. But on the tenth day of the ninth month, in the year of 2028, a plan of action was decided upon during a weekly discussion of the current theories at the Cribb compound. Ozone is an allotropic form of oxygen, formed when a silent, electrical discharge passes through oxygen. As a result, it is present in minute quantities in the atmosphere, owing to the occurrence of electric storms. It was agreed that

they would build giant lightening rods where the
rain forests used to be. This would attract electrical storms, and form the gases of the Ozone Layer.
The lightening rods would take a year to install.
They estimated the process would take ten years
to complete.

On the sixth day of the tenth month, in the
year 2028, the order of priorities had changed
again. Cheyenne's Dakota Moon had been ordered
to eliminate the Black Marketeers. They had become a thorn in the President's side. Crime was a
major campaign issue, and he could not risk the
upcoming election. This would be the last campaign for Stone and Cribb. They would have to
spend the next four years grooming Rameses Cribb
and Tyler Samuel Turner for the Oval Office. And
that was their first priority.

On the tenth day of the eleventh month, in the
year 2028, the black market and organized crime
were eliminated three days before the elections.
Because of its priority, Cheyenne's Dakota Moon
personally took charge of the mission. Rameses,
Tyler Samuel and five of soldiers of the Special Force
of Five Thousand comprised his strike force. The
mission was easier than it sounded. They operated in the open without fear of government inter-
vention. The election was won by a landslide; Stone
and Cribb had a mandate to maintain the world
order. The President appointed Rameses and Tyler
Samuel to the Cabinet. Rameses was appointed
Secretary of State, Tyler Samuel, Secretary of the
Treasury, and Canyon Mesa was appointed Chairman of the Board of Infectious Diseases. Once
again, Stone and Cribb had set the stage for the
continuance of their control of the world order, and
the nations of the civilized world applauded.

"Of all the lessons that you learn in life, none are more valuable than the ones you make use of"
George Lee Jr.

Chapter Thirty-four

The Training

The year was 2029. Juan Pablo and Arabesque were in the Royal Bed Chamber of the Palace in Oman. George Lee Jr. and Jasmine were at the compound of Moses Cribb, under the safety of the Dome. They had agreed to live in Oman, for six month intervals, rotating the Royal Families between Oman and the compound. A Dome was being erected over the Royal City, and when completed, the city would be invulnerable to an assault from external forces. The Royal Families would then rule jointly and simultaneously.

There was a guard outside the door of the royal bed chamber. He was not a member of the Force of Five Thousand. He wore the uniform of the Palace Guard and was trained by them. Beneath it, he wore a suit of Body Armor. These guards were formidable opponents for anyone who chose to challenge the Throne of Oman. Their loyalty to the Throne was unquestionable, but it remained untested. The lives of the Royal Families were in the hands of those few men, and they guarded their charges with a savage jealousy. The palace grounds were protected from intrusion by a curfew which was in effect every evening after dark. The penalty for trespassing was death, without benefit of trial or defense.

The desert was cool that night, considering the temperature had been 155 degrees before the sun had set. It was only 98 degrees now. Everything

that had once happened in the day, now took place
at night. The extreme heat from the sun had
changed the population, in this part of the world,
into nocturnal beings. The night air carried the
sounds of the merchants and the people trading at
the bazaar three miles away.

Arabesque lay naked under the veils covering
the bed where she and Juan Pablo slept. Without
the dome, there was no climate control, and eunuchs fanned the room. They took little notice of
the royal couple. Juan Pablo began to lick the nipples of Arabesque's firm, little breasts. With long
strokes of his tongue, he continued down to her
stomach. The sounds of her pleasure broke the
silence, and her legs parted as his head approached
the pubic area between her thighs. He inserted his
tongue into her vagina, licking the drops of moisture she began to secrete as her legs tightened
around his head. He cupped her buttocks in his
large hands, and started to move his head up and
down between her legs, in search of more. She
opened her legs again, allowing him the movement
he needed to regain access to his quest. He used
his strong hands to hold her legs apart, as she
thrashed about wildly when he thrust his tongue
deeper and deeper, letting up only to lick away the
emitted drops of moisture from the lips of her vagina. In the heat of passion, she seized his head
and shoved it toward the thrust of her pelvis. He
broke her grip just in time to draw a breath and
continue the pursuit of their pleasure. She reached
a climax that left her spent. She spoke to him un-
intelligibly, in the long forgotten Arabic dialect of a
lost tribe in the deep desert.

Despite the heat, she slept close to him that
night. The sweat from their bodies left the bed wet,
and they awoke in a pool of water. The eunuchs
bathed them in cool water taken from the bathing

pool, and massaged their bodies with perfume and myrrh, brought from a land once called Persia. Members of the Palace Guard entered their chambers to be sure their charges had arisen. The guards prostrated themselves before their masters, thanking Allah for giving their Lords another sunrise. Juan Pablo had little tolerance for this God. He allowed his wife her deity, as King Solomon had done, and he prayed that her decision would be a wise one.

Since the defeat of United Oriental Petroleum, all of the desert nations of the Middle East bowed at his feet. The oil from these nations was sold to, and refined by, Oman Petroleum Enterprises Unlimited, the company controlled by Ny Li Tu and George Lee Jr., the other King of Oman. As a direct result of the loss of the Jihad, the children of Allah now enriched the coffers of the infidels. This monopoly was created by the family business of Ny Li Tu. It was for this reason that no matter how low they bowed, they would always be the enemy. Juan Pablo would always remember that; his training ensured it.

In his capacity as President of Oman Petroleum Enterprises Unlimited, George Lee Jr. traveled to the land of Syria to attend a summit meeting of the leaders of the oil producing nations. He left his wife, Jasmine, at the compound, under the safety of the Dome. She was three months pregnant, and he did not want to risk the life of the unborn child. She reluctantly agreed to stay behind. He travelled without a bodyguard, and for the first time in years, without wearing his Body Armor. After kissing Jasmine good-bye at the door to their suite of rooms at the mansion, he was driven to the airport by one of the chauffeurs. He boarded the plane armed with the knowledge of who he was and why he was going, and with the training he had received as a

youngster from Master Soo Sing Wong. He knew
he would not need more. He was one of the Kings
of Oman, tested in battle, and trained to live forever.

As the plane landed, a chill ran down his spine.
It was as if he had been touched by the hand of
death; only death could have been that cold. He
knew that if he could die, and he was not sure that
he could not, he would come close to his death
before this trip was over. At the airport, he was
met by a Syrian bodyguard who drove him to the
summit meeting. The bodyguard kept glancing at
him in the rear view mirror as he drove, but George
Lee Jr. shrugged it off, telling himself it was paranoia. The bodyguard got out of the car and opened
the door for him, and another Syrian bodyguard
escorted him to the conference room where he was
greeted by the other leaders of oil rich nations. They
seemed to be going out of their way to make him
feel comfortable.

The summit meeting lasted for what seemed to
be most of the day. George Lee Jr. was not scheduled to speak until the next day. He sat and listened to hundreds of complaints about the monopoly of his company on the oil refinery business
in the East. He listened as they referred to his company as the infidels who stole the oil profits, and
robbed Islamic women of their virtue. As he listened to them silently and sardonically, he realized they spoke to him openly, and without fear of
his wrath. The same chill he had felt upon landing, returned. He was now fully aware of the impending danger of the situation. If he was going to
be able to survive, he would have to rely on his
training.

He began to search the room with his eyes and
ears. He closed his eyes, recalling the expressions
on the faces and the scent of each man who had

greeted him. He separated his mind from his body and gave himself the inner peace that would allow him to get through the rest of the meeting without giving in to paranoia. He was now ready to confront his adversaries, and face his destiny, with the calmness and serenity of a man unaware of his future.

The meeting adjourned, and the Arabic leaders who had spoken of him and his family so harshly bid him good evening, acting as if the comments of the day had not been made. They bowed respectfully and kissed his signet ring to let him know that he was still the King of Oman for as long as he lived. The Syrian bodyguards who had escorted him there returned to take him to his hotel, as expected. He watched them come through the door with their hands out of sight. They walked with the determination of men on a mission. The Arabic leaders moved aside to make way for them as they approached him. Their path was as clear as the one Moses made when he parted the Red Sea. George Lee Jr. looked fearlessly into the eyes of his assassins, putting himself into the same healing trance he was taught as a child, and awaited death. Unnerved by the young King's lack of fear in the face of death, the assassins hesitated long enough for him to complete the ritual. They regained their composure and shot him in the head, as they had been instructed to do. The head shots ensured that he would die, even if he had been wearing Body Armor. The bullets ripped into his face, tearing away one of his eyes, splintering his jaw bone, shattering his left ear drum, leaving him unrecognizable and unquestionably dead. He lay there, faceless, in a pool of blood.

"Allah be praised!" the assassins screamed. Six bodyguards of the Arabic Leaders assassinated the assassins, sending them to glory in reward for the bloody deed. With the assassins dead, the plot could not be traced back to any of them. They placed the distorted body of George Lee Jr. on a conference table and sent word to Juan Pablo of his cousin's death. Upon receiving the news, Juan Pablo made arrangements for himself and three members of the Special Force of Five Thousand to go to Syria and retrieve the body. Then Juan Pablo sent word to the compound of the treacherous deed.

On the flight to Syria, Juan Pablo could think of only one thing: had George Lee Jr. remembered the training? The ancient art of self-healing had never been tested by any of them. The plane was met by the American Ambassador to Syria. He took them to the corpse that had remained in its original condition since the assassination, late the day before. Tears came to Juan Pablo's eyes when he saw the faceless corpse of his cousin. He knew then that he could not take the body home with the bullets still in him. Dismissing all but his entourage, he began to remove the bullets that were continually poisoning George Lee Jr.'s body and retarding the self-healing process.

If his cousin had, in fact, remembered the training, he would have to be taken to Soo Sing Wong at once. If he could be saved at all, Soo Sing Wong was his only hope. Immediately after the surgery, they flew to the compound, where the family was waiting. They were relatively calm considering the circumstances. They understood that they must wait for an evaluation by Soo Sing Wong once the body arrived. Jasmine had been kept under sedation since the news of George Lee's assassination had reached the compound. She knew nothing of the training that everyone was talking about. She only knew that her husband was dead, and her baby would be born without a father.

By the time Juan Pablo arrived from Syria with

George Lee Jr., a room had been turned into an infirmary. Once George Lee Jr. had been rushed there, Soo Sing Wong checked for life signs and anything that could be retarding the self-healing process. Juan Pablo proved himself an excellent surgeon, having removed all the bullet fragments from the body before they arrived at the compound. Soo Sing Wong found the slightest heart beat he had ever heard after examining the body for an hour. It was like music to his ears. He sent word to the awaiting family that George Lee Jr. was alive. His body was in the self-healing trance, and it would take several months for him to completely recover.

The next day, Juan Pablo flew back to Oman, where Arabesque was waiting. He had not been able to send her news for fear of spies that may have been planted in the Palace. George Lee Jr.'s self-healing process had to remain a secret known only to the family. Arabesque was sent to the safety of the compound to comfort her sister, and Juan Pablo made arrangements for a mock funeral to keep their enemies at bay. The ten members of the Special Force of Five Thousand who were assigned to him replaced the Palace Guard. This move ensured George Lee's safety while he was in the self-healing trance at the compound. Juan Pablo had no love, and certainly no trust, for the followers of Allah.

Meanwhile, at the compound, Jasmine sat with her husband in the infirmary. She watched him as he lay in his self-induced coma. For the first time since George Lee had arrived home, she realized his conscious mind was with her, and that his body was slowly returning. He, like his father before him, had gone to live among strangers, with strange customs, in a strange land in order to reach another level of maturity that he might fulfill his destiny. So she sat there, and waited, as his heartbeat grew stronger and his faceless body regained the features of the man she once knew to be her husband. The baby in Jasmine's womb seemed to understand the metamorphosis its father was undergoing, and it moved within her to the rhythm of his heartbeat.

In Washington, D.C., Cheyenne's Dakota Moon wrote a letter to his father explaining the wide range of emotions that he felt about George Lee Jr. having entered the spirit world through the self-healing trance. The younger Moon would have given up all his earthly possessions to go in his friend's stead.

My Dearest Father,

I hope this letter finds you and Mother in good health. The job of leading the Special Force of Five Thousand is, to say the least, the most important thing in my life. However, upon hearing of the plight of George Lee Jr., I was overcome with jealousy that he had the opportunity to enter the Spirit World before me. I have dreamed of travelling into that realm all my life. I have prepared myself for the trip. I have always been the best candidate for the trip, with the best chance of returning safely.

In closing, please forgive my infantile tantrum and give my love to Mother.

Your Son, Cheyenne's Dakota Moon

George Lee Jr. lay naked in a glass topped coffin with a loin cloth covering his genitals. It was easier to watch his progress while he was unclothed. He had regained all of his features and the shiny new skin on his beautiful face gave him the aura of an angel. He was even more handsome than Jasmine had remembered. The last picture of him that she had in her mind was from the day he left her to go to the summit meeting in Syria.

He had kissed her passionately on the lips and told her he would return within the week. She never dreamed he would come home in this condition, and Jasmine watched him impatiently for signs of consciousness. He breathed, but he did not open his eyes. She kissed his lips, a gesture she recalled from a fairy tale she had once read, hoping that would rouse him from his sleep.

"Please, my prince, come back to me," she said to him almost inaudibly. Although he gave no sign of it, she knew he had heard her. She also knew that if her love had not responded, then there was some unknown reason why he could not respond. She called for Soo Sing Wong who came at once. No words passed between them, but he read the expression of anguish on her face. The anxiety in her eyes told him how close George Lee was to coming back. He examined him closely and saw that he had come as far as he could. Jasmine would now have to come to him.

Soo Sing Wong explained the situation to her very carefully. When he had finished, she knew what had to be done. He told her that he had no idea what effect the journey would have on the unborn child, but Jasmine's decision was already made. She had no intention of having this baby without her husband.

"I should inform the others of what we intend to do," Soo Sing Wong said to her.

"I must go now," Jasmine pleaded with him. "George Lee needs me to complete the journey now, or he will be lost to us forever." Soo Sing Wong knew that the urgency in her voice could only have been communicated to her by George Lee Jr. himself. He put her in a trance using hypnosis .

Ten seconds later, deep in the trance, Jasmine was on her way to her love. She travelled back in time to the day they first met. She watched the short courtship that her father and Ny Li Tu had arranged, and saw, as a voyager, the love that she and her husband had shared at first sight. She watched as they consummated their marriage on their wedding night in Brazil. She watched as they made love on the day that the unborn child had been conceived. She saw the sperm travel up the birth canal and fertilize the egg within her. She gasped as she watched the speed at which the egg started taking on the form of the child. She watched all the days of their lives as they passed before her, including the assassination. The self-healing trance, the trip home, the wait for him to return, and the exact time at which he was healed all passed before her eyes. She grabbed his hand and guided him back to consciousness. When George Lee Jr. opened his eyes, Jasmine was the first person he saw. He smiled at her knowingly, and she smiled back and hugged him. He tried to rise, but he was still very weak. Soo Sing Wong told him to lie still. He would need much rest. While Jasmine was going to him, Soo Sing Wong had summoned the family. They were all there waiting when the couple returned home.

Suddenly Jasmine screamed in pain. Holding her stomach, she fell to the floor. She had started hemorrhaging and her water had broken. Her sister Arabesque and Soo Sing Wong reached her first. Soo Sing Wong picked her up and carried her to the bed. While he was getting sheets and water, Arabesque removed Jasmine's underpants and positioned her on the bed with the soles of her feet down and her knees up. Now she could push when the contractions came. Arabesque timed the contractions while Lula Ann, George Lee Jr.'s mother, checked to see how much Jasmine had dilated. She could see the head of the baby coming out.

"Push, Jasmine, push", she said.

"I am pushing, I am pushing," Jasmine replied, screaming at the top of her lungs.

"Jasmine, the baby is here, but it needs another push from you," Lula Ann said in a frantic plea.

"I can't push anymore," Jasmine screamed. "It's killing me. Oh God, help me!" "Jassy, we will all push together," said Arabesque. "Come on Jassy, on the count of three. I'm pushing with you, one, two, three, push, push, push."

Jasmine screamed in pain as she felt the baby slide out of her.

Lula Ann caught the baby as it moved from between its mother's legs, and said, "Jasmine, it's a girl. Jasmine, you have a beautiful little girl. She held the baby upside down and struck her on the buttocks to clear her lungs by making her cry. At that moment, Arabesque placed the palms of her hands on Jasmine's stomach, and pushed with all of her might. Jasmine screamed in pain as the afterbirth came flowing out.

"It's over now, Jassy," she said. "It's all over now." Lula Ann washed the baby in the afterbirth, dried her off and handed her to Jasmine.

Jasmine said, "Oh mother, she is beautiful. Isn't she beautiful, Arabesque, isn't she?" For an instant Arabesque was consumed by jealousy.

"Yes Jasmine, she is the most beautiful baby I have ever seen," she then said, in all honesty. Jasmine, with the help of Arabesque, carried the baby over to her husband, "Look George Lee, it's a girl," said Jasmine. But George Lee Jr. was too weak to respond. He just smiled, closed his eyes, and drifted out of consciousness. That night, they were moved to the second floor of the third wing of the mansion, where the nursery was. They were given a three room suite next to Canyon, Greta and Tomorrow, and Ali, Maria and Millennium. A nurse stayed in the room with them. She bathed George Lee Jr., Jasmine and the baby, then put them in the bed together. The baby was in the middle, wrapped in an electric blanket which was turned down low to keep her warm. The nurse watched them as they slept. She was from the Special Force of Five Thousand and would protect them with her life. They slept safe and sound in her care.

Arabesque spoke to her husband on the videophone that night.

"Juan, I helped to deliver Jasmine's baby tonight," she said, with tears streaming from her eyes. "Juan, I want one. I want a baby, just like Jasmine's. Please Juan, can I have one?"

"My love," he said. "you can have anything that is in my power to give you. You have but to ask."

"Juan, I want to come home. Please come and get me."

"Arabesque, my love, I miss you dearly, but it is not safe here as of yet. Stay there with my family. Please, Angel, do not ask me to risk your life for the comfort of your love. I will come for you soon. Go to bed and get some rest, and I will call you in the morning."

Reluctantly, she gave in to his wishes and turned the videophone off. When she went to bed, she dreamed of her love and of her new love, their baby yet to be.

On the second day of the twelfth month in the year 2029, the family of Ny Li Tu came together at the compound of Moses Cribb, under the safety of the dome, to celebrate the recovery of George Lee Jr. from his mortal wounds. Ny Li Tu had Juan Pablo inform the Eastern Powers that no inquiries would be made into George Lee's assassination. She was convinced that her family would not be safe from these attempts on their lives unless the world was made to believe that they had achieved immortality. She made this known to the family in a short monologue ending with a short prayer.

"God forgive us, your faithful servants, for this vain blasphemy, but it is necessary in order that we may continue to serve you."

"Amen," the family responded in unison.

George Lee Jr. was living proof that they had achieved everlasting life. He would appear in public, before his enemies, and the sight of him would make them all living gods. They would reconvene the summit meeting that had ended with the tragedy of George Lee Jr.'s assassination. The invitations would go out from the King of Oman. No one would dare to risk his wrath, so soon after his cousin's death, by refusing his hospitality. Such a refusal would be interpreted as fear, a sure admission of guilt. The Royal House of Oman would call and all would come. The just and the unjust would all gather together under the same roof to meet the master of Oman face to face. They would look him straight in the eye and honestly proclaim that they did, or did not, kill his cousin. It came to pass, on the day of the summit meeting, that they all stood united, the guilty and the guiltless, ready to answer for the death of George Lee Jr., the King of Oman. They assembled in the coliseum built by the Romans during the days of their conquests and occupation of Egypt and all the lands of the East. There, seated in the middle of the arena on a dais, was Juan Pablo, the King of Oman. Beside him sat a man of similar size, dressed in a robe with a hood that covered his face. The hooded man seemed somehow familiar to them, and they wondered if it was his presence that they recognized. He sat there faceless, silent, and still, like the grim reaper. Every voice became mute in his presence.

They all sat in silence, for sixty seconds, until Juan Pablo spoke. He spoke of the discontentment among them. He spoke to them about the price they received for the oil they sold to Oman Petroleum Enterprises Unlimited. He spoke to them of his father-in-law, the old Sultan of Oman. He spoke to them of Arabesque and Jasmine, the Sultan's daughters who had married him and George Lee Jr. He spoke of the peace that the unions had secured for the world and about the Jihad which had started after the Sultan's death. He told of how he had been overcome with sadness after the battle, upon seeing all the pointless death. He spoke of the assassination of his cousin, the other King of Oman. He told them that he had made no inquiries then, and would make none now.

"All of the members of my family are immortal," he finally said to them. He said it, as if it were common knowledge and that he was just repeating it again for their benefit. "We will be with you until the end of time. We harbor no ill will toward you; it is not necessary, my cousin is still among us. He lives." As he said this, George Lee Jr. stood up, threw his hood back, and removed the robe. The crowd gasped in surprise. They fell upon their knees in awe of him, exalting his name and praising Allah for his life. They cursed his enemies as their enemies and pledged their loyalty to the Throne of Oman. That is how it came to pass on the twenty-fifth day of the twelfth month of the year 2029. All of the Middle Eastern nations united and swore allegiance to the god kings of Oman. The dome over the Royal City was completed in 2031, and in that year, both of the royal families began to rule jointly again. A sign outside of the domed city read: "Welcome to the Royal City of Oman. The people who reside here have no enemies. They are protected by the Gods." In that same year, a boy was born to Juan Pablo and his wife, Arabesque. They named him Emanuel. He was betrothed to the girl born the year before to George Lee Jr. and Jasmine. They had named her Odessa.

These children were raised in the light of Islam and trained to follow the path of Mohammed. This union strengthened the bonds of the United Nations of Oman, as the Middle East came to be known, under the reign of Emanuel and Odessa. Peace in that part of the world is still maintained by the Royal Family of Oman.

In the year 2030, all of Asia was at peace. China had signed a treaty making her an ally of the god Kings. After China realized that her enemies would be the enemies of Oman, all of the other Asian countries fell in line behind her. The idea was not foreign to them. Not so many centuries ago, their Emperors had been considered living gods. They had been at war with each other for centuries, and peace was a pleasant change. They also enjoyed the benefits of the New Trade Agreement which allowed them to utilize the principles of capitalism. Asia was quickly becoming an industrial continent with an inexhaustible work force.

The power of these god Kings was self-evident. Southeast Asia was still uninhabited as a result of the Germ Warfare. The Eastern Alliance enveloped all of Asia, including the countries that once had been part of the Soviet Union, and all of northern Africa. It could have been extended, but that would not have been in the best interest of the European allies and World Peace.

*"Love and War are connected by
a common thread: Romance"*
Roman Micheal

Chapter Thirty-five

The Twins

During the same year, Roman Micheal and Mica Mark were in South America. The South American countries were engaged in civil wars again. Civil war seemed endless there. The indigenous populations had been engaged in battles and wars since Spain and Portugal had claimed and colonized the continent with the Treaty of Tordesillas when they had come in search of gold in the year 1494.

President Maxwell Mason Stone had given the order to Cheyenne's Dakota Moon, personally, ten years before.

"Send the twins to South America. Divide the continent between them and bring me a united South American continent before my term is up and Rameses comes to power," he had said. A plan of action was already in progress. It started with the marriages of Tyler Samuel, Roman Micheal and Mica Mark to the Salvestia triplets in Brazil. Roman Micheal controlled the North of the continent: Brazil, Bolivia, Peru, Ecuador, Colombia, Venezuela, Guyana, Surinam and French Guyana, with headquarters in Brazil. Mica Mark controlled the South of the continent: Argentina, Chile, Paraguay and Uruguay, with headquarters in Argentina. The twins and Tyler Samuel personally trained hand picked men who then trained revolutionaries in every country on the continent. When the time was right, they would assassinate the current heads of state, overthrow the governments, and bring order to the continent through a series of treaties. Unlike the Middle East, they were told not to use chemical or biological warfare.

The mission was successfully completed in the year 2030. Roman Micheal and Brillante had a baby boy that year, in Brazil. They named him Constantine. Tyler Samuel and Brillosa lived in the compound of Moses Cribb. Tyler Samuel was Secretary of the Treasury, so he had to be close to Washington, DC. Brillosa was in her seventh month of pregnancy. They were expecting a little girl. A newly developed pregnancy test had not only revealed the pregnancy, but also indicated the sex of the unborn child. Her name would be Conzeula.

Their sister Brillantez in Argentina had found that she was unable to conceive, and she did not want to tell Mica Mark. He had been very unhappy about not having a child. In fact, he spent every spare moment with her, trying to conceive. She knew that if he found out, their marriage would be over. She was no longer able to contain her secret. For the sake of her own sanity, she confided in her sister Brillante by videophone. These two had always been close, and remained the best of friends. Either one would have done anything to ensure the other's happiness. After giving careful thought to the conversation she had with her sister, Brillante called her back.

"Come and visit with me for awhile in Brazil," Brillante requested.

"I don't know," said Brillantez. "Mica is so busy with the treaties these days. Maybe a vacation will do him good. I'll talk to him this evening, after the dinner hour." Before the ordeal of his sexual ritual, Brillantez convinced Mica Mark that a change of scenery might help her conceive. He was willing to try anything to have a baby, so he made arrangements to take a thirty day leave of absence from the Ministry. Brillantez had not seen her sister in over a year, and she was anxious to leave immediately. The twins saw each other more frequently. Matters of state had always kept them in close contact.

In Brazil, the girls talked privately. Brillante has a plan.

"Brillantez, you know I love you. How much do you want a baby?" she asked her sister.

"I love Mica Mark and he wants a child. What can I do? I must tell him and take my chances with the marriage," Brillantez responded. Very seriously, Brillante lowered her voice and whispered, to her sister.

"They are identical twins. Their mother has a hard time telling them apart. The only way I know my husband from yours is the slight scar he has on his right forearm. He received it years ago while on training maneuvers before the Extermination Campaign. We, dear sister, are two members of an identical set of triplets. I have no blemishes, do you? There is no way they can tell us apart."

"Brillante, are you suggesting we trade places?"

"Yes. You stay here and take care of Constantine and Roman Micheal. I will return in your place and havě a baby for you. Once I deliver, I will come back and trade places with you again. They will be none the wiser."

"You're serious, aren't you?" asked Brillantez.

"You did say this could ruin your marriage, didn't you? Do you have a better idea?" questioned Brillante. Brillantez shook her head. They hugged each other and began to sob.

"Do you think we can really pull it off, Brillante?"

"Of course we can," answered Brillante, "but it will be harder for me, I have never been to your home. I don't even know where your bedroom is."

"Maybe this is the reason I have not invited you sooner," said Brillantez laughing. Brillante laughed with her, and yet she knew there was some truth in what Brillantez said. They heard their husbands coming down the hall and tried to contain their levity before the men entered the room. Roman Micheal walked over to Brillante and kissed her.

"Is this a private joke, or can anyone get the punch line?"

"No my love, it is only girl talk, but you will get it soon enough." The girls broke into uncontrollable, contagious laughter which caused their husbands to join them without understanding the comment.

That evening, the sisters chattered all through dinner like two schoolgirls who had not seen each other since summer vacation. Brillantez described each room of their villa in Argentina to her sister with such pride that Mica Mark stopped talking to his brother and listened. He watched Brillantez as she talked and laughed with her sister. She had not laughed in a long time. He knew this was his fault. He had created tension between them with his insane obsession about having a child. It had even made their lovemaking a chore for her. Now he noticed Brillantez's relaxed mannerisms return. He realized that he should have brought her down here to visit Brillante last year, but affairs of state had kept him tight and tense. He owed her an apology, and he could not wait until they were alone to try to make amends. They both needed this time with family, away from business, to rekindle the romance he had almost let die. He sat there in a trance, looking at her as he had when they first met. She didn't have a care in the world back then. She had enjoyed being one of the three most beautiful women on the continent. Fortunately for Mica

Mark, his family's influence had won him her hand in marriage.

His daydream was cut short when his brother said, "Earth to Mica, do you read me?"

He turned back to him and said, "I'm sorry Roman, where were we?"

"I was here all the time, my brother," Roman answered. "I don't know where you were." They laughed as they had when they were children. Laughter. In a house with laughter, he thought to himself. Suddenly, he missed his mother. Just like when they first went away to the Academy. He had felt so sad that day. He remembered Roman putting his arm around him, saying, 'don't worry Mica, it's not forever.'

How wrong my brother was, he thought. It was forever, and mother knew it. That was why she was crying when we left. She knew it was forever. It seems that Roman was the only one who did not, and if he did? How brave he must have been. Maybe that is why I am drawn to him during every crisis in my life. He is my strength.

Once again, Roman caught his brother deep in thought. This time he put his hand on Mica Mark's shoulder. "Don't let it get you down, Mica. We have a big responsibility here. We can handle it; we were trained for this from birth. We are the Masters of the world. We are immortal. You hear how they refer to Juan Pablo and George Lee Jr.. They are gods. Are we less than they? We, my dear brother, have conquered a continent and we have done it without using the Germs. We fought like they did in the old days, hand to hand, man to man. We are the true warriors in this family. Why do you think they sent us to South America, with so many of our cousins to choose from? We are more like the old Ghost Shadows than any of them. Through our veins runs the blood of James Edward Magee, our father—a true warrior in every sense of the word."

Tears filled their eyes, and for a brief moment, they were still Mai Lee's little boys. Their youth had been snatched from them and replaced with responsibility, a code of honor, and a choice of arms.

They all remained at the table, talking as the servants cleared the dishes. Each was engrossed in his or her conversation, and they carried it into the evening. As the night wore thin, they grew weary and gave in to their bodies' need for rest. The next day, the girls dressed alike, something they would do until it was time for them to part. Brillantez would stay and Brillante would go in her place to bear Mica Mark an heir. Happy and yet sad, Brillantez was after all a woman and she knew that every man needed at least one child.

The charade began with simple things, like answering to the others name. They spent a week getting used to being called by the other's name. When this went undetected, they began the switch. First, they interacted with the other's husband on a non-sexual basis. By the end of the third week, they were ready to take the charade into the bedroom. From that point on, there was no turning back. Unaware of what was taking place, Roman Micheal was kissed by his wife for the last time. When she walked out of their bedroom, her sister Brillantez returned in her place.

"Brillante, what is taking you so long to get to bed?" he asked.

"I went in to kiss Constantine goodnight," Brillantez lied.

"How many times are you going to put that child to bed? You spoil him. Who do you think will put him to bed when he goes to the Academy?"

"I don't know, Roman. I guess for now, I just want him to remain a baby."

She said it with such sadness that Roman asked her, "Is there something wrong with him that I should know?"

"No Darling, the boy is fine," she said. "I guess I am just a little sad tonight. Soon he will be grown, and if I know you, he will be a soldier just like you and Mica. I will lose him, just as your mother lost you." She disrobed and sat on the bed next to him. Roman sensed her mood. She wanted him to make love to her, and yet she was apprehensive, like a virgin bride on her wedding night.

"Are you all right?" he asked.

"Yes," she said. "I am fine. Don't I look all right to you?"

"Yes," he answered while removing his pajama bottoms. He pulled her close to him and kissed her with a tenderness she had not felt in a long time. She responded by kissing back. At first she felt guilty, but then she felt alive again. Her tongue probed his mouth. He moved his kisses from her lips to her neck. She trembled with desire as his index finger penetrated her vagina. She rolled on top and straddled him, guiding his penis into her vagina and arching her back. She moved her pelvis in a rhythm that caused him to moan in pleasure. She put her feet flat on the bed, and rode him until he ejaculated. Feeling his penis tense before he was spent, she accelerated the motion and came with him in a heated frenzy. Still on top of him, her lips found his, and they stayed in that position. He picked her up in his arms and carried her to the bathroom. They showered, and went back to bed. He felt closer to her that night, than he had felt in all the time that they were married. Brillantez recognized the point of no return, and she did not want to go back. She was now Brillante. Roman was her husband and Constantine was her son.

Brillante went into the guest room where her

sister and Mica had been staying. She heard the water running in the bathroom. Mica was just stepping out of the shower when she opened the door. He was the same height as her husband, with exactly the same physique. He looked like the statue of a Greek god. Her eyes followed the contour of his body from head to toe. She gasped when she saw the size of his penis and stood there gawking at his manhood, trying to look at him as if she had just seen him naked that morning. He looked at her strangely.

"I was waiting for you to shower with me. What were you doing all this time?"

She lifted her eyes to meet his and their gazes locked. "I was with Brillante. We were saying goodnight to Constantine," she said nervously. The truth was, she had been putting Constantine to bed for the last time.

"Get undressed," he ordered, then added in a much softer tone, "I will bath you if you like." There was something sexy and exciting about the rugged way he ordered her about in private. Brillante had never heard him talk like this before. She undressed quicker than he remembered her ever doing before, leaving her clothes laying about wherever they fell. It struck him as unusual; she was normally as neat as a pin.

He turned the shower on again, and she stepped in. She let the back of her hand brush against his penis. It stiffened to her touch. This unusual flirtation from his wife excited him, and his penis grew a size larger. Her eyes were still fixed on it as he stepped into the shower with her. He rubbed a bar of soap over her body, scrubbing her as if she had been working in the fields, and he expected to remove dirt. The rough manner in which she was handled excited her to the point of coming. He rinsed her off, this time gently. Her nipples hardened as the water rolled down her body. He turned the water off and dried her with a towel the size of a blanket. He picked her up and carried her to the bed, putting her on the edge so he could kneel on the floor and still have most of his body cover her. He cupped her buttocks in his hands and pried her legs open so he could insert his tongue between them.

Brillante locked her thighs around his head as if trying to consume him with her vagina. Then she relaxed her legs. As they opened, he slid up her body, putting his tongue in her mouth and his penis into her vagina at the same time. She bit down on his tongue as she felt what she imagined to be a tree trunk stretching her vagina to what seemed to be its limit. Yet the hurt felt so good that she returned the thrust to his body rhythm until they came simultaneously. They lay there, breathing heavily, neither of them believing the experience they had just shared. It was the day before her menstrual cycle and she started to bleed. Mica thought it was because he had finally broken her hymen. She was too exhausted to explain. He seemed so pleased with himself. She was sure the truth would somehow effect their relationship. She calmly got up and went into the bathroom. His male ego made him follow her, as if he could be of some help. She smiled at his genuine concern.

"Darling," she said, "hand me the sanitary napkins under the vanity please." He picked them up as if they were alive, handed her the box and stepped into the shower. He didn't know what had come over his wife that night, but he was pleased with the change. He even changed the bedding while she showered. When Brillante returned to bed, he was asleep. All through the night she kept touching his penis and marveling at the size. A lesser woman would have been split in half.

Poor Brillantez, she thought, *we certainly picked the wrong brothers. Between now and next year, I will find a way to keep him.*

The next day, the Salvestias, Brillante and Brillantez's parents, came to dinner. This was an unexpected test of their deception, but a test welcomed by them. Both girls agreed that this was what they really wanted. They had inadvertently married the wrong men, and now they had come up with the perfect solution to their problem. They were determined to either deceive their mother, or make her an accomplice. Deception was the first choice.

Mother Salvestia watched the girls closely all evening, waiting for a chance to talk to them alone. There was something different about her girls, but she could not put her finger on it. There was no question of their happiness, that was evident. However, they hadn't dressed alike since they turned seventeen.

"Brillantez," she asked, "how do you like living in Argentina?"

Brillantez answered, "You would not believe the villa Mica bought for me. You and Daddy have to come down and visit us," Brillantez answered.

"Visit," her father said, "I don't have time to visit your sister and she lives right here, in Brazil. When will I get a chance to come down to Argentina? But I will gladly send your mother," he added, jokingly.

"Don't worry. When Brillantez needs me, I will be there. When she decides to raise a family, I will go and help her, just like I did for Brillante. You will see, Baby. I will be there when you need me the most," their mother said, pinching her daughter's cheek.

Roman whispered to his brother. "Yes, you will see. The woman moves in and takes over."

Mica smiled and said under his breath, "I am sure I will see." He looked over at his wife and thought of all the pleasure they would have making a baby.

At the end of the week, they left to go home. So far, the plan was working and everyone seemed happy. The vacation had worked wonders for Mica Mark. He left ready to take on the world and all the responsibilities that went with it. His newfound Brillantez conceived. They had twin boys which they named Damon and Damien. Brillante did go back, but they never traded places. The deception continued the rest of their lives.

"I believe in Democracy. I cannot be a king. I am the Lord of the Alliance."

Rameses Ryan Cribb

Chapter Thirty-six

The New Year

Rameses started his Campaign for the White House in the year 2033, and he chose Tyler Samuel as his running mate. They ran on the Fusion Party ticket, but contrary to the wishes of President Stone and Moses Cribb, they were running on their own merit. They held an innovative record and were very popular among the voters. They had managed to get the Legal Tender Act of 1933 repealed, and changed the United States of America's monetary system. A computerized card replaced coins and paper money. The card allowed the bearer to draw as much credit as deposited in an account, which was protected by the individual's hand print. Rameses made the following remarks during a speech at a fundraiser in December of 2033:

The Democratic process is a pendulum. Once it has swung to the right, as far as it can go, it swings back to the center, and then proceeds to the limits of the left. Somewhere in the middle are the checks and balances. I am an American in the truest sense of the word. I believe in the democratic process, and I will govern by the will of the people. The pendulum will swing in the other direction whether I am elected President or not. Half of the planet is led by men who claim to be gods. If this is true, it is imperative that I be your leader. Who else can make that claim? Who else can ensure the peace and hold the Alliances together?

Only me. I can, and I will.

This was no idle boast; it was true. He was the son of Moses Cribb.

The sixth day of the eleventh month of the year 2034 was Election Day. The family was in the compound of Moses Cribb. They had cast their ballots that morning and awaited the election results. Tyler Samuel and Brillosa were in their suite of rooms while Conzeula took a nap in the next room.

"Do you think we can win?" Brillosa asked Tyler Samuel.

"We always win," he answered. "The question is, by what margin?"

"Tyler," she asked, "why is that always the question?"

"Each election the margin grows less, and one day we will lose."

"Does that bother you, Tyler?"

"No," he responded.

"When will we lose?"

He kissed her and answered, "One day we will lose, but not in our lifetime." "Good, then we will be President forever. This will make you happy?" she asked.

He answered, "Only you can make me happy," kissing her passionately. She returned his kisses, unbuttoning his shirt as he unbuttoned her blouse. As the blouse fell off, he fumbled with her bra until it unhooked.

There is no graceful way for a man to remove a woman's bra. It unhooks with a will of its own. On the days that it is willing, a man thinks to himself, 'I'm getting good at this,' but then in the next encounter, he fails. This was a day that the bra was willing, and he threw it on the dresser as if it was always this easy. She helped him wiggle out of his pants as the skirt he just unzipped fell to the floor around her ankles. They remained locked in each other's arms, lips glued together. Tyler picked her up and carried her to the bed. As he put Brillosa down on the bed, his fingers found the elastic waistband on her panties, and in one swift motion, the panties were off and dangling on his index finger. He shoved them under the pillow as if they were going to play a part in the encounter and he didn't want to lose them. He kicked out of the shorts that she had just slipped below his knees. He was at the point of penetration when a knock on the door broke their concentration. They moved with the speed of two teenagers caught by the unexpected arrival of a parent home sooner than anticipated. Brillosa ran into the bathroom, picking up the scattered articles of clothing as she went. She tossed Tyler his robe and went into the bathroom to do whatever women do that takes longer than men in the same situation.

A little voice from behind the door, not yet fully awake, called out, "Mommy, Daddy I have to use the toilet."

"Okay, Baby, Daddy is coming," Tyler answered her, as he opened the door. He picked her up, carried her into the bathroom, and gave her to Brillosa, who was laughing at the pun, 'Daddy is coming.'

"I am glad you think it's funny," he said, laughing to himself as he lay on the bed. The girls came out of the bathroom, and lay down beside him. They still had a few hours before they would go down and join the rest of the family before dinner. They used it to sleep. This was not Tyler's first election night celebration. In this family, Election Night was the beginning of a new year. The family would be arriving from every part of the world today, and sleep was not a part of the ritual.

Canyon, Greta and Tomorrow were the last to arrive. They came home while Tyler and his family were asleep. Canyon was darker than his mother had remembered. He had worn little to protect himself from the sun. The hole in the Ozone Layer was shrinking; the average temperature on earth was ninety degrees. The ice caps at the ends of the earth had stopped melting the previous year, and were now holding their own. A large portion of the earth's population had migrated to the polar regions to escape the deadly heat of the sun. Canyon and his family had just returned from a trip to the South Pole. They had been away for three weeks, and were glad to be home. Before going to their rooms, they went to pay their respects to Ny Li Tu. She and Moses never left their rooms on Election Day, until the last return was in. Ny Li Tu greeted them with hugs and kisses. She marveled at the deep tans the girls had developed, and said that the house had been empty without her dark-skinned, golden-haired beauties around. They ran into Rameses, and Elizabeth Susan, on their way up to the suite."

You guys are looking more and more like family every time I see you," teased Elizabeth Susan, hugging the girls and kissing Canyon.

"See you at dinner," said Rameses.

Roman Micheal heard them in the hall and poked his head out of the door saying, "Welcome home."

"Same to you. I'll buy you a drink at dinner," Canyon replied.

"You're on," Roman said, and went back into his room to rest until then.

They entered the suite, promising never to leave home again as they always did after returning from a trip. They fell on the bed, and went to sleep fully clothed. This was not their first Election Day either.

Mica Mark, Brillantez and their boys, Damon and Damien, slept undisturbed by the new arrivals. Ali Khan and Maria were in their suite with Millennium, who also was asleep. They were speculating about what new role Rameses had for them to play in the New World Order. They had gotten wind of a plan for them, but they had no idea what it could be; they would be happy to serve Rameses in any capacity. They waited impatiently for the festivities to begin. Finally, they fell into the last sleep they would get before the end of the celebration.

While the family was asleep, resting before the start of the celebration, the servants rushed about, in preparation for the glorious event. Everything had to be perfect. Ny Li Tu was a hard task mistress. Her words could cut deeper than the lash, and none of them wished to incite her wrath. The servants had been with the family since before the children were born. They loved and respected Ny Li Tu more than they feared her. She had always been a friend as much as an employer to all of them. What they did that night was a labor of love, as their mistress knew well.

Canyon entered the living room with Greta on his arm and Tomorrow a step behind. The others had just come down, a family or two at a time, so Canyon's arrival was a grand entrance. They applauded them in jest as they walked into the room. Greta blushed, embarrassed by it all, while Canyon bowed and played the clown.

"I have an acceptance speech written that will cover any appointment in the New Administration that Rameses might have in mind for me," he said with mock formality. Rameses did not find this amusing and would have said so, had not Elizabeth Susan interceded. She announced that her husband had no sense of humor as of late. He was taking everything entirely too serious. The statement eased the potentially tense situation, and

Rameses changed the subject. He went on to say how much he admired the way his cousins, Roman and Mica, had handled the job of bringing the South American continent into the fold. He asked Roman to describe the feeling of hand to hand combat, as opposed to using chemicals on the enemy. Rameses said the use of chemical warfare would be outlawed in the new administration. The side effects it had on the environment, necessitated the decision to ban its use. There was a silence in the room. Roman used the opportunity to speak.

"I have participated in both types of warfare. Hand to hand combat is my choice, but I would not want to go into an extended war without the threat of the chemicals. I am not in favor of giving up our chemical capabilities." Seeing that Rameses was listening, he went on, "Today, we hold the world in our grip. The hold is secure in different parts of the world for different reasons. Asia and the Middle East are held by the awe the people of the region have for the living gods that rule them. We have married their daughters and our offspring have embraced their deity. These people have become an extension of ourselves. We will reign there in perpetual peace.

"South America is held by a series of treaties, and an armed force of three million. The South Americans believe us to be invincible, but more than our armies, they fear the chemicals. I say that we agree amongst ourselves to ban the chemicals; but the world should know nothing of our decision. Our strength is in the threat."

"My cousin has the wisdom of Solomon. It is agreed," Rameses said, without asking for approval from the rest of the family.

"Another Cribb has come to power," Canyon Mesa said under his breath.

Rameses continued. "There are millions of displaced people living in refugee camps all over the world. People of every race and religion. Collect these people and deliver them to Southeast Asia. Separate them from their clans. Mix them thoroughly so that they may interbreed, intermarry, and homogenize harmoniously, bringing forth a New Race to that region. This New Race of people shall be my people, and all of you will embrace them as your people. Ali Khan will carry out this mission and rule over them as their king."

Ali Khan and Maria walked over to him, bowed their heads and bent down on one knee. "We can do it. We will do it," Ali Khan said.

Rameses put his hand on Ali's shoulder and guided him to his feet. Maria rose along with him. Standing in front of them, Rameses put his arms around their necks. First he kissed Ali, and then he kissed Maria. "You will be given your choice of a thousand of our best people," he said. "Use them well and fulfill your destiny."

Rameses then walked over to Canyon. "You will be my Surgeon General, and you will not need an acceptance speech, Canyon. This is in addition to your duties as Chairman of the Board of Infectious Diseases."

"That's good," Canyon answered. "I probably would not have agreed with your choice of replacement for me. I hate fighting over appointments that I don't really want."

"I know, my cousin, that you would rather retire in '38, when the Ozone Layer is restored, but I need you, so I can't allow that," said, Rameses.

"I know, so I'm here," said Canyon, "and here I stay as long as you need me." Later that night, the election results came in. Rameses and Tyler had captured ninety-eight percent of the vote. The celebration of the New Year began, and ended a day later.

Sometime during the night, Rameses said to Cheyenne's Dakota Moon, "Ninety-eight percent of the vote. Does that make me a king?"

"Every knee is bent, and every tongue calls your name," Cheyenne's Dakota Moon responded.

Two weeks later, Ali and Maria started selecting the thousand members of the Special Force of Five Thousand who would follow them into Southeast Asia. When this was done, they collected the refugees around the world and delivered them to Southeast Asia. They began to rebuild and re-populate the countries. In time, the races, and languages, began to mix and blend into one. One country, one language, one race, one god, one king, one queen, and one allegiance: Rameses.

In the year 2038, Rameses was in the first year of his second term as President of the United States, and Lord of the World Alliance, a title he bestowed upon himself with the blessings of the New World Order. The hole in the Ozone Layer had been repaired and the World Alliance had appointed Canyon Mesa as Lord Protector of the Environment.

Everett Jr. and Marion Matilda had a baby girl. She was called Myrrah, named for the moon goddess of the ancient Alboes, a tribe of albino Indians who once lived along the banks of the Amazon River. Rameses and Elizabeth Susan had a boy child. His name was Trojan. The third generation of the Ghost Shadows numbered ten: six boys and four girls. The legend continued.

*"Behold a pale horse and his
name that sat upon him was
death and Hell followed with him."*
Revelations 6:8

Chapter Thirty-seven

The Passings

It was the second month of the year 2043. Maxwell
Mason Stone lay on his death bed. The remainder
of his life numbered in days. He was dying of one
of the many diseases he had ordered unleashed
on his enemies, and his body was weak, but his
mind was still sound. Visitors paraded in and out
of his room all day. But Tara sat at his bedside,
holding his hand and bravely waiting with him to
greet Death, one of the Four Horsemen of the
Apocalypse. Their son, Canyon, stood with his
hands on his mother's shoulder while Greta fluffed
her father-in-law's pillow on the other side of the
bed. The child, Tomorrow, sat at the foot of her
grandfather's bed. Although the disease had left
him thin and weak, he was still a handsome man.

Greta watched as the old couple held hands,
and thought how beautiful they must have been in
their youth. They were certainly a handsome, elderly couple. Canyon looked at his father and wondered why the innoculation had not worked on him.
He had saved so many other lives, why not his father's? Tears came to his eyes briefly, and he
quickly remembered. It was only a passing, and
the passing was inevitable. Even he would one day
pass away. Tomorrow saw her grandfather through
the eyes of a child. To her, he was ancient, and the
ancient ones always passed away.

Dakota Moon had come to see him earlier that
morning, before the children arrived. They spoke

of their days in Southeast Asia when they had tested the Chemicals and Germs on the unsuspecting enemy. They spoke of the old days when they first decided to Exterminate the Ku Klux Klan. They spoke of the War in Vietnam, and America's decision not to win it.

"That," Maxwell said, in a feeble voice, "was the turning point in my life. It was then that I decided to take the Presidency, the Country, and then the World. Dakota, old friend, I could not have done it without you and Moses." He continued, coughing in the middle of every sentence. "You fought off all of my enemies and kept me alive. Now, in this final battle, even you cannot save me." He looked at him, as if to ask, 'can you?'

Dakota Moon leaned over, without fear of the illness, and kissed him on the cheek, answering the question that he had not asked. "If it were possible, I would be your champion. I would mount my horse and ride out to meet Death face to face, and fight him for your life."

Maxwell smiled. "Farewell old, friend. I will see you on the other side of the Passing."

Moses and Ny Li Tu came in as Dakota Moon was leaving.

"Are we in time?" they asked him.

"Yes," he answered, "he is strong enough to last until nightfall. Has everyone come?"

"No," answered Ny Li Tu. "They're on the way."

"Good," said Dakota Moon. "He will need them to help him pass."

Maxwell perked up as soon as he saw Moses and Ny Li Tu enter the room. Ny Li Tu went over and embraced Tara. They talked quietly about Maxwell's condition while Moses went to his bedside.

"Did you see Dakota Moon?" asked Maxwell.

"Yes, we ran into him as he was leaving," said

Moses.

"The man has not changed in sixty years. He is as muscular as he was when we were in Southeast Asia," said Maxwell.

"Yes," Moses agreed. "If it were not for the gray hair, I would say he has a portrait that is aging for him." On that note, they shared a laugh, causing Maxwell to go into a fit of coughing. Tara brought a towel over to wipe his mouth. The coughing always brought up phlegm.

"The doctor said you were to stay calm, and then this would not happen," she said, looking at Moses as she spoke.

"Moses," Ny Li Tu said crossly, "he cannot stand all that excitement and still last until everyone has seen him."

Maxwell came to the rescue of his old friend. "The doctor said, the doctor said. What the hell does the doctor know? That son-of-a-bitch never died before. I want a laugh before I go." He was barely able to finish his sentence before the coughing made his last words unintelligible. Tara caught the phlegm in a clean towel as he was spitting up, and Ny Li Tu gained a new respect for her. She, herself, had seen all the horrors of the wounded and dying during the War. But Tara was the spoiled, rich, brat from the suburbs of middle America. Now Tara was cleaning phlegm and heaven knows what else off of her dying husband.

This is a quality I would not have attributed to you, Ny Li Tu thought to herself.

It was at that point in time that Canyon and his family had arrived. Moses and Ny Li Tu went out to host and await the arrival of the other family members, while Tara stayed with her husband. The others arrived in family groups: the Valdezes: Alexandro, Carmella, Juan Pablo, Arabesque and Emanuel; the Joneses: Everett, Betty May, Everett

Jr., his wife Marion Matilda, the daughter of Calvin
Chipman who came with them, and their daugh-
ter Myrrah; Elizabeth Susan, her husband
Rameses, the son of Moses and Ny Li Tu, and their
son Trojan; the Turners: Samuel, Janie, Tyler, his
wife Brillosa and their daughter Conzeula; the
Browns: George Lee, Lula Ann, George Lee Jr., his
wife Jasmine, and their daughter Odessa; the
Magees: James Edward, Mai Lee, Roman, his wife
Brillante and their son Constantine, Mica, his wife
Brillantez and the twins Damon and Damien; and
the Wongs: Soo Sing, Lin Lee, Ali Khan, his wife
Maria, and their son Millennium. Cheyenne's Dakota Moon arrived last. The family was united once
again— this time for the passing of Maxwell Mason Stone. In the final hour of his life, he spoke
the words that they had all come to hear—the passing speech:

I do not regret a day that I have spent on earth
among you. From a small circle of friends, we have
evolved into a large family circle, multi-racial, multi-
cultural, and of many faiths. We have successfully
recreated the family of man. We have amassed a
fortune of wealth that we cannot even count. We
have conquered the World and orchestrated the
Peace. The result is a symphony of prosperity. We
did that, and we did it together. If we are to hold on
to it, then we must hold on to it together, each
generation adhering to the same principles, and
improving on the formula that has made us what
we are. We have made some mistakes along the
way to this place where we are, but the second
generation corrected them and saved us from ourselves. You who have saved us will also make mistakes. I pray that you will be fortunate enough to
raise a third generation with the same competence
and ingenuity that you have shown. Educate them

well, and this family will live forever in a world per-
petuated by the peace and prosperity that we have
created. They are the future to you as you were the
future to us.

He said it all without coughing. His last words
were, "the end will justify the means," and he died
with those words resounding in their heads. When
it is our time to pass, we will not be afraid to go.
Maxwell went before them—the advance party, the
forward observer, and he would guide them to the
crossing, and take them to the place beyond. Over
the next five years, three others joined Maxwell;
Everett Henry Jones, the father of Everett Jr. and
Elizabeth Susan, Calvin Coolidge Chipman, the
father of Marion Matilda, and Samuel Nathaniel
Turner, the father of Tyler Samuel. The world
watched as they passed and came to the conclusion they were not the gods they professed to be,
but the Alliance held strong. The world forgave them
the blasphemy. The Lord of the Alliance tightened
his grip and they forgave the world their doubt.

BOOK III

Preface

This third and final book will lead you into the lives of the third generation. This generation will maintain all that was accomplished by their ancestors. They will bring nothing new to the Alliance because they are the keepers of the legend, the custodians of the monuments, the preservers of the wealth. In the year 2050, Ny Li Tu relinquished her seat as Chairwoman of the Board to Elizabeth Susan, who is now the head of the family. She orchestrates the third generation in the same manner that Ny Li Tu orchestrated the second generation. She betrothed Tomorrow and Millennium. They will eventually lead the New Race in Southeast Asia. She did the same with Emanuel and Odessa, a move that solidified the rest of Asia, Russia and north Africa. Constantine is betrothed to Myrrah; they will rule one of the halves of South America. Damon and Damien will rule after Roman and Mica. Trojan and Conzeula are betrothed. They will become the new Lords of the Alliance.

Odessa has a special gift. When her mother went into the Spirit World to lead her father back, she went with her. This resulted in her ability to see into the future and have complete knowledge of the past. Elizabeth Susan took her under her wing and past mistakes were never repeated.

Canyon Mesa claimed the world's vast wastelands of the polar regions for his domain. He erected thirty-two domed cities at the North Pole and twenty-nine at the South Pole. These became the world's new frontier. The climate-controlled Dome Cities offered the world's tourists a winter wonderland.

As the political pendulum swung back to the left, the issue of crime and punishment was resurrected. Rameses, the Lord of the Alliance, ordered Everett Jr. and Marion Matilda to construct penal colonies on the floor of the Atlantic Ocean to contain the increasing population of the convicted. This project would be paid for by the convicts. They would spend their prison terms mining the many underwater caves on the ocean floor.

*"Marriage is the alliance, love is
the adhesive by which it is bound,
true love is its only defense"*
                                    Emanuel

Chapter Thirty-eight

Emanuel and Odessa

The year was 2092 and change was blowing over
the Desert of Oman. The god Kings had abdicated
their thrones in favor of the heir children Emanuel
and Odessa, the light of Allah. The incestuous
marriage of the two first cousins would not taint
the family genes. They would not have children of
their own. They would adopt a child, an orphan
from the streets of Oman, who would become king
when his parents passed on. This had been foretold by Odessa to Elizabeth Susan, which was why
she had decided to betroth them as children.

The subjects of Oman celebrated for three days.
They did not dislike the god Kings, but the children were of their faith and they had long awaited
this coronation as a religious event. Emanuel and
Odessa had been away at school and had returned
for the occasion. Their parents would remain in
power, as figure heads, until their children graduated. There had been rumors, spread by the fundamentalists, that Muslims would never rule the
Eastern Alliance. The early coronation put that
rumor to rest. Much of the success enjoyed by the
Eastern Alliance was due to the ability of its rulers
to anticipate and avert unrest among their subjects, a skill at which Emanuel and Odessa were
unequalled by any other member of the Alliance.

In the year 2069, in China, Lo Fu Chu, a descendant of the Ming Dynasty and a prince of the
Eastern Alliance, had been named ambassador to

the court of Oman. He had the ability to veil the
future from those who were able to foretell it. He
had come to Oman in order to further the interests of his nation by casting a shadow of infidelity
on the marriage of the royal couple. His intention
was to seduce or rape the queen, impregnate her,
and then expose the affair. Under Islamic law infidelity is a death warrant. The bastard child would
be next in line to the throne because they had no
natural children.

China would then step in and protect the
mother and unborn child from their fate. To prevent a war, Emanuel would have to divorce Odessa
and marry one of the Chinese princesses. Even if
Emanuel refused to marry a Chinese princess, the
bastard child would still be heir to the throne. Add-
ing insult to injury, Emanuel would not be able
rescue his wife and bring her back to Oman since
Islamic law would call for her execution. The bastard child would be living proof. The result of such
a plot would eventually lead to China's domination of the Eastern Alliance. On the bright side, all
of this would be accomplished without a war.
Odessa herself predicted that there would be peace
in the East for one hundred years. The plot was a
double-edged sword, and China was holding the
hilt.

The new ambassador entered the throne room
where he was given audience with the king and
queen of Oman. He was a tall man (considering he
was an Oriental) of five feet eleven inches. He approached the throne and bowed down on one knee.

"My lords," he said. He remained on one knee
until Emanuel told him to rise. "How are my allies
in China?" The way Emanuel posed the question,
it could have had a double meaning.

Lo Fu Chu responded like a true diplomat saying, "all in my humble country who serve you, serve

you well." He lifted his eyes up to look at Emanuel, then eyed Odessa from head to toe, visually disrobing her as his eyes caressed her body parts, one at a time.

"My lady, you are as beautiful as my predecessor promised," he said boldly, but openly, so that it would be taken as a compliment instead of the flirtatious remark that it was meant to be.

Emanuel spoke before Odessa could respond. "My countrymen," he said, "have a way of saying to a guest in their house, 'all that I have is yours'. I am not that hospitable. When my father ruled here, such a bold remark would have cost you your tongue. Since then, we have become more civilized, but please remember I am my father's son."

"If I have offended you, my liege, my tongue is offered freely as appeasement," Lo Fu Chu said. Sweat formed on his forehead as Emanuel considered his offer. Odessa sat quietly, wide-eyed and in partial shock, as she witnessed the scene that could possibly end half of the Eastern Alliance. She waited silently, in morbid fear, for her husband's answer.

Emanuel looked at his wife, and without as much as a glance toward the ambassador, he said, "I have no need of your tongue, the audience is over." He extended his hand to his wife, she took it, and they exited the room leaving the ambassador still kneeling, without permission to rise. The royal couple had been gone for at least ten minutes before a palace guard went over to him.

"Your excellency, I have arranged transportation for you to return to your embassy."

He followed the guard without responding. *She cannot be seduced,* he thought to himself. *I must cloud her vision so that I can get her alone, then I will rape her.*

He was visibly shaken by the encounter with

Emanuel. All he wanted to do right then was sleep. He would get some rest and work on the second part of his plan the next day. The ride back to the embassy was long and silent, not that he ever would have conversed with the chauffeur under any circumstances. He was not in the habit of making small talk with servants. It was the length of the ride that disturbed him. Obviously, the chauffeur had been told to take the scenic route. In Emanuel's place, he himself would have given him the extra time needed to remember that he was not in China—a point well-taken, and he would never allow himself to forget it as long as he was away from home. He was in Oman, and for now it was Emanuel who ruled the Eastern Alliance.

The limousine came to a halt in front of the embassy. The chauffeur got out, came around, and opened the door. Lo Fu Chu walked by him without speaking a word, trying to resist the urge to strike him in place of his king. A doorman from the embassy came out to meet him. The doorman prostrated himself on the ground before him. Lo Fu Chu was confident again. Here, in the sanctuary of the embassy, he was home. He breathed deeply, as if the air was different and said inaudibly to himself, "China."

There was more of a chill in the desert air that morning than Odessa had ever experienced during that time of the year. She felt strange. She had slept well, but something had happened to her last night that had never happened to her before. She had not dreamt; it was as if her mind had been erased. She could not see the past or the future. She was like everyone else. To her, seeing nothing but the present was like being blind.

Blind, she thought as she was bathing, *I will not think about it. When I wake up tomorrow I will be able to see again. There is no need to alarm Emanuel. He gets so upset about things that affect me.* She remembered that when she had first gotten her period, she told him she was ovulating. He made her stay in bed until it was over. He was very excitable where she was concerned. That was just Emanuel's way of expressing his love. First her, then the Alliance, but she was always first. He asked her about the new ambassador at breakfast that morning. He said that he did not like him, that he was nothing like his predecessor. She told him that was easy enough to understand. His predecessor had been ninety-two years old and this ambassador was barely thirty.

"Nevertheless, he bares watching," he said.

She smiled. Em*anuel my love,* she thought to herself, *I am glad you could not read his thoughts. We would have been at war this morning, the Alliance would have been shattered and Rameses would have become our enemy. Nothing is more important to Rameses than maintaining the Alliance. Nothing.*

Lo Fu Chu arose early that morning and put himself through a series of exercise routines. After running five miles, he had a breakfast of protein, dairy and starch supplements. He never stopped thinking of how close he had come to death the day before. The previous ambassadors had always known how dangerous the father was, but until now, the son was untested. He wrote of Emanuel in a report to his superiors, "the fruit does not fall far from the tree."

Word of what had transpired between the young king and the new ambassador reached the ears of Cheyenne's Dakota Moon. It came via his network of spies in the court of Oman. Rameses had insisted on him placing spies throughout the Alliance. It was not that he didn't trust his allies, he just wanted to know what they knew as soon as they knew it. Cheyenne's Dakota Moon knew there was a problem. One of his spies had been found dead in the Chinese Emperor's court. This had happened prior to Lo Fu Chu replacing the old ambassador to the court of Oman. He wrote a report to Rameses.

My lord, there is a problem brewing in the Eastern Alliance that goes undetected by Odessa's foresight. The Chinese Emperor has replaced the old ambassador in Oman with a much younger man. I cannot believe it has anything to do with diplomacy. I have also lost my ear in the Emperor's court. I fear for the safety of our family in Oman. I will keep you appraised of the situation on a daily basis.

Rameses wrote back to Cheyenne's Dakota Moon in coded message:

Make no move to assist the Royal House of Oman. Emanuel rules the Eastern Alliance. If he is to remain king, then he must settle this affair alone. No matter what the outcome, the Alliance will remain intact.

Emanuel and Odessa were in the gymnasium with their fencing instructor. They practiced three hours a day, each morning between nine and noon, six days a week. They were both quite good. They had started the lessons at college. Then they brought the instructor, and his family, to Oman to be their private tutor. Fencing together had developed their camaraderie as soldiers-in-arms, the same camaraderie that Moses Cribb had shared with Ny Li Tu years ago in Southeast Asia. This was part of the glue that held their marriage together. This, and the fact they were each other's best friend. Every afternoon, they would return to the palace, bathe, and rest before taking care of the affairs of state.

The hot water of the bathing pool was soothing to Odessa's over-stretched muscles. Emanuel rubbed the soapy sponge across the back of her neck. Her nipples hardened as he lightly rubbed the soapy sponge across her breasts and down her stomach, terminating in the wedge of soft pubic hair between her legs. She parted her legs, turned around slowly.

"Mannie, do my back," she said, as if she had to ask.

They developed a love ritual that was an essential part of their foreplay. Both partners knew exactly what the other needed to enhance this erotic, orgasmic, sexual journey they were about to embark upon. Unlike their parents and grandparents before them, they had been intimate since they were eleven and twelve years of age. After all, they were betrothed very early. This meant marriage, and sex was a vital part of marriage. They learned from their training that practice made perfect, and consequently they became perfect lovers. Even though polygamy was permissible in their religion, neither could imagine anything less than monogamy in their love relationship. This had absolutely nothing to do with trust. They truly loved each other. They were the best of friends.

A gift arrived from the Chinese embassy, addressed to the royal couple from the new ambassador. Odessa opened it, tearing the wrapping paper, and discarding it on the floor like an excited child on Christmas morning. She loved receiving gifts.

"Mannie," she exclaimed, "a pair of golden doves. Oh Mannie, can I keep them?" She knew her husband was still angry with the presumptuous young ambassador from China. She put on her best if-you-say-no-I-will-die-of-disappointment expression. Emanuel tried not to look at her, but she held the expression until he did.

One look at her face and he conceded, saying, "keep the birds, Odessa, keep the damn birds."

"Mannie, we will have to invite him back to court, to thank him properly," she said to her husband, "or afternoon tea, maybe." He said,

"Court, no. Tea, okay."

"Oh Mannie, you're so good to me. I tell my mother all the time, Mother, Mannie is so good to me."

He smiled at her attempt to stroke his ego. Even though it was in jest, it was amusing.

"When?" she asked.

"Whenever," he responded.

"Tomorrow," she said. They looked at each other, and said at the same time, "after we make love," and they kissed to seal the bargain.

It was the third day at his new post for Lo Fu Chu. He sat at his desk in the Chinese embassy in Oman. The golden doves had been a gift to him from the emperor himself, and the new ambassador had not parted with them easily. But he had incurred the wrath of Emanuel. This would make his mission in Oman virtually impossible if he could not get back into the palace. The golden doves would be a small price to pay for the success of his mission. The knocking on his door proved to be the royal messenger from the palace of Oman. He reported that Emanuel and Odessa had extended an invitation to the ambassador to accompany them for tea in the sitting room of the palace at three o'clock the next afternoon.

The Gods have looked favorably on me again, he thought. *The gift of the golden doves has reo-*

pened the palace gates. Once again his fate was in his own hands. This time he would hold onto it with a firmer grip.

On the day of the tea, Emanuel and Odessa awaited the arrival of Lo Fu Chu in the sitting room. They were cooing like two lovebirds, reminiscing about the previous two hours of love making, when one of the servants announced, "his Excellency, Lo Fu Chu, the Chinese Ambassador to Oman." The ambassador entered the room. His short steps and the long robe that nearly touched the floor which he wore made him appear to be floating on air, just above the ground. The soft slippers on his feet masked the sound of his footsteps. Giving further credence to Emanuel's suspicion, the man did not walk, he slithered like a snake. He knelt before them—this time down on both knees. His head bowed and his eyes locked on Emanuel who would have left him in that position had not Odessa motioned for him to rise.

"Come sit with us. Do you enjoy the herbal teas?" she asked.

"Yes," he said in response to her question. Careful not to take his eyes from the gaze of her husband, the insidious Lo Fu Chu sat unnerved by Emanuel's stare. He was visibly uncomfortable sitting across the table from them. He spoke cautiously, careful not to offend them and jeopardize his mission in Oman.

"In my country, we not only drink tea socially, but also use it for medicinal purposes." For the first time since entering the room, he looked at Odessa as he spoke. He looked nervously at her husband, searching Emanuel's face for an expression of approval to carry the conversation with the queen any further. Pleased with the ambassador's discomfort, Emanuel picked up his cup of tea to take a sip. In their society, this was permission for a guest to partake also. Lo Fu Chu was familiar with all the languages and customs in the Alliance. This was one of the reasons he had been chosen for this assignment. He also had the obvious traits of his youth, good looks and sophistication. Lo Fu Chu continued the conversation, looking at both of them as he spoke, pretentiously exhibiting his knowledge of the herbal teas. Odessa changed the subject when she saw Emanuel looking at his time piece as if he had placed a limit on the amount of time he would spend with the ambassador.

"The golden doves are beautiful. I will cherish them forever," she said to the ambassador. This made Emanuel a bit more hospitable. Odessa was getting to the point of the visit—thanking him for the doves so he could leave. The ambassador went into a short history of the doves, telling them that they were a present to him from the emperor and how happy he was to give them to the royal couple of Oman as a token of his eternal friendship to the King and Queen of the Eastern Alliance. He went on to say that the birds were the only pair ever made, and the mold had been destroyed. They were priceless.

Lo Fu Chu left the tea feeling that he had made a friend in the queen, but he would still have to earn the trust of the king. In one of the many communications Ambassador Chu had with his emperor, he indicated that it was imperative that he have time alone with Odessa. In order to make the plan work, Emanuel had to be diverted or called away on an affair of state, one that would cause him to leave his wife behind, perhaps a dispute of some kind in the Alliance. He further stroked the emperor's ego by saying it was something only a man of his status could accomplish, and that it must be done soon.

This logic must have worked. Three weeks later,

Emanuel was called away to China. A border dispute had erupted between the Chinese Emperor and his cousin. He, as King of the Eastern Alliance, was called upon to settle it, but Emanuel was suspicious. The Chinese had always settled their own problems in the past, especially when it involved family. However, as King, it was his duty to resolve any problem that might disrupt the Alliance.

It was at this time that Odessa informed Emanuel that she was blind. He tried to make light of the situation. "Here we are, knee deep in Chinese. and you tell me that we are blind." He smiled. "Don't worry, we'll be all right. How long can blind be?"

Then came the foreboding feeling when Odessa did not answer. With her foresight gone, she had no way of seeing the outcome of his trip, or the scandalous plot that was beginning to take shape. Soon they would both be thrown into circumstances that only their superior intellect could bring them through unscathed.

Like a bad omen, on the day Emanuel left for China, Lo Fu Chu went to see Odessa on the pretense of speaking to her about her husband's impending peril. He told her that there was a plot to assassinate the king as soon as he interceded in the dispute between the Emperor of China and his cousin. Odessa told him that she did not believe anyone would have the audacity to attempt another assassination against the royal family of Oman. History had proven this to be a futile effort. The Eastern Alliance had been formed because of their family's immortality. She then asked him if he was informing her, that the emperor was behind a plot to overthrow the Eastern Alliance. He said he was sure that it was without the emperor's knowledge. She ordered the Palace Guard to go after King Emanuel and defend his life. This was the opportunity Lo Fu Chu was waiting for. The queen would be unguarded.

Several hours had passed since Odessa was informed of Emanuel's alleged danger. As of yet, there had been no word of him or from him, and the queen was frightened for his life. All that kept her from being frantic was the Training. The Training was what separated the members of this family from ordinary man. She would weather this crisis in text book form, as learned from the history of her family. History was the only frame of reference from which she could draw. She was totally blind.

Lo Fu Chu had put a sedative in a glass of wine and suggested she drink it to calm her nerves. In a matter of seconds, she was out like a light. He picked her up, carried her to the bed chamber, and placed her on the bed. The sound of his heartbeat filled his head with a loud pounding that to him seemed audible throughout the palace. Odessa's body emitted a faint, but intoxicating aroma of Persian Myrrh. He was no longer in control of his emotions. He removed her clothes with premeditated care, calculating the risk of her regaining consciousness before he was done. She lay there, a nude sleeping beauty with eyes closed and breasts moving as she breathed. She was a visual feast for a depraved degenerate in the service of his emperor. He had been ordered to sire a child, to rule the Eastern Alliance.

He savored her beautiful young body with all his senses as she slept exposed. His penis erected as his eyes travelled from her firm, upright breasts, to the mound of pubic hair below her flat abdomen. He kissed her full lips, then licked the nipples on each of her breasts until they stood erect. Convincing himself that she was responding to his

205 CHOICE OF ARMS

advances, he used his tongue to lubricate her vagina before penetrating the emotionless body of the unknowing queen. His hips moved up and down, and he breathed like a man who had run a marathon. If he could have had anything in the world that he wished for, then at that moment he wished that she was awake and responding. His head began to spin. His thoughts began to race. His body went limp as he ejaculated. Suddenly, it was over. He had reached a climax, actually an anticlimax, not at all sexually satisfied, but thoroughly happy the mission was complete. He could return home in triumph. He wiped away the excess sperm, redressed her as best he could and left her there until the sedative released its spell.

When Odessa awoke the next morning, she had a slight headache and she felt drained and soiled. She bathed longer that morning, scrubbing herself in places she usually washed with gentle care. Her dreams were returning. She was not sure, but she thought last night she had dreamed. The dream was not clear and she could not remember what it was about. She sat there in the water, trying to recall it. She knew it was not a pleasant dream, but she knew it was important for her to remember. Her vision was returning. Soon she would be able to see the future again and end the mystery of the past few months. Two hours later, a scream of horror was heard coming from the royal bed chamber. But no one came to assist the queen. She was alone. She had sent all the guards to save Emanuel.

Later that day, she learned that the ambassador had been recalled to China. Emanuel had told her on the videophone. He asked her why she had sent the Palace Guard to protect him. She said it was a long story. She told him that she loved him, and to hurry home. She told him that her vision had returned and that some of the things she recalled were nightmares. She kept repeating that she loved him. He did not doubt her love, but he detected something new in her voice. Fear. Something neither one had ever known.

Two days later, Emanuel returned. That morning, they fenced, bathed and made love. She clung tightly to him, as if seeking his protection. He sensed this and vowed never again to let her out of his sight. In the safety of his arms, she revealed to him what she now knew to be true. His grip tightened and he drew her closer to him as he listened to the story. His blood began to boil as she told him of Lo Fu Chu's deception. His heart sank when she told him that it had worked, and she was pregnant. Emanuel reacted unlike any other man in the same position. He did not act as if it was he who had been violated. He shared the pain of her degradation, and he shared the joy of the new life she carried within her. He held her close.

"This baby is my baby. We will get through this together," he said, kissing her. Then they fell asleep.

When Odessa was in the ninth month of her pregnancy, stories about Odessa's unborn child grew like wild fire. Some said the baby was that of the young Chinese Ambassador, Lo Fu Chu. The Chinese Emperor claimed the unborn child would one day rule the Eastern Alliance. He claimed that since China was the largest country in the Eastern Alliance, it was fitting for one of her people to rule.

Meanwhile, the Fundamentalists gathered outside the palace gates. Every day their numbers grew.

"The Queen is an adulteress. Islamic law demands that she die," they chanted this over, and over, day after day. Emanuel would have used the Chemicals to extinguish the discontented in the textbook manner, but Rameses, the Lord of the Alliance, forbade it.

"The Alliance must hold together. It matters not if you hold it or China does," Rameses told him point blank, "All that matters is that it holds."

The young King and his Queen were in their bed chamber when a messenger arrived from the Chinese embassy. The emperor had offered Odessa asylum at the embassy, warning that if any harm should come to the Chinese heir to the Alliance, there would be war. Reconnaissance verified the report of five hundred thousand heavily armed Chinese troops at the border of their country. They were waiting for orders to attack. The situation looked bleak, but Emanuel would not turn his wife over to the Islamic fundamentalists. Alliance or no Alliance, he would defend her. He ended a letter to Rameses with the words: "Odessa's life is at stake. Damn the Alliance, damn you for not taking your place at our side and damn the family for not condemning your decision."

He secured the inside of the palace using his personal guard. The Palace Guard surrounded the exterior. They pushed the demonstrators back to a barrier two hundred feet from the gate, and Emanuel declared it as a no man's land. Anyone caught in between the two security forces would be shot on sight. The subjects of Oman supported their king. The armies of the Eastern Alliance stood ready, awaiting his command. The fate of the Alliance was in his hands, as was the life of Odessa and the unborn heir. Emanuel's options were bad and worse. If he eliminated the fundamentalists, it would mean civil war in Oman. If he marched against China, it would mean the end of the Eastern Alliance. If he turned his wife over to the fundamentalists for trial, it would mean certain death. The child would certainly be half-Chinese, meaning it was the product of infidelity.

Emanuel sat on the edge of their bed, talking to Odessa. In Odessa's mind the solution was clear; she must accept the invitation from the emperor. The fundamentalists would not violate the sanctity of the embassy. She would be safe there for the rest of her life if necessary. The important thing was the birth of the baby. Odessa would have to be smuggled into the embassy, and it would have to be done soon. The baby was due anytime. Delivery would be within hours.

Two hours later, the royal limousine pulled in front of the palace entrance door. The king and queen got inside. The guards walked along both sides of the vehicle. When the gates opened, the crowd outside parted, allowing the car to leave. The crowd followed behind the limousine at a safe distance. It rolled to a stop at the front door of the embassy. The king and queen got out, and the guards surrounded them for protection. The queen moved slowly because of her condition. The crowd began to chant again when they saw her. They chanted louder as the doors of the Chinese embassy opened. They went into frenzy as they finally realized that the embassy was a sanctuary. Emanuel breathed easier when the doors of the embassy closed behind them.

"She is safe now," he said to himself, "after the baby is born, I will negotiate for her life."

Odessa went into labor immediately upon arrival at the embassy. The child was female, Chinese of course, with black hair and slanted black eyes with deep black pupils. Her skin tone was not yellow, but a light tan. Her nose was like her mother's, and her lips were thin, like her father's. She was as beautiful at birth as her mother had been. Emanuel left two of his personal bodyguards with Odessa and the baby before returning to the palace to make plans for his next move. The immediate threat was still the fundamentalists. They were religious zealots who lived by the letter of the law, and Emanuel knew he would have to prove Odessa's innocence to them before she would ever be safe again in Oman.

Emanuel sent an emissary to China. He wanted an audience with the emperor and he wanted the audience on neutral ground, outside of the Eastern Alliance, where they would both feel safe. The emperor agreed, reminding him of the fact that the Alliance was controlled by his family. There really was not a safe place for him to meet Emanuel outside of China, but he would. After all the baby made them almost related.

Emanuel had no desire for revenge; his only concern was for the safety of his wife. Tomorrow suggested to Odessa that Emanuel speak to the one member of the family who was a prince of the Alliance, but remained his own man—the son of Maxwell Mason Stone, her father. He controlled the polar regions of the world, the last frontiers on earth. The emperor agreed. He would trust the Canyon Mesa Stone, Chairman of the Board of Infectious Diseases, United States Surgeon General, and Lord Protector of the Environment. They would meet at one of the domed cities near the South Pole. Canyon Mesa would personally guarantee their safety. The emissary contacted Canyon Mesa and explained Emanuel's plight. Canyon Mesa told the emissary he had orders from Rameses himself not to interfere in the affairs of the Eastern Alliance. However, he would be in the First Domed City of the South Pole on Friday week with his wife.

"If the gentlemen will join me and my family on the slopes, I would be glad to guarantee them a safe holiday," he said. This was all the emissary needed to know. The date was set, and one of the most important conferences in the history of the Alliance secretly took place under the protection of Canyon Mesa. A winter storm raged outside of the domed city, but inside the climate-controlled structure, the temperature remained a constant forty four degrees. A light man-made snow fell in the skiing area, giving it the appearance of a winter wonderland. All of this was the brain child of Canyon Mesa. Here, he was king. Some of the residents referred to him as the Snow King. Canyon Mesa had accomplished all this without the aid of the Alliance. Even though he was a member of the Alliance, he owed Rameses nothing except the loyalty of family.

The emperor met with Emanuel for the first time that day. He told Emanuel that when he brought China into the Eastern Alliance, he had thought that one day one of his daughters would marry an offspring of the god Kings. Such a marriage would only strengthen the Alliance. When Emanuel and Odessa were married, he had realized that there was no chance of this happening in his lifetime. A Chinese descendent would never be on the throne in Oman. He had devised his plan solely for the procreation of a Chinese heir. They both agreed that was what they had. Emanuel told the emperor of the danger Odessa was in from the Islamic fundamentalists. He told him that he held no grudge about the rape of his wife; his only concern was to save her from the rigid Islamic laws. He explained that the only chance she had of freedom was a trial proving her innocent of infidelity. He wanted the ambassador, Lo Fu Chu, to return to Oman under diplomatic immunity and testify at her trial.

"What of the child?" the Emperor then asked.

"A child of Odessa is a child of mine. The child will be heir to the throne of Oman. To this end, you have been successful, but you cannot have the life of my wife," said Emanuel.

"It was never my intention that she should die," the Emperor said in his own defense.

"Then you will send the ambassador back to Oman for the trial of Odessa?" asked Emanuel.

"Yes I will," promised the Emperor. "You have but to tell me when."

Odessa was in her suite at the Chinese embassy in Oman. Emanuel entered the room with a smile on his face. He had not seen her since the day the baby was born. While he was away, she had named the child Omania. She was nursing the baby when he arrived.

"Do you think that kid will save some for me?" he asked her, as she looked up to see who had entered the room. He could see the delight in her eyes at the sight of him.

"Look, Mannie," she said. "See how big she has grown?"

"The only thing I see is that she likes that breast as much as I do," he quipped.

"Oh, Mannie," she said seriously, "it is only hers for now. It is yours forever."

He leaned over to kiss her and the baby. "Odessa," he said, "I went to see the emperor."

She smiled at the way he said, "emperor." It was like the way they used to talk when they were children—when they shared a secret. "He is a fine man, you know, really he is. He is going to help us," said Emanuel.

"He already has, Mannie," she said referring to the child. "Isn't she beautiful?"

"I am glad you like her. I told the emperor that a child of Odessa is a child of mine." Emanuel paused and then said very seriously, "Odessa, I am going to let you stand trial. The Emperor is sending Lo Fu Chu back to testify to your innocence. I am granting him diplomatic immunity."

"Mannie," she said, "that is a very practical solution. I am so proud of you. I was never worried that you wouldn't find a way out of this for me. Never."

Emanuel decreed that the Queen Odessa would stand trial, but she would not be arrested. She would attend the trial while staying at the embassy, until a verdict was reached. The ambassador came back from China. He avoided seeing the royal couple face to face. He preferred to see them in court, testify on behalf of the Queen, and when the trial was over, leave immediately for China.

The courtroom was crowded with spectators on the morning of the indictment. Testimony would be heard that day to determine if the evidence against Odessa warranted an indictment. A hush came over the courtroom when the queen arrived, escorted by her husband, the king. Everyone rose and bowed their heads in acknowledgment of the royal couple. Emanuel nodded his head, and court was in session. The prosecutor carefully and meticulously presented his case, concluding with the most damaging evidence, the child Omania. The courtroom spectators raised there voices in anger, asking what more proof could be needed. In their eyes, the queen was guilty as charged. The judge rapped his gavel several times before the courtroom came to order. The prosecution rested its case. It was now the defense's turn, and Emanuel defended his queen. He stood and looked angrily into the crowd. They sat silently as he glared at them. He broke the silence when he called his one and only witness to the stand.

"The defense calls Chinese Ambassador Lo Fu Chu," he said. Lo Fu Chu stood, and then walked silently in his soft-soled, slipper-covered feet to the stand, raising his right hand to be sworn in.

Emanuel asked him what had happened on the day the king left for China to settle the alleged border dispute between the emperor and his cousin. The ambassador told the court of the story he had concocted to get an audience with the queen. He told them how he had sedated her after getting her to send the guards away to defend the king. He then told them of what he described as the insemination of Odessa.

"The queen was not only unwilling, but unconscious the entire time the incident was taking place," he concluded.

The fundamentalists in the crowd stood and shouted foul. They said the Crown had invented the story and bribed the witness in order to save the queen. The judge rapped his gavel until they came to order. He announced he would clear the court room upon the next outburst and then ordered the jury out for deliberation. He told the jury that they, and they alone, would decide Odessa's fate. The jury deliberated for three hours before returning a verdict. Their decision was unanimous. The only person who could possibly know the truth was the baby's father, Lo Fu Chu. In light of his confession, the queen was exonerated.

The royal couple held each other close as the verdict was read. The ambassador was quickly hustled away by the Palace Guard. He was given safe passage to the border, where Chinese army officers took charge of his safety. Emanuel and Odessa had withstood the challenge of religion verses absolute power. They were forced to make their choices alone, without the benefit history as a guide. Love was their strength and marriage was their alliance. The war they had fought was the battle of wills, a war as consequential to the world as any fought by their ancestors. The only difference was their choice of arms. Later that year the king and queen adopted a son, who they had discovered on the palace grounds in a basket. Evidently, he had been abandoned in a place where they would find him. They named him Obalah of Oman and betrothed him to Omania in the year 2071. Their marriage united China and Oman, forever sealing the breach in the Eastern Alliance.

"If it were possible for man to be perfect, then it would be my daughter, with all her imperfection"
Canyon Mesa Stone

Chapter Thirty-nine

Millennium and Tomorrow

In the year 2092, Millennium and Tomorrow came to power in Southeast Asia. Ali Khan and Maria, Millennium's parents, had ruled the New Race of people since 2034. They had held this part of the Alliance intact for the last fifty-eight years, without even the threat of a war. They maintained a small, but powerful army, trained by the Special Force of Five Thousand under the leadership of Maria Theopopulous, Millennium's mother. Now Millennium would be the commander-in-chief of this deadly force.

We find him speaking to Rameses on the videophone in his office.

"Why have you allowed the emperor to intimidate Emanuel with those ridiculous maneuvers on the Chinese border?"

"Believe me, Emanuel is not intimidated by the Emperor's show of force," Rameses responded. "The emperor has informed me that he is reassigning his ambassador, Lo Fu Chu, to Oman."

"Yes, I know. I am getting the old guy from Oman assigned here. My army is ready to go in and support Emanuel if the emperor puts one toe across his border," said Millennium.

"You will not do anything without my orders. Not now, not ever," said Rameses. "I am still the Lord of the Alliance, and as long as that is true, I will lead and you will follow." This was not the first time he had put the young Millennium in his place.

The angry Rameses raged on. "I will not chance a breach in the Alliance based on emotions. My first responsibility is to the Alliance. When will your generation learn that I must support world peace above all other interests, including family ties? If China pulls out of the Alliance, we will lose a third of our strength in the East. That is, every allied country not ruled by a family member," said Rameses.

"My lord Rameses please forgive my youth, but history tells me that was not always our priority. I recall your mother claiming most of the world's wealth for what she referred to as the future generation. Well sir, I am that future, and so is Emanuel," said Millennium.

By this time Rameses was enraged. He said, in no uncertain terms, to Millennium, "if I may be so bold as to point out to you, young sir, at that particular time in history, wealth and power were the priorities of the day. Now it is the Alliance. Do I make myself perfectly clear?" He did not wait for Millennium to respond before cutting off the transmission, without saying good-bye.

Millennium would have sent troops to the aid of Emanuel, had not his father interceded. He explained that Emanuel must settle his problem with the emperor without outside interference.

"I hope I never need the support of this family. I see what happens if you are not second generation," Millennium said to his father. Ali Khan could see it was futile to continue the conversation with his son. He was glad that it was Emanuel and Odessa who had to face their choice of arms, and not Millennium and Tomorrow.

Odessa was in her eighth month of pregnancy when she spoke to Tomorrow by videophone. After listening to Odessa's story, Tomorrow knew the only person that could help them was her father, Canyon Mesa. He was the one person who could intercede without incurring the wrath of Rameses. Tomorrow was right. When Rameses heard that Canyon Mesa had offered the Emperor and Emanuel a safe place to reconcile their differences, he smiled, and said, "that is his job. Lord Protector of the Environment. War is a threat to the environment, isn't it?" The third generation of rulers of the Alliance had learned a valuable lesson from Emanuel and Odessa: discretion is sometimes the better part of valor. In their situation, this had evidently been true.

In that same year of 2092, Damien, the son of Mica Mark Magee, came to the Southeast Asian Alliance with a force of one thousand troops. He came in support of Millennium's decision to fight the emperor of China if he invaded Oman. The arrival of Damien in the Southeast Asian Alliance convinced Rameses that the third generation of his family had no respect for their elders or the preservation of the Alliance. Elizabeth Susan did not take their defiance of her husband's orders personally. She realized they were still immature, and prone to make impetuous moves. She reminded Rameses that they had not been much different. Wars had hid most of their mistakes, and they did not leave their critics alive to judge them. Now it was the third generation's time. They would rule. They would make mistakes, and they would suffer the consequences. They would learn as they had. The past was the only frame of reference.

Millennium greeted his cousin Damien with open arms. They embraced and talked awhile about old times. Damien had not seen Tomorrow since she and Millennium were married. Tomorrow walked into the room where the men were talking.

"Tomorrow," Millennium said, "Damien just arrived."

"Yes, she replied, "and from the look of things, he's ready for war."

"These are uncertain times, dear cousin, I do what I must," Damien said.

"So I am told," she said. "War is a little boy's game, and boys will be boys."

Millennium was annoyed by his wife's statement. "There was a time when you supported anything I did without question," he said.

"There was a time when you would never have defied the Lord of the Alliance," she responded.

"That's your mother talking. Besides, this is different. Rameses is wrong. The emperor must be stopped at his border or he will seize control of the East, and we will lose the entire Eastern Alliance. I, for one, will never serve him," said Millennium.

"Or anyone else," she remarked as she left the room. The fragrance of the myrrh she was wearing lingered for a few seconds after she was gone. Damien inhaled the scent of her as if he were trying to get a contact high from marijuana. He stood there in a hypnotic trance, looking at the door she had just gone through while Millennium made excuses for her behavior. Damien did not hear them.

"I don't know what has come over her. She seems to be a stranger in my life since this trouble in Oman began," he said. When Damien did not reply, Millennium dropped the subject and stared at the man staring at the doorway. Damien sensed the silent chill, of Millennium's gaze as his attention returned to the room.

"I'm sorry, Cousin, you were saying?" he asked.

"It was not important, and certainly not something I should be talking to you about, or anyone else for that matter," Millennium responded coldly.

Damien pretended that the episode had gone over his head as he inquired about his room. He said he would like to shower before dinner. Millennium had a servant take him to the guest rooms on the other side of the courtyard. They were directly across from the suite that he and Tomorrow shared. Damien entered his suite and walked over to the window. Across the courtyard, he could see the window of Tomorrow's suite. He stood a moment watching the window, hoping to get a glimpse of her as she passed. His heart skipped a beat when he saw the shadow of a woman cross the room. His imagination gave the shadow a face and a body. His desire gave her life. It was at that moment he finally admitted to himself that he coveted his cousin's wife. Coveting was a sin, a sin for which he may burn in Hell. But the fires of Hell could not be any hotter than the lust that fuelled his desire. For her love, he would chance the fires of Hell and Damnation.

At that moment in time, all he had ever wanted in life would have been granted if Tomorrow but gave him a sign that she felt the same. That she loved him. That she would face Hell's fires standing by his side. He walked away from the window, thinking.

Why would she, he wondered. She already has a kingdom. All I could offer her is the flames of Hell. That, and a love affair that would last until the end of time.

He removed his clothes and stepped into the shower. The soap and hot water washed away the contemplation of sin. This was his cousin's wife. She was beyond his wildest dreams, and even if she succumbed to his desire, the fruit of their love would be a civil war. It would be a love that would destroy the family and end the Alliance as they knew it. Suddenly he was overcome with fatigue. He lay naked across the bed and fell into a deep sleep. When Damien did not answer the knock on the door, Tomorrow let herself into the suite.

"Damien, we are waiting for you at the dinner table," she called out softly. She walked into the bedroom where he was asleep. She wanted to call out to him that dinner was ready, but she dared not. How could she have explained the intrusion? She wanted to leave the room, but she was compelled to stay and look at his naked body. Tomorrow studied his handsome physique. He was long, lean and muscular. She massaged the muscles with her eyes, coming to a rest on his penis. It was all she could do to resist touching it. She panicked when he stirred in his sleep and ran out the door.

The door slammed, and he awakened. When he sat up, he realized it was dinner time. And he then became aware of Tomorrow's scent in the room. He had gone to sleep with the scent of her myrrh in his nostrils. He inhaled deeply to make sure he was awake. The blinding desire returned, and his penis became erect at the thought of her. He brushed his teeth, dressed and went down to dinner.

Millennium greeted him, "Sleeping beauty, I presume. My wife went up to get you. She said you were sleeping so soundly that she did not want to wake you." Tomorrow purposely did not look at him for fear he would say something about his state of dress. It all became clear to him then. She was really there in the room while he was asleep in the nude. The scent had been real. Their gazes met briefly. Her eyes pleaded with him to drop the subject.

"What's for dinner," he asked as she breathed a sigh of relief. Millennium watched them through dinner. Although he was not suspicious, he did notice the uneasiness of Tomorrow whenever her eyes met Damien's. Damien was amused by her predicament. They knew something her husband was not privy too. At the end of the meal, Damien announced he would be sleeping in the field with his men for the next two weeks.

"After all," he said, "I am not a king, I am a soldier and my place is with my men. In the field." He pushed his chair away from the table and got up. "By your leave," he said to them both, looking at Tomorrow.

She lifted her eyes to meet his gaze. "Sleep well, my cousin and prince of the Alliance." She said cousin, as if to remind him that they were related.

"My cousin's wife," he said, kissing her hand, as if to remind her they were only related by marriage.

Damien woke up early the next morning and joined his troops in the field. He thought about Tomorrow. Much of what he was going to do about how he felt would depend on her. His days were spent in thought, and at night, she occupied his dreams. Her scent tantalized his senses, making his dreams of her a reality. His thoughts of her possessed him. A possession from which only an exorcist could set him free. He wished the threat to Oman were over so he could go home. He cursed the day he came there. If he had not, he would not be in love with his cousin's wife. If he had not, he would not be in danger of damnation. Even if he were, coveting would not be the sin.

It had been one week, one day, one hour, ten minutes and thirty seconds since Tomorrow had last seen Damien. She knew that because on the day that he had left, she had watched him as he walked across the courtyard to the limousine that drove him to the place where his troops were waiting. She happened to look at the clock that morning and saw that it read five a.m. She remembered that she had been restless that night and could not sleep. She had been enveloped by thoughts of Damien. When she made love to her husband that night, she closed her eyes and it was Damien who was holding her, kissing her, nibbling on her neck, caressing her breasts and satisfying her unfulfilled hunger for him, a hunger that seemed to have consumed her since that first evening she had seen him naked, asleep on the bed. Watching him lie there, she had remembered the story of Adam and Eve from Sunday School classes. It was like being a voyager at the scene of the Original Sin in the Garden of Eden when the serpent had offered Eve a bite of the forbidden fruit from the Tree of Knowledge. Unlike Eve, Tomorrow resisted the temptation. Yet she fell into the abyss. Her sin was the desire. The desire to see him again. The desire to touch him. The desire to be touched by him. The desire to have him. She, without having tasted the fruit, had already committed the sin of coveting him. Tomorrow had made her decision. If Damien would have her, she was willing to be his lover. Secretly or openly, whatever he wanted, she wanted. For his love, she was willing to risk hell and damnation.

On the Friday of the second week, Damien returned from the field. He did not wear the uniform of a soldier this time. He dressed in the attire of a prince of the Alliance, and around his waist hung a short sword. Tomorrow's eyes lit up when she saw him. Her face took on the glow from the light of her eyes.

"I could hardly wait for your return," she said with a flirtatious smile, and inaudibly to anyone but him. Millennium had moved within earshot. Damien acknowledged that he understood with a nod of his head. They were standing next to each other silently, looking around the room. Both were satisfied that they had communicated their true feelings. Both felt the excitement and danger that went with this kind of deception. Their hearts pounded furiously, leaving them short of breath and speechless as Millennium approached their side. He extended his hand to Damien and welcomed him back with a firm handshake. The guilt felt like a heavy mantle thrown across Damien's shoulders, and his knees felt as if they were going to buckle under the weight.

"I must say, you don't look well, Damien," said Millennium. "With all that talk of being a soldier and sleeping in the field with your troops, I think your health has paid a heavy toll. Look at him, Tomorrow. The man is without color."

Tomorrow pretended to look at him and responded to her husbands concern by saying, "Perhaps he should be in bed. Lord only knows what a man could catch in the field. Why don't you go up to bed? I will bring you up a hot toddy. It works wonders. It always works for Millennium. Don't you agree, darling?"

"Yes," Millennium agreed. "You probably need a good night's rest in a real bed. The hot toddy will put you to sleep."

Damien agreed with them and started upstairs. He turned to Tomorrow, and said, "Rum."

"Rum?" she asked.

"A jigger of rum in my toddy."

"If it's a jigger of rum you want, then a jigger of rum you shall have. Now run along. Millennium and I shall be up in a minute."

"No," protested Millennium, "I can't chance catching anything. You take the toddy up to him. I must meet with the new Chinese Ambassador, the one that was transferred here from Oman. I want to see if he has any word on the situation in Oman, from the Chinese point of view."

Tomorrow looked at Damien, trying to read his thoughts. He gave no indication that he understood the implication of what Millennium's statement could mean to them. He simply turned and went upstairs, leaving her and Millennium alone in the room.

Tomorrow went to mix the rum toddy, but she did not take it up to Damien until after Millennium was gone. She climbed the steps slowly, anticipating that Damien was waiting for her in the suite. She opened the door of the room, went inside and used her foot to close it behind her. She called to him as she had in her first encounter with him in this room. This time Damien answered her. He came through the bedroom door into the parlor of the suite where she was waiting. He had made no assumptions; he was fully dressed. She was nervous and unsure of herself, alone with him for the first time. It was easy for him to see that this was not something she had done before. She stood there with the hot toddy in her hand.

"Is that for me or do you intend to spill the rest of it on the floor?" he asked her, laughing nervously.

"I guess my hand is shaking more than I noticed."

They started to talk at the same time.

"You go first," he said.

"No, you first. I insist," she replied.

"You know you don't have to go through with this."

"I know. I want to. I guess I'm just scared."

He walked over to her and stroked her long, blond hair with both of his hands. He drew her face to him and kissed her softly on the lips.

"What you must think of me," she said. "Being here with you like this. I'm married to your cousin and alone with a man who is obviously lonely and far from home."

He looked into her eyes and said, "It's true, I am a long way from home. But I am not lonely. I'm a soldier. I have spent most of my life away from home and loved ones. I have grown accustomed to this life. There has never been any time for a woman in my life. I have not been looking for one. Not until I met you. I fell in love with you the first day I arrived here, two weeks ago. I knew then that I could not live without you. I left here in hope of forgetting you, but it didn't work, so I came back. I'm too weak to leave you now that I have found you. Before you came up, I was hoping that you would be strong enough for the both of us and let this feeling go before it destroys everyone and everything around us."

She answered him soft, seductive and sexy, "I can't. It's too late for me. I love you." Her deep, blue eyes drew him to her like a pool of water on a hot summer day. She opened her arms as he moved to her like a piece of metal drawn to a magnet, and they kissed.

"Whatever happens will have to happen. I can't let you go now. We will face this thing together," he promised. Damien picked her up and carried her into the bedroom. She seemed weightless with her arms around his neck and her head on his shoulder. She remembered that her father had carried her that way when she was a child. She would fall asleep in her parents' room on purpose, just so he would have to pick her up and put her to bed. He was a strong man, her father. Until now, no other man had ever measured up to him. Actually, she never had given anyone a chance to try. She, like all the girls in the family, had married young. Millennium had been her childhood friend. They were married because they had been betrothed. They were never given a choice in the matter. That was the way it was in the family, everyone married someone else's choice. Now she was in the arms of a man of her own choice, for better or worse.

Damien laid her on the bed. They had no idea how much time they had before Millennium returned, so they didn't remove any of their clothes. He lifted up the skirt that she was wearing, fumbled with her panties, and finally in frustration, ripped the crotch out. He unzipped his pants, and penetrated her. She was frightened by the abrupt way he handled her underwear, but he kissed her until she was at ease again. She moved her body to the rhythm of his until they climaxed. They held on to each other for a few minutes before she went into the bathroom to clean up. Then she went downstairs, leaving him lying on the bed.

"Drink the toddy. I'll come back for the glass," she said before going down.

He must have been tired. He was asleep before the door closed. If she returned that night he didn't know it. She must have returned; the glass was not there when he awoke in the morning. He took a shower and went downstairs for breakfast. She and Millennium were sitting at the breakfast table. Dishes were being cleared. They had already eaten. The servant set another place for him, and he drank a glass of orange juice while he waited to be served. She greeted him with a smile, but she didn't say anything. Millennium asked if he felt any better. Damien replied in all honesty that he had never felt better.

"The toddy is a secret recipe contrived by her father while he was searching for a cure for the Disease Without a Name," Millennium said.

Tomorrow's father was a legend and his fame extended far beyond the Alliance. Since he invested most of his wealth in the development of the polar regions, he had shown little interest in politics. He had brought the polar regions into the Alliance, but only as a show of solidarity to Rameses. He ruled those regions without any outside interference. His only interests were his family and his domain. Other than his wife Greta, his only love was Tomorrow. This fact weighed heavily on any decision made by his daughter. She knew her father would take her side over anyone in the Alliance. She would tread lightly on the issue of her new love, only because of the injury it would do to Millennium's ego. She had nothing to fear from her family or the Alliance. She was the daughter of Canyon Mesa Stone. When it came to her, adverse opinion could be fatal. This was a fact that everyone in the Alliance was aware of.

Millennium was leaving on a three day tour of the borders. Security had been a priority in this part of the Alliance since the trouble in Oman. Millennium's border patrols were ready to give sanctuary to Emanuel and Odessa if they had to flee their country. He had been making these trips once a month since the trouble started, so Tomorrow was not surprised. An hour later, he was saying good-bye to them at the gate. After kissing Tomorrow, he said to Damien, "Look after her while I am gone." Damien said he would. He and Tomorrow watched until Millennium was out of sight before they went back inside. They would have three days and three nights together before Millennium returned.

That day, Tomorrow wanted to go into the jungle. She liked to watch the wildlife, especially the young at play. They set out on the excursion that afternoon; Damien, Tomorrow, her servant. and a bodyguard. A little more than ten miles into the jungle where Moses Cribb and Ny Li Tu had found each other in the mid 1900's, Tomorrow took pictures of the wildlife young at play. She swam in the waters of the Mekong Delta as Damien watched. All too soon it was time to return home.

That night after dinner she came to his room.

There could be no doubt of her intent. She only wore a sheer nightgown with nothing under it to resist his advances. He was lying in bed, nude as usual. His penis stood erect at the sight of her. In this encounter, time was not a factor. Tomorrow had come to spend the night. She let the night-gown fall to the floor at her feet before getting into bed. She knelt on the bed, leaned over, and kissed him, using her tongue to probe the inside of his mouth. Then his tongue moved into her mouth, back and forth. She turned her attention to his neck. If she had not, she would have suffocated; he inhaled her breath as he was kissing her in re-lentless pursuit of her essence. Breathing heavily, she bit his neck in self-defense, sending sensations over his body that he had never experienced be-fore. She took his penis in her hand while sucking on his neck like a vampire, leaving a red mark that would soon turn blue. In a move executed as if she had practiced it, she replaced her hand with her mouth on his penis without losing the rhythm of her movement. He let out a sound somewhere be-tween pleasure and pain. She muffled it by plac-ing her hand over his mouth. She whispered in his ear, "don't come," as if it were a threat. Then she mounted him, impaling herself on his long, thick penis and moving her body in a frenzy that could have been mistaken for a deranged fit of lunacy. Together, they unleashed a river of body fluids. Her body went limp as she felt the force of his semen erupt inside of her.

Her head was spinning when she rolled off of him. She lay there next to him, watching the ceil-ing go around until it stopped to let her off. She went into the bathroom. When she came out, he was asleep. She cleaned him up and laid herself down beside him. She watched him as he slept, and suddenly her sanity returned. There was no doubt. If there was a list of things that she must do before she died, this was on it. But to leave Millennium, to leave her kingdom... I think not, she said to herself.

When Damien awoke the next morning, she was not in bed. He showered and went down to breakfast. She was drinking her orange juice when he sat down. The servant poured his orange juice and they were served at the same time.

"Damien, I like, no, I love making love to you, but I can't leave my husband," Tomorrow said when the servant was out of earshot.

He smiled at her and said, "I knew that when you were not in bed this morning. Let's just take it as it comes. If you change your mind before I leave, you come with me. It's as simple as that. In the meantime, I want to make love to you every minute of the time we have left."

"I know I'm not going to change my mind, but you have a deal on the lovemaking part," she said. They made love once more before Damien left. After that they never spoke of it again. He moved into the field with his men when Millennium came back. Four months later, the threat of war in Oman had ended and he went home.

In the months that followed, Tomorrow came to know why she stayed with Millennium. He was safe, he was predictable, he was strong. To him, Tomorrow was the sun and the moon. He was the man most like her father. Seven months later, Tomorrow gave birth to a girl. She and Millennium named her Marisol. It would be a long time before Damien married. He took a consort from the European Alliance named Grecian. She was a beautiful young girl with pale, white skin and long blonde hair. They had a son they named Franc. Tomorrow shared her secret with her father five years later. At the end of her story, she asked him to forgive her.

"For what?" he asked her. "How else would you have fallen in love with your husband."

"Oh, Daddy, in your eyes I can never do anything wrong," she said.

"And I dare anyone to beg to differ," he responded in jest.

"The difference between making love and taking love is being loved in return"

Damien

Chapter Forty

The New World Beneath the Sea

In the year 2092, far away from the Alliance and the rumors of war, Everett Jr. and his wife Marion Matilda went about their work. They were building a penal colony under the sea, somewhere in the Atlantic Ocean. The project was almost completed. They had the old weather satellites that had circled the earth, controlling the condition of the atmosphere. The satellites were originally weapons of war, but the Lord of the Alliance had banned them ten years before. Everett Jr. and Marion Matilda were given total control of their use, thus some of them were under the sea. These were called Inner Space Stations.

Twenty-five of these satellites were sitting in a circle, with three forming an inner circle. All were connected by above-ground tunnels made of the same material. On the outside of the two circles, sitting alone, was a single satellite that controlled the air supply and pressure for the colony. It held a solar power plant with two giant generators and an emergency switch to prevent power failure. Inside this satellite lived six scientists and their families. The only access to them was from the outside through a pressure chamber. There was no corridor leading from the other satellites for security reasons. These people held the lives of the entire colony in their hands.

Rameses and Elizabeth Susan attended the ribbon cutting ceremony. With them were one hun-

dred miners and their families along with
Cheyenne's Dakota Moon and one hundred members of the Special Force of Five Thousand. They
would serve as temporary guards after the inmates
arrived. The mining engineers and their families
were to occupy the Inner Circle of the satellites.
The Outer Circle would house the inmates, ten
thousand of them, all together. The first two thousand were to arrive in two weeks. They would set
up the mining operation. The rest would come down
two thousand at a time, over a period of one year.
If all went well, the one hundred members of the
Special Force of Five Thousand would not be
needed. The inmate colonists would be joined by
their families and would live in the underwater
community, mining the under-sea caves.

Rameses talked to Everett Jr. about how long
he thought it would take before the colony could
be fully occupied and the mining operation showed
a profit. They were in a suite of rooms in the Inner
Circle. Their wives walked in just in time to join
the conversation.

"I was hoping the settlement of the colony would
take precedence over the mining profits," said
Marion Matilda. Rameses was not surprised that
she would think so. He expected her to oppose the
establishment of a mining operation before a form
of government was established by the penal colonists.

"Why, Marion, do you refer to these people as
colonists instead of as inmates?" he asked.

"You said yourself that they are people, convicted criminals, but nevertheless people. If this
experiment is to work, they must have a form of
government and a governing body, comprised of
them, by them," she answered.

"That's all well and good, Marion, but our family financed this project, and I would like to see an

immediate return on the investment," said Rameses.

"Profits, profits," she said. "The success of this experiment is not about profits. The mining profits are the byproduct. A whole new world is opening up for us down here, a new civilization beneath the sea. The colonists just happened to be convicts which is not a very original idea. In time it may just be profitable, but until then we will form a governing body to administer law and order."

After seeing that it was fruitless to carry this conversation any further with Marion Matilda, he turned to Everett Jr. and said, "I am holding you fully responsible for the mining profits. She is your wife, you reason with her." He turned away from Everett Jr. before he could answer. Rameses took Elizabeth Susan by the arm and left, thus ending the discussion as abruptly as it had begun.

The next day Rameses and Elizabeth Susan returned to the surface by way of the submarine transport. The first wave of convicts went down two weeks later. They discovered that there were no chains or shackles. The outer circle was their domain. They had recreation facilities and plenty of hard work. There was no question that it was a prison, and there was no way out, but it was heaven compared to the institutions they had come from. On the first day, they had an orientation. There was no warden, so Marion Matilda gave them the rules and regulations by which they would live.

She gave them the timetable for reuniting their families, the timetable for self-government and the schedule of wages, which were equal to the free miners on the surface. She gave them the seven day work schedule, consisting of three shifts, four days on and three days off. Ninety percent of the convicts would be miners, the other ten percent would maintain the satellites in the outer circle.

These people would be trained by the scientists before the arrival of the last wave of convicts, all of whom would be miners. The convicts did not fully understand what the future held for them, but for most, this was the next best thing to freedom. All of them were serving life sentences. The first two thousand convicts and their families would form the prototype society for the new world beneath the sea. Marion Matilda emphasized the importance of the mining operation. The mining products would be the main exports of their new world. Their survival would depend solely upon the trade agreement they would establish with the Alliance once the mining operation started to show a profit.

The families of the first wave of convicts came down three weeks later. This was definitely an added incentive. The men were working longer, harder and with fewer complaints than anticipated, considering the conditions in which they were expected to work. The caves were unexplored, uncharted and underwater. Manpower became a problem, and the second wave of convicts was brought down sooner than scheduled. Their families came with them. Marion Matilda insisted on this, based on the increased performance of the first wave after the arrival of their families.

It was the one hundred and sixtieth day of mining in a cave seven miles from the colony. Marion Matilda was inspecting the findings of a crew on the third shift, one mile inside the cave. While digging, they had hit a geyser. The hot water gushing from the geyser created a spa-like effect in the cave. The water temperature in the cave had risen to eighty degrees Fahrenheit, and was still rising at each hourly check. By the end of the shift, the cave walls began to crumble around them. They were in the middle of an undersea earthquake. The cave floor was moving and the falling rock revealed new cavern corridors. The water swept the miners into the new caverns, bouncing them off the walls with such force they were knocked unconscious for an undetermined amount of time. Finally, they all made their way to safety.

Despite the ordeal she had just suffered, Marion Matilda stayed outside with the first shift until the second shift came to relieve them. She re-entered the cave with the second shift after the quake ended and the water inside the cave cleared up. The walls of the newly revealed caverns sparkled with streaks of pure gold. Some of the veins were thirty or forty feet wide, and heaven only knew how deep. They had made their first find, and Marion Matilda had been there when it happened. She stayed outside with the miners until the shift ended, and even then she was reluctant to leave. In her excitement, she had forgotten her husband. She returned to the colony with the second shift to tell him of the rich strike.

Everett Jr. was with the scientists in the power plant, evaluating the effects of the tremor created by the earthquake in the cave. The satellites were not damaged, but many of the connections from the power plant to the colony were. This temporarily interrupted the air and pressure supply. Everett Jr. had been working two shifts with the maintenance crew, repairing the damage, and Marion Matilda found him and the scientists together, discussing the long range effects on the satellites resulting from the decrease in pressure. The worst case scenario was a complete shutdown of power which would cause the colony of satellites to implode, the outside pressure being greater than the inside pressure. This would crush the satellites like tin cans. The problem was, the emergency switch had taken thirty-five seconds to turn on. This had created the imbalance in pressure.

The scientists rose when Marion entered the room. Her husband looked up from the blueprints that were spread over the table and greeted her with a smile. "I understand that you were swimming in the deep for the last two shifts," he quipped.

She smiled and said, "I see you all were busy saving our world," making light of the near disaster that could have ended the entire experiment. He noticed that her arm was limp. He walked over to her and touched it lightly. "I got that during the earthquake, rocks were falling all around us. Or maybe it happened when the water washed us into the new caves that were opened by the quake. I am not sure," she said before he could ask.

He put his arms around her, drew her close to him and said, "Let's go see the doctor. The danger is over." He kissed her on the forehead as if she were a little girl who had gotten hurt doing something she was not allowed to do, and the kiss was forgiveness.

Annoyed by his assumption that what he did that day was more important than going into the mines, she said sarcastically, "Everett, we struck gold today."

He was suddenly embarrassed by his patronizing, chauvinistic gesture. She was a capable individual who could take care of herself under the most extreme circumstances. Realizing the mistake, he said, as if it never happened, "Gold?"

"Yes, gold," she responded. "A vein so rich and wide it could be a highway."

As the magnitude of the revelation struck him, Everett Jr. began to display the relief he felt. The last words spoken by Rameses before he left for the surface still echoed in his mind: "I am holding you fully responsible for the mining profits. She is your wife, you reason with her." Those words were to be his cross to bear, but now one word had relieved him of his burden. When his wife spoke that word, he was able to stand upright again. "Gold," he said to himself inaudibly. "God, how I love that woman."

They left the room without saying good-bye. Halfway to the infirmary he said, "Marion, I think they understand, and if they don't, who cares? Down here, I am..." he changed the thought mid-sentence, "we are in charge."

A smile crossed her lips as she realized that Ny Li Tu had always been right about the men in this family.

And you, my husband, are the epitome of male ego, she thought. *You would never have even gotten through the Academy without me.*

Three weeks had passed since the first strike, and twenty-two more veins had been discovered. The remaining miners and their families had come down from the surface. The colony was at its utmost capacity and it seemed like a beehive. The miners, working around the clock, gave the colony the appearance of a city that never slept. The gold was ninety-nine percent pure. It took very little heat to melt it and mold it into bricks. They stored it a mile from the colony, in open sight of the submarine port which was the only transportation to the surface.

Everett Jr. would have reported their success to Rameses immediately, but Marion Matilda would not hear of it. She believed that news of their newfound wealth would bring the whole Alliance down upon them. Although Rameses was the Lord of the Alliance, they could not depend on his protection. As of late, he had exhibited a wait-and-see-how-it-works-out attitude, remaining neutral in the last three crises. The colony was too small to survive that kind of a policy, especially since it had no army. What they did have was gold, and that would buy an army. Their only hope was to locate Damien and send for him. He made his living as a mercenary and they were sure he would support their cause. The last time anyone had heard from him, he was in the Southeast Asian Alliance with Millennium and Tomorrow. The story made no sense because he was there in support of Emanuel and Odessa, who are in Oman facing China's threats of war. The situation, however, had finally been remedied without the help of Damien, Millennium or Rameses. Living so far away from the Alliance, they didn't get news first-hand. Down there, they were lucky to get any news at all. The decision was made. They would send a messenger to seek Damien's help, wherever he was.

The next morning, one of the scientists left on a journey that would take him across three continents in ten days. He carried a secret coded message in a microscopic disk implanted under his left eyelid. He found Damien in Germany. He was in a a tavern in a tiny hamlet on the outskirts of Dresden, drinking with two of his officers. One drink away from intoxication, he was challenged to a duel by one of the barons of the European Alliance. He had been told that Damien was making overtures to his wife. The accusations, true or not, left the baron no choice but to kill Damien if he was to hold his head up and maintain his self respect. The baron took advantage of Damien's intoxicated condition, demanding immediate satisfaction. Unfortunately, he had chosen swords for weapons, and Damien was one of the best swordsman in the Alliance.

Damien had already sobered up for the duel when the messenger entered the tavern. He recognized Damien immediately, and asked permission for an audience. Under the circumstances, it was granted; the duel would be to the death. The messenger introduced himself and gave Damien the coded message. After reading it, Damien gave the message to one of his officers who verified the seal.

"You have caught me at an uncertain time in my life," Damien said to the messenger when they were sure of his authenticity, "The way I feel, coupled with the situation I am in, I may not even survive the day."

The messenger said to Damien, "I am a doctor. Will you trust me with your life?"

"In my condition, I am as good as dead already," Damien answered. "Either the baron kills me or you kill me. I will take my chances with you, unless somewhere in my travels I have met your wife." He looked at the messenger suspiciously.

"I doubt that you have," the messenger replied. "We spend all our time underwater."

Damien laughed as the messenger mixed a potion from some herbs and gave it to him to drink. Damien fell on the floor and went through a series of convulsive fits. In a matter of minutes, he got up off the floor under his own power and said, "I need a drink of water." The messenger nodded his approval, and Damien was given the water. "What was that stuff?" he asked the messenger.

"I don't know, but it seems to work."

They laughed as Damien picked up his sword and began to test his strength.

"What are they waiting for?" he said to his second after a series of exercises.

"For a swift and merciful death, my lord," the second answered.

"Then I hope it is he who is waiting," Damien smirked. He went into the street to meet his fate, sword in hand, with the confidence of an executioner prepared to execute the condemned. The baron stood in the middle of the street with his second, waiting for him. The baron began to lose the color in his face, when he looked into Damien's cold steel eyes. He was sober, and his hands were steady. The baron recognized the executioner.

"Do you love my wife?" he asked him.

"Sir, I can't even remember your wife," said Damien.

"I invoke the rule of the duel of honor, where a woman is involved," the baron said in a panic-stricken voice. The duel was delayed for the explanation. Damien was aware of no such rule.

"The woman whose honor is at stake in such a duel will not lose her benefactor. She will either retain the one she has or gain the survivor," the baron's second quoted.

"That rule must have been written by a woman of questionable character," Damien said to his second, under his breath, "It's better than a divorce. Is she at least beautiful?" "As fair as the lady Tomorrow," his second answered.

Damien smiled and said to him, "Then the baron is as good as dead. I will honor this rule."

Damien's second conveyed the message to the baron through his second. They touched swords, and the duel was on. They fought for a half hour. The baron gained some confidence when he drew first blood, cutting Damien across the crest in a sweeping motion. It was a move that caused him to leave his guard down, and it cost him his life. As Damien thrust his blade deep into his heart, the baron made a sound like a punctured rubber ball as the air is let out. He fell down on both knees. The weight of his body was supported by Damien's sword through his heart. Damien pulled the sword free, and he fell face down in a pool of blood.

The baron's blood-soaked body gave the false impression that he had died a horrible death. Damien had seen many dead bodies in his short lifetime. Many of them he had killed, but he had never experienced guilt before. This one he had killed for his woman, a woman Damien could not even remember, yet he knew that he must keep her. He had been told that she was as fair as the lady Tomorrow. He made up his mind, before seeing her, that she would be all that his true love would have been. He sent one of his officers to collect the dead baron's wife, the lady Grecian.

When she arrived, they went to the New World Beneath the Sea. The journey was long for her. She was used to a life of luxury and everything that went with it. This man who had killed her husband was unrefined and crude. She wondered why he had evoked the rule to keep her. She had never seen him before. One of the servants had told her that her husband was dead, and that Damien would come to claim her. She was packed and ready to go when his officer arrived. The lady Grecian knew she had no other choice. She went, but not before swearing that she would never love the man who had killed her husband.

Now they were alone in a room somewhere in the New World Beneath the Sea. They had arrived in the middle of the night and they were assigned quarters in the power plant with the scientists and their families. Everett Jr. and Marion Matilda would see them in the morning. This was the first time that Damien and Grecian had been alone together, and there was only one bed. If they were going to sleep, it would have to be together. The lady Grecian walked through the rooms, nervously looking for alternatives to the sleeping arrangements.

Damien saw the problem and said to her, "I don't intend to share my bed with you. I will ask for separate rooms in the morning."

She was stunned by his statement. *He does not want to share his bed with me. The nerve of this murderous bastard. He kills my husband to get me, and then he doesn't even want me,* she thought to herself. The longer she thought about it, the angrier she became, until her anger forced her to confront him. "Who the hell do you think you are?" she asked. "I am a Baroness of the European Alliance. Don't you think that because I am only nineteen years old I don't understand the rules of the duel you fought with my husband. I am entitled to all that you have and anything you acquire. I will not be abandoned by you. You are going to live up to your responsibility, and that is me, forever, or my father will have your head. Don't think I won't call him!" she said in a huff, as she started turning the bed down. She went on like that for the length of time it took her to prepare herself for bed. Her last remark to him before she went to sleep was, "You may sleep anywhere you please. But remember this, I will be right there beside you. Good night to you, my lord Damien."

"Good night my lady Grecian, Baroness of the European Alliance." he responded. He showered, and crawled into bed beside her. *I'm glad at least one of us knows what my responsibilities are. I was worried that you did not come with instructions,* he thought to himself. He slept in one spot that night, without moving. When he awoke the next morning, he sat upright abruptly, startled by the cold stare of the woman lying next to him.

"How long have you been lying there, awake?" he asked her, with some concern for his well-being. She smiled, when she realized she had made him nervous. She didn't answer his question. She had questions of her own.

"Where are all of the servants around here?" she queried.

He shook his head. "How would I know? We arrived last night together, remember?" He rolled out of bed and went into the bathroom. She followed him, and watched as he urinated.

"I observed that while you were sleeping," she announced.

"You observed what while I was sleeping," he responded, irritated by the intrusion on his privacy.

"That," she said, pointing to his penis.

He rolled his eyes and said, "Well don't observe it anymore while I am sleeping. It makes me nervous."

"I'm not surprised" she said. "The size of it would make anyone nervous."

"The size of my penis does not make me nervous. Just leave it alone while I am sleeping," he said, annoyed by the statement.

Seeing that he was getting agitated, she changed the subject. "I need a servant," she said to him, as if he could produce one upon request.

He rolled his eyes again, and said, "Get into the shower so we can dress."

"I have already taken one. Thank you just the same," she replied.

"Without a servant?" he asked in jest.

She stood there with a serious look on her face as she answered. "Of course. My servant did not bathe me."

Again he rolled his eyes. He stepped into the shower and turned on the water. "Of course. My servant did not bathe me," he mimicked as he soaped his body. When he opened the shower door, she was standing there with a towel.

"I heard that," she said as she handed him the towel. "Don't think I am not telling my father."

Damien dried himself off while thinking about her husband, the dead baron. It's a small wonder *why the son-of-a-bitch committed suicide, at the point of my sword,* he thought. *Between her and her father, life must have been hell.* If there had

been any way to bring him back to life, he would
have done it. A knock on the door called them to
breakfast. Damien answered that they would be
along in a minute. They dressed in the same clothes
they had arrived in the night before. Grecian complained about having to wear them. He opened the
door, took her by the hand and dragged her one
step behind him while she complained about her
clothes all the way. The corridor widened into a
foyer, from which the dining room could be seen
straight ahead. When they entered, Marion Matilda
rose to greet them.

Before he could cover her mouth with his hand,
Grecian blurted out, "Are you a servant?"

"I'm sorry, lady Marion," interrupted Damien.
"This is my..." He was suddenly lost for a word to
describe his relationship to Grecian.

"His intended," finished Grecian. "I am the lady
Grecian of the European Alliance," she said, introducing herself to everyone in the room at the same
time. They all rose and said good morning. Damien
pulled out one of the unoccupied seats, and she
sat down at the table.

The conversation at breakfast was different that
morning. The young lady Grecian did most of the
talking. She told them she was going home with
Damien, wherever that was. He had not told her
yet. She was sure that he was saving it for a surprise. Damien interrupted her several times during the conversation, but she chattered on to the
delight of the scientists. They had not met anyone
so carefree, and without responsibilities before in
their lives. The morning, spent with her, took their
minds off the reason for Damien's visit. The subject of servants came up again, and Marion Matilda
told her there were no servants down there.

"That's terrible. However do you get things
done?" Grecian asked.

"We do it ourselves," Marion Matilda said.

"You mean everyone down here is on their own?"

"Yes," said Marion Matilda. "In the sense that you mean. Everyone is self-sufficient."

"Well," said Grecian, "as long as it works." She changed the subject. "Do you know where Damien can buy some clothes for me? He brought me here with only the clothes on my back." Damien's head dropped to his chest as everyone at the table roared with laughter.

"Damien, she is precious. I think we will be able to find something to fit her down here," said Marion Matilda, "and if not, we will send someone to the surface." Embarrassed by the fact that everyone in the room was aware of how he and the childlike lady Grecian came to be together, he thanked them and excused himself and Grecian from the table.

"Damien, I will send someone for you in an hour," Marion Matilda said to him before they left.

He nodded to indicate that he understood, and they went back to their quarters. One of the scientists came to get him soon after. They met in a round room with an oval table and eight chairs in the center of the floor. The room was in the middle of the satellite—it had no windows. The walls were made of the clear plastic manufactured by one of the family owned factories in Taiwan. The insides of the walls were filled with sea water, and each wall was inhabited by several schools of multi-colored, tiny fish common to the Atlantic ocean at that depth. The lights in back of the wall illuminated the room as the fish of many colors swam around, creating a kaleidoscope of images that stimulated the brain cells. It caused normal thought patterns to accelerate into an erupting volcano of original ideas. It was here that all decisions concerning the New World were made. Marion called it "the room of raw material thought patterns."

When the others arrived, Marion Matilda gave Damien a detailed report on the problem they faced. Damien sat with his eyes closed. Suddenly his body became erect, his hands tightly clutching the arms of the chair. His body was in motion, his movements involuntary; he was in a trance. Armed with the facts, and influenced by the room of raw material thought patterns, his mind sorted the information like a computer, searching for the solution. Then his body lurched forward, leaving his head resting on the table. The others watched as he returned from the transient state in which the room had placed him. When he lifted his head from the table, his face had a glow. His eyes were clear as he sat erect again in his chair. Unaware of his previous experience, he began to speak to them as if nothing had happened. He uttered the revelation they were all waiting to hear: the solution to the problem that only his military mind, in conjunction with the room, could have come up with.

"My army will protect you from the surface. You will arm the satellites with lasers as they were intended, weapons. Then you will give the surface world a demonstration of your power. Your strength shall be your salvation. They will have no choice but to secure a place for you in the Alliance, if for no other reason than for the sake of their own security," he concluded.

Marion Matilda smiled at him and said, "We will care for Grecian while you are on the surface." Addressing the others, she said, "Arm the satellites."

Damien left for the surface without saying goodbye to Grecian. He spared himself the speech she would have given him about trying to desert her and his responsibility. He thought about her on his ascent to the surface. He loved her. He could hardly wait to return and tell her of his love. He had a new commitment to his, as she put it, "responsibility".

With his army in place, he went to seek an audience with Rameses, the Lord of the Alliance. He informed Rameses that he had been hired as a mercenary to protect the New World Beneath the Sea.

As usual, Rameses tried to intimidate him, roaring, "From whom are you protecting them! Me? I financed that experiment with family funds. Up until now, all I have to show for it is ingratitude," he said to Damien.

"My lord Rameses," said Damien. "If you will listen, I will explain that my mission here is not one of adversity. Lady Marion Matilda seeks only to protect the New World Beneath the Sea from an invasion. This will also protect the family's investment in the experiment." Seeing that Rameses was calming down, he proceeded with his mission. "The experiment was successful. They struck gold three months ago. They were afraid of reporting the find for fear of an invasion from the surface. The Lady Marion Matilda had reason to believe they would be invaded by the European Alliance. The European Alliance has a history of colonialism. They also know that you would not jeopardize the Alliance by trying to stop them, for fear of a war. They saw how you handled the problem in the Eastern Alliance. They have no fear of you. The Lady Marion requests that all the members of the Alliance meet at the point of descent into the World Beneath The Sea to witness a display of power."

"Power?" asked Rameses. "I am the only power on earth available to them. What nonsense is this? Your lady Marion Matilda takes liberties from me that I am unwilling to grant. She is testing my patience with this unorthodox request."

"Unorthodox or not, I suggest that you grant the request. The demonstration will commence with or without you. It would be wise to show your support. A show of support for the actions taken by Lady Marion Matilda is a show of support for your investment in the New World Beneath The Sea," said Damien.

"I will be there, at the lady Marion Matilda's invitation. Don't embarrass me in front of the Alliance. Do you understand me, Damien?" Rameses threatened.

Damien rolled his eyes, and said, "Yes my lord, I understand you perfectly. If it works, you will take all the bows. If it does not, I will take all the blame."

Rameses smiled, "I have been misled about you. They say you are slow-witted. I hope this proves them wrong." Rameses dismissed him with a wave of his hand, indicating the audience was over. Damien bowed his head in respect, turned and went back to his army.

If I am right, he thought as he left, we will be independently wealthy, Grecian my love, independently wealthy. Free of Damon's purse strings. Damon, my level headed brother, I will never have to ask you for another penny of our father's money. Grecian my love, we will be able to live anywhere in the Alliance that we choose.

On the trip back, Damien daydreamed of Grecian, the gold, and what he would say to Damon when he arrived home with Grecian on his arm. He regained his sense of reality when the limousine came to a screeching halt. He had arrived. His men were awaiting his orders. Three Battalions stood at attention. Their job was the same now as it had been in the Southeast Asian Alliance. They were to look threatening and intimidating.

The demonstration of power came a day later. It was witnessed by all of the leaders of the Alliance. An airship towed a zeppelin, the kind used for target practice, on a three hundred foot line. A laser beam shot out from beneath the sea, demolishing the zeppelin. The leaders of the Alliance watched as the remains of the target fell from the sky into the ocean. The penal colony had armed the satellites. They had violated the disarmament treaty, and now they possessed the power to destroy the Alliance.

Later that month, at an emergency meeting of the leaders of the Alliance, Rameses made a speech to the members:

My fellow members of the Alliance. The penal colony, which was funded with my own money, has been a tremendous success. Firstly, there is the rehabilitation of long term, incarcerated career criminals. Secondly, the mining operation has struck gold, as well as other sources of wealth. This has made the entire experiment profitable. However, fear of colonization by members of the Alliance, no matter how unwarranted, has motivated them to arm themselves against us. I was appalled, as I am sure you were, by the blatant display of force shown by the newcomers. This is the issue that we have met here today to resolve. Members of my own family have conspired against the Alliance. Members of my own family have been hired as mercenaries to protect the revolutionaries from the wrath of the Alliance. This is a different world in which we now live. Unlike us, they have no sense of discipline or honor. We are forced to make a decision here today that will affect the order that we have struggled to preserve. If the decision affected me alone, without risk to the Alliance and the lives of the masses that depend upon our sound judgment, then I would not hesitate to go to war. However, in the interest of world peace, I suggest that we embrace the New World Beneath The Sea as brothers and invite them into the Alliance. The choice is yours: war or peace.

You would have had to be a fool to believe anything Rameses said at that meeting. The entire Alliance, except the Europeans, were family. They began to look around the room. For the first time they felt alone in the mist of the world leaders. They were the last of the pure, white race. The world had homogenized. They alone remained unmixed. Suddenly, the Europeans realized what this was all about. They were the last threat to peace in the Alliance. Their leaders, one of which was Grecian's father, made a motion to bring the New World Beneath the Sea into the Alliance. Another one of them seconded the motion. The New World Beneath The Sea was welcomed into the Alliance with a single united "yes". Damien returned to the New World Beneath The Sea with an ambassador from each country of the Alliance.

He went to the quarters he shared with Grecian as soon as he arrived. She was sitting on the bed with her back to the door, painting her toenails. He entered the room. She turned toward the door when she heard his footsteps. Her face lit up with a smile, as he crossed the room.

"Damien," she said. "Damien you're back. I knew you didn't leave me."

"Why would I leave you?" he asked. "I love you."

Damien took her into his arms and she held on to him as if he were trying to run away. She wrapped both her arms around his neck and her legs around his waist. She kissed him, probing his mouth with her tongue. He walked over to the bed and knelt down on it with her still wrapped around his body. She released the grip her legs had around his waist so he could lay her on her back. He removed the skirt she was wearing while she clung tightly to his neck, her mouth never leaving his. Grecian positioned her body to allow him to remove her panties, and unsnapped her bra as she released him long enough to remove the blouse she was wearing. Then she began to help him undress, unbuckling his pants, then removing his shirt. He kicked off his boots and she slid his pants off, removing his socks at the same time. He never wore an undershirt. Grecian dug her fingernails into his bare chest, hard enough to leave nail tracks, but not hard enough to break the skin.

When she reached Damien's stomach, her fingers caught the waistband on his briefs and pulled them down below his knees. She rubbed him slowly while helping him to remove his underwear. He lay on his back, naked. She straddled his shins with her mouth covering his penis. Grecian's long, blond hair covered the upper half of his body, while her head bobbed up and down, trying to extract the semen, over which he seem to have developed full control. She moved her body up and mounted his penis, and it slid in without resistance. She was wet with excitement from the foreplay and the abstinence from sex, and this was the first time he had penetrated her. Impaled upon his penis, she rode him in a heated frenzy, like an urban cowgirl on an electric bull. She moved faster and faster until she screamed in ecstasy, releasing the pent-up emotions she had stored away while waiting for him to come back for her. She lay there on top of him, panting, spent, exhausted, asleep and still impaled on his rock hard penis. He had not ejaculated, but he was completely satisfied that she was pleased with his performance. They fell asleep in that position for the rest of the night.

They went down to breakfast together the next morning, holding hands. Her face revealed the pleasure of having him back. They sat close and whispered through breakfast, touching each other at every opportunity. Damien ran his fingers along the outline of her lips. He stroked her cheek with the back of his hand. He hung on every word Grecian uttered, digesting them before responding. Then they returned to the room, and made love again.

"Don't ever leave me again," she said to him.

"I never left you, I just went away," he responded.

"The next time I go with you," she warned.

"There won't be a next time," he said, kissing her. "Wherever I go, you go." They released their body fluids together. The sounds of their pleasure must have been heard throughout the satellite.

They went to meet Marion Matilda that afternoon. She told Damien that it had been decided. He could name his price. They would send the gold wherever he wanted it shipped.

"Home," he said to her. "I'm going to take Grecian to meet my mother."

> *"The real power in our family has always been the women. We work clandestinely in the shadows of our men, giving them the aura of gods. If they are gods, then we are god-makers"*
>
> Myrrah

Chapter Forty-one

Myrrah

In the year 2092, Roman Micheal retired from government. He left his son, Constantine, the absolute power in the northern half of the South American continent. Constantine wed Myrrah, his betrothed. She was the daughter of Everett Jr. and Marion Matilda, and one of the most beautiful women in all of the Alliance. Myrrah's complexion was as black as ebony, and the enamel on her teeth appeared whiter because of her deep dark skin tone. She had long, black, silky hair and pale green eyes. Like all of the girls in the family, she was of amazon proportions, standing six feet tall, barefooted. Like her mother, she was a scholar. She had graduated from college at thirteen. She spoke every language in the Alliance fluently, and had spent much of her childhood in the lands ruled by the family. Now, at the age of twenty-six, she and Constantine had come to power. The natives referred to her fondly as Negrita.

It was a beautiful morning in late July. She and Constantine were visiting his family in Brazil. They had just finished breakfast and the servants were clearing the table. Brillante, Constantine's mother, was speaking to Myrrah about starting a family. Constantine and his father, Roman Micheal, had left the two women alone in the room, using the pretense of state business. Myrrah was annoyed with Constantine for leaving her alone with his mother. Brillante detected the change in her tone of voice as soon as the men left the room.

Myrrah had noticed that Constantine seemed distant as of late. He and his mother were always whispering over the videophone, and the conversations ended abruptly whenever Myrrah entered the room. At first, she had thought herself paranoid. Then she overheard the words, "divorce her." The words had rolled off of Brillante's tongue, crisp and clear, "Divorce her and remarry. This is a new day and age. It is being done all over the Alliance every day." The subject of Myrrah bearing a child was not a new conversation between her and her mother-in-law. She was obsessed with the idea of having a grandchild before she died. Myrrah placated the old lady with the same story she had been telling her since the first week after the honeymoon.

"We are not doing anything to prevent having a baby," Myrrah said to Brillantc. "Be patient. One day I will be pregnant, and you will have your grandchild."

Meanwhile, outside on the verandah, Constantine was telling his father of the fruitless relationship he was having with his wife. He complained that his wife was barren and could not conceive a child. Worse than that, if she was not barren, then she was using a contraceptive without his knowledge. Roman Micheal could see from the sound of his son's voice that a childless marriage was not the only problem. His son no longer loved the beautiful Negrita.

"Barren or not, you cannot carelessly cast her aside," Roman Micheal said to his son. "She is the daughter of the newest and most powerful nation in the Alliance. Divorce her and it may mean war.

My son, a war with them would tear the South American continent apart. They are allied with my brother's son Damien. That would be a civil war, brother against brother. I will not let you do that." The thought of civil war in the family was enough to make Roman Micheal shiver. The thought of him facing his brother, Mica Mark, on the battlefield brought tears to his eyes. The thought of his son being the cause brought on an emotion he had never before had to deal with: depression. He would commit suicide and doom himself to hell rather than take up arms against his brother. Surely feelings that strong would dissuade his son from war.

That night Roman and Brillante lay in bed, talking about the past day.

"Our son is not happy," Brillante said to her husband.

"There are millions of unhappy people on the planet. Concern yourself with your own happiness," he said to his wife.

"If my son is unhappy, then I am unhappy," she responded to Roman. She continued, "It is Negrita. She is not trying to have a baby for us."

"For us?" asked Roman. "What do we have to do with it?"

"Negrita," she said, "she is not good for him."

When he heard her say this, Roman realized his wife was part of the problem. He looked at her in disbelief. "How long," he asked her, "have you been talking to my son about this?"

She knew she was in trouble, by the tone of his voice. She tried to shift the blame on him. "Now, he is your son. You never used to talk to him when he was a child. Naturally when he has a problem, he is going to bring it to me," she said.

"I am not questioning your right as a mother to counsel your son. But dear heart, I do question the advice," he said in a threatening manner.

Sensing the danger of being struck by her husband, Brillante covered her head with both arms and said, "I did what any mother would do. I advised him to get another wife."

He pulled her hands away from her face. His first instinct was to smack her, but more important than that, he had to make himself understood. "Do you know that if he divorces her, there could be a civil war?" Then he struck her with his open hand. "Mind your own business. You will be the destruction of the Alliance," he said.

She ran off sobbing, more scared than hurt. In all their years of marriage, he had never raised his hand against her. He had threatened to, but he never did. She laid on the bed in their room, crying and feeling sorry for herself.

All I did was protect my son, she thought. *Any mother would do the same given the circumstances.*

Roman Micheal walked over to the closed bedroom door. He put his ear against it and listened to her cry. He wanted to go in and comfort her, but he resisted the urge. This was a serious matter. She had to be made to understand the consequences of her decision to interfere in the lives of the children. Her crying became more audible when she heard him at the door. Again he overcame the urge to go to her. He turned from the door and walked away without looking back. His wife would have to learn. In a choice between his love for her and his duty to the Alliance, he would choose the Alliance every time. He was first and foremost a soldier. The only choices he ever made in life concerned his choice of arms.

Constantine and Myrrah returned home the next evening. They were discussing some of the things that had happened at the home of his parents. Myrrah was not happy about the subject of divorce. She questioned her husband about his mother's attitude toward her.

"Why is your mother always talking to you about me, behind my back?" she asked Constantine.

"My mother said nothing to me that she would not say to your face," he responded.

"Then why hasn't she mentioned a divorce to me? I overheard you talking to her about it."

"My mother is concerned about my happiness," he said to Myrrah.

"Your happiness?" she retorted. "Perhaps you would be happier married to your mother?"

"Are you suggesting an incestuous relationship between me and my mother?" he asked angrily.

"Constantine, I am only suggesting that your mother mind her own business," Myrrah replied.

"This marriage is my mother's business," he said.

"Your half of the marriage is your mother's business. Keep her away from me. If you were any kind of a man, you would not allow her to blame me for not being pregnant. It takes two fertile people to have a child. You remember that much from biology, don't you?"

"There is nothing wrong with me," he said. "I am as fertile as my parents. No man in this family has ever been impotent. We have always had superior genes and produced superior children."

Myrrah cringed to think that this invertebrate, who called himself a man, had the audacity to also be a chauvinist. The only qualification one needed to rise to his position was a phallus, and all that proved was the gender. She stared at him with a blank look, the animosity raging in her head, screaming, and shouting for his blood. She had wasted her adolescence with this sterile mamma's boy, and now they were at the breaking point. He stood there in silence, watching her stare at him with her teeth clenched. Constantine wondered what she thought and how he would respond to Myrrah when she spoke. The cold stare sent a chill down his spine. He wished his mother were here. She always had the right answers. Constantine knew he should never have come back, once he had decided to do this.

Finally, Myrrah spoke. He felt immobilized with her gaze locked on him like a tractor beam. He felt powerless to do anything except listen. She made no demands. She said calmly, "You and your mother may have your divorce, but the terms will be mine." With this, she turned and went to their bedroom. Constantine followed instinctively. When he reached the door, she went inside and closed it quietly in his face. From the other side of the door he heard her say, "Find another place to sleep. This room is mine." He turned and left the scene of the closed door, like a little boy who had been locked out of his parents room so they could perform some secret ritual he was not allowed to witness. He walked away slowly, in search of a sympathetic servant. They had always been his surrogate parents.

Myrrah did not sleep that night. She thought about the revelation Odessa had made when they were children. It had been about Constantine's parents. She had seen their past in a dream. His mother was really his mother's sister. His mother had once faced the same problem Myrrah was having, conception under pressure. That was all Odessa would tell her, and she was sworn to secrecy about it. Myrrah believed this to be the reason her mother-in-law insisted on the pregnancy. She had never given birth to a child of her own. Myrrah lay awake that night thinking.

The nerve of him. It is he who is sterile. Divorce me for being sterile, she thought over and over

*again. We will see who is sterile, me or you. I will
expose your impotency to the entire Alliance, and
show them what kind of man you really are. In the
morning I will go to Oman to visit Odessa for a few
weeks.*

She and Odessa had been best friends since
childhood. They shared all of each other's secrets.
Odessa had predicted that she would one day marry
a descendant of James Edward Magee, and it did
not surprise her when she was betrothed to
Constantine. Later, Odessa told her she had given
that same information to Elizabeth Susan, and that
was why Elizabeth Susan had betrothed Myrrah
to Constantine, thinking he was the one. At any
rate, Elizabeth Susan would never be the woman
Ny Li Tu had been in these matters, even if she did
leave her as heir apparent.

Constantine slept in one of the guest rooms
that night. It would be more accurate to say that
he occupied one of them that night. Sleep did not
come easy. He lay awake, thinking about Myrrah,
her threats and his future. He fell asleep just before sunrise. Myrrah went to Oman without leaving word of where she was going, before
Constantine woke up that day. He only found out
about her whereabouts from a spy working for
Cheyenne's Dakota Moon in Oman. The network
of spies was the only thing that remained of the
twentieth century form of government. The old
Central Intelligence Agency was irreplaceable.

Meanwhile in Oman, Odessa greeted Myrrah
with open arms and a heavy heart. She was aware
of the problem. They had been talking for hours
when Emanuel arrived home. He smiled when he
saw Myrrah. She was his favorite cousin in the
Alliance. They, along with Odessa, had spent many
pleasant summers together as children, playing in
the desert of Oman. Emanuel could see that Myrrah

had been crying from the redness in her eyes. She tried to conceal her unhappiness from him as she ran to leap into his arms. But she broke into tears when Emanuel kissed her on the lips, as he had done so many times when they were children.

"Why," he asked, "does my ebony doll cry?"

She laughed through her tears when she heard him refer to her as his ebony doll. He had not called her that in years. "Oh Mannie, am I still your ebony doll?" she asked, crying and laughing at the same time. She clung to him for dear life and squeezed his neck. He picked her up in his arms and walked over to Odessa, while she sobbed with her head on his shoulder.

"If he has hurt you, I will..."

His wife stopped him in the middle of the sentence. "You will do nothing. I have seen the outcome in a vision."

"You mean her father kills him before I do?" he asked in earnest.

"No, nothing so violent is necessary Mannie. It is an affair of the heart. They are getting a divorce."

"A divorce?" asked Emanuel. He could not fathom anyone being so unhappy that they would pursue such an extreme measure.

"Emanuel, it is a divorce. Not the end of the world. You were about to kill him and plunge the Alliance into a civil war. Surely you can see this is the lesser evil," said Odessa.

"No," said Myrrah, "Mannie will kill him and I will kill his mother." They both broke out in a burst of laughter. He was still standing there holding Myrrah in his arms, and she had both arms around his neck.

Failing to see the humor, Odessa said, "Emanuel put her down. She has an excuse for being crazy. You're a king. You are supposed to display the wisdom of Solomon. Instead, I find I have married the court jester."

With that outburst from Odessa, they all began to roll with laughter, just like when they were
children. Myrrah had come to the right place. Suddenly she was alive again. Myrrah knew exactly
what path she must take to regain her self-esteem.
During the next three weeks of her stay in Oman,
Myrrah contacted the highest ranking officers in
the armed forces. They pledged their loyalty to her.
In the event of a divorce, Negrita would take the
reins of government. With the army on her side,
she would have a choice. She could be a president
or a queen.

Myrrah returned home to find that Constantine
had moved into the home of his parents. He had
taken the opportunity, while she was away, to petition the courts to allow him to divorce her on the
grounds of desertion. Myrrah did not protest the
petition and the divorce was finalized thirty days
later. Three days before the divorce was finalized,
Myrrah inspected the armed forces. Neither
Constantine, nor his father Roman Micheal, were
aware of the loyalty the officers of the armed forces
had sworn to Myrrah. She trained in the field with
them every day since her return. Both the armed
forces, and the public supported Negrita. The next
day, the armed forces would swear allegiance to
her in a public ceremony, televised throughout the
Alliance.

Once again, the Alliance was threatened by war,
but this time a civil war that could destroy all that
had been gained in the blink of an eye. Myrrah
knew this to be true. But she also understood that
war would be avoided at all cost. She knew her ex-
father-in-law could not afford to allow his son to
be the instrument of the Alliance's destruction.
Under the circumstances that she had set, with
the armed forces in her control, Roman Micheal

would be her most powerful ally. Myrrah understood what Constantine and his mother could never
understand: his father was first a soldier. His first
loyalty was to the Alliance that he had helped build.

Roman Micheal sent a message to Myrrah, asking for a meeting before the televised broadcast.
He planned to have Negrita assassinated, using the
same poison Maxwell Mason Stone had used on
the C.I.A. prior to the election that swept him and
Moses Cribb into power in the 1990's. Before accepting the offer to meet with him, Myrrah called
her mother, the lady Marion Matilda, to seek her
advice. The conversation between the two women
was one of mother to daughter, ally to ally. It was
the most important conversation Marion Matilda
ever had with her daughter since the age of puberty.

"Mother," Myrrah said, "how is Daddy?" It was
as if the eight month lapse in communication had
been a day.

"If all goes well, he will live forever," said her
mother.

Myrrah laughed lightly at her mother's response.

They played the cat and mouse game for a few
minutes before her mother came to the point. "What
is the matter? I know something has to be wrong if
my independent baby takes time from her busy
schedule to call me. Talk to me, Princess. What is
the matter?" Marion Matilda had learned of the
problems her daughter was having from the spy
that was planted in her country since her wedding
to Constantine. She wanted to hear it from Myrrah.
She always came for advice after the fact.

"Mother," she said without going into an explanation, "I got a divorce."

"And," said her mother, as if that one word was
a sentence.

"Mother, don't you listen? Constantine has divorced me."

"Listen, Myrrah, I hear more about you from my clandestine sources than you have ever told me," said her mother. "Don't you dare to tell me to listen. You talk to me. Tell me everything right now."

Marion Matilda could hear her daughter sniffling back the tears, just as she used to do when she was scolded as a little girl. She told her mother the story, including every minor detail. And at the end her mother asked, "Is Roman going to meet with you alone?"

"He did not say," said Myrrah. "What are you thinking, Mother? What would you do in his place?"

"In his place, there are no choices," her mother answered. "You threaten all that he has spent his life working for. I would have you killed."

Myrrah gasped at the answer. But she knew it was true. "Mother, what shall I do?"

Her mother spoke very sharply and firmly. What she said was not a request, but an order. "I will contact Roman Micheal. Do nothing until you hear from me." Marion Matilda ended the transmission without so much as a farewell.

She then called Roman Micheal on the videophone. She gave him no salutation, but came right to the point of her call. "My daughter is going to grant your request for a meeting. She trusts that you will not harm her. I wish to make one thing clear. Be sure the room is warm. If she should catch a draft from an open window, I will hold you personally responsible. That means the fate of the Alliance is in your hands. I would not hesitate to destroy the Alliance. I did not build it, you did. Think carefully about your next move, my cousin. I place my daughter's life in your hands."

Roman Micheal remained silent for a long time. When he spoke he said, "Negrita shall inherit an empire. All that I have fought for is hers. She has my support. Farewell my cousin. Your daughter is my daughter. When we speak tomorrow, it will be about adopting her. Then when she comes to power, the government will not be lost, it will remain in my family."

Marion Matilda smiled for the first time; Roman Micheal returned it.

"The solution is a reasonable one. I will inform my daughter she has another father."

Again he said, "Farewell, my cousin."

Marion Matilda called her daughter back and gave her the terms of the compromise. Myrrah would be the only female world leader in the Alliance. The next day Myrrah met with Roman Micheal and signed the adoption papers. The divorce, the adoption, the public support of the armed forces and the people made Negrita the new president. Roman Micheal used his influence with his new daughter to have her appoint Constantine ambassador to the southern half of the South American continent, which was ruled by Damon, his nephew.

Damon had come to power in the same year Constantine and Myrrah succeeded Roman Micheal. He was known for his statesmanship, and for the adage, "war is never an option." He was the only leader in the Alliance who remained a bachelor. For him, there was only one love, a secret love whose name he had shared only with his brother Damien when they were children. It was a secret because she was betrothed to his cousin Constantine. He had sworn on a Bible that he would never marry anyone but Myrrah. He had kept that vow for the last ten years, and remained unwed. When word of Constantine and Myrrah's divorce reached him, he was in the bathroom of the presidential quarters. A servant had delivered the message from his brother Damien. A smile crossed his face as he read the letter.

Dear Brother, I hope this is the first time the news I am about to give you has reached your ears. I know you do not concern yourself with gossip, but I was sure you would want to hear this bit of news. Your true love is available. Myrrah and Constantine are divorced. My brother, a union between her and you would unite the continent. May God continue to smile upon you. Your brother, Damien

Damon folded the letter carefully, as if it would someday be a priceless antique, and put it aside to read over again later. If this was true, he would have to move quickly. Soon she would have more suitors than Penelope, when Odysseus failed to return home from the Trojan War.

In the Brazilian presidential palace, Myrrah was reading the mail. Hundreds of thousands of letters had flowed in from around the Alliance. Some congratulated her as the new president. Others were letters from admirers hoping for her hand in marriage. Then came the suitors. They came by the hundreds. She dared not insult the finest families in the Alliance by turning them away, so she indiscriminately gave them each an audience. They came bearing gifts, the like of which she had never witnessed before. The gifts filled a room. Each one was acknowledged individually, with a separate audience for the bearer. She had grown up with most of these men while attending school. All claimed to have been enchanted by her rare beauty, but had never dared to speak because of her betrothal to the son of Roman Micheal. All seemed pleased just to have her acknowledge their presence and be allowed to leave a token of their undying affection for her. Myrrah did not plan to remarry, especially since the prophesy of her first marriage, to a descendant of James Edward Magee, had gone so badly. However, she did feel obligated to act as if she were interested in the proposals. She entertained her suitors with a banquet befitting kings, all at the same time. None could say he had been slighted, but none could claim an advantage.

Damon arrived on the day of the banquet. He brought her no token of his affection. He claimed no privilege of rank, and he requested no audience. At the banquet, each of the suitors were announced before they were seated. All were titled gentlemen from titled families. Finally, the servant announced Damon, "defender of the Alliance, and descendent of James Edward Magee." The room was silent as the man, who made this unexpected claim to one of the most famous heroes of the Alliance, was ushered to his seat.

The room started to buzz with unintelligible chatter among the suitors. Someone could be heard saying, "It is Damon." The name began to spread around the banquet hall like wildfire. Each of the suitors with a single thought in his mind, but none with the audacity to voice it: What right had he to be there? Hadn't his cousin *done enough to make Myrrah's life miserable? The nerve of him.*

Myrrah sat silently watching the chain of events as if she were a voyager, unattached to the reason that had inadvertently brought these men together. The tension in the room was thick enough to cut with a knife. To make an enemy of someone of Damon's rank in the Alliance was suicidal. The risk of making an enemy was also as great for Damon. Everyone there had families capable of starting a war. Damon disarmed the potentially dangerous situation with his broad smile. He proved himself once again to be a statesman instead of a soldier, announcing that he was there to fulfill the prophesy foretold by Odessa. Myrrah would marry a descendant of James Edward Magee. And he concluded by saying, "Eat, drink, and think of other women. This one has been spoken for."

Myrrah could not believe this man had walked into the banquet hall and tried once again, to take away her right to decide whom she would marry. "Damon, how dare you think you can tell me who I will marry. I will marry anyone I damn well please. You, sir, are in my country. I rule here. If you wish to keep your head I suggest you remember that. You there," she said, pointing to the fair-skinned young man from Switzerland in the European Alliance, "you may escort me to my quarters." The young man looked at Damon for his approval before rising to do her bidding.

The look did not go unnoticed by Myrrah.

She then asked, "Is there a man among you who will escort me to my quarters without Damon's permission?" When the offer was not accepted, she turned and proceeded to her quarters unattended.

Damon followed at a safe distance, several steps behind. He realized now that he did not win her heart by presuming she would fall in love with him, just because of Odessa's prophesy. The next day he sent Myrrah a dozen giant roses from the Asian Alliance. In the note accompanying the flowers, he threatened to send her a dozen roses each day until she promised to marry him. He showered her with gifts of jewellery from every land in the Alliance. He made her every possible promise a man could make and still be taken seriously. He was the first person she saw in the morning and the last person she saw at night.

Myrrah was not to be swayed so easily. Her

mind was made up; she would not marry a man who took away her choices. She was determined to remain her own woman, and she believed Damon to be like all other men who wanted only to possess her. She would never allow that to happen again.

When Myrrah refused to accept Damon as her husband on his last proposal of marriage, he went back to his country. He was to meet with one of the leaders of the European Alliance, Grand Duke Wilfred III, Grecian's father. The meeting had been scheduled months before he went to visit Myrrah, and there was no way he could explain why he could not keep the appointment. Regretfully, he tore himself away from his courtship of Myrrah to honor his commitment.

Damon and the grand duke arrived on the same day. Fortunately, for the sake of good manners, Damon arrived an hour earlier. They met in the conference room of the presidential palace. Grand Duke Wilfred was accompanied by an aide, a captain of his personal guard. The captain poured the grand duke a glass of brandy from a decanter offered to him by Damon's servant. The captain insisted on this. Under different circumstances, he would have tasted it first, but that would have been an insult. Damon met them alone, unarmed and unguarded. He overlooked the brandy episode, giving the young captain's overzealous behavior the benefit of the doubt. His servant waited until Damon dismissed him, only then leaving him alone with them. The Grand Duke noticed the servant's reluctance to leave. He dismissed his aide so he and Damon could speak confidentially.

Grand Duke Wilfred began the conversation with, "Your brother Damien killed my daughter's husband in a duel several months ago."

Damon listened, wondering what this had to do with him. Damien's business was his own. He let the him go on without interruption.

"Your brother has taken my daughter out of the country without my permission, and to add insult to injury, he has yet to marry her," he complained.

"My dear duke and ally, what is it you would have me to do? Damien is a grown man over whom I have no control. I can only assume, since I have never met her, that your daughter is a consenting adult," said Damon.

Pretending not to have heard Damon's apathetic words, the Grand Duke went on. "Like all fathers, I was very happy when she was married to the late baron, the man your brother killed," he interjected with tears in his eyes, "a man of the European Alliance, one of her own kind. You understand what I am saying. A real European from a good European family."

"Yes, of course I do. One of her own kind," Damon repeated sarcastically.

Grand Duke Wilfred thought about what he had said and quickly added, "It is not that your brother isn't good enough for her, or that your family is not acceptable in the European Alliance. In fact, if she is going to marry someone outside of the European Alliance, I am pleased that it will be your brother."

"Sir," said Damon, "you came here with a two-part grievance. Am I to understand that my brother has abducted your daughter and asked for her hand in marriage?"

"Not exactly," said the grand duke. "What I would like for you to do is press the issue of marriage. Coming from me it would sound more like a threat, and for the sake of peace I would rather it not be misinterpreted."

Damon smiled. Grand Duke Wilfred was indeed a diplomat. He had just threatened a war, and he was using Damon as an emissary. "I will deliver your message to my brother," he said. "The hour grows late, and I am sure you are weary from your travel. If you will excuse me, I beg your leave."

The Grand Duke bowed his head in acknowledgment that the audience was over. He returned to the guest room in which he was staying.

Damien, Damien, thought Damon, *how do you manage to weave such tangled webs?* Damon sent a message to Damien and returned to Brazil in pursuit of Myrrah, not waiting for an answer from his brother. To him, Myrrah was much more important than the threat of another war.

Damien received the correspondence the same day by courier. He was in the south of Argentina, where he and Grecian were having a house built. They were temporarily living in a pavilion, much like the one Damien had used when he slept in the field with his troops. Grecian was inside when he received the dispatch, and he was still reading it when he entered the huge tent.

"Is that a coded message?" she asked. Then in the same breath she asked, "Damien, when are you going to teach me how to read the secret code?" She asked him this question every time he received a communication. This time he surprised her.

"It is not coded. Here, read it," he said handing her the dispatch. As she was reading he said, "It seems your father is concerned about us living in sin."

"Uhmmmm," she sighed, "if he only knew how delicious it is, he would not be so worried."

"Shameless hussy," he teased, walking over and patting her on the buttock.

"Stop, Damien," she whined. "I'm reading." After reading the message from Damon, she asked,

"Damien, does this mean that if we don't get married Daddy will go to war against us?"

"Well, it does imply that," he answered.

"Damien are you going to marry me?" she asked.

"One day. Remember you are my responsibility," he jested.

"And don't you ever forget it," she said, laughing. Her mood became very serious. "Damien, I don't want you to marry me because of Daddy. I want you to marry me because you want me," she said.

"Well don't worry about that. I will always want you," he responded.

"Good," she said as she rubbed her body against his until she felt an erection. She then pushed him away and ran off. This was a game she played with him. Tease and Run she called it. Damien was a big kid himself. And off they went, chasing about like dogs in heat.

In Brazil, Myrrah had to literally wade through a sea of roses to get from one room to another. Damon kept his promise to send her a dozen giant roses a day until she agreed to marry him. Actually Damon was growing on her. With each dozen roses he sent a card. Today's card was the most endearing.

I loved you since my first consciousness in the womb of my mother. I have wanted you since my hormones screamed out to you in my puberty. I loved you when you were promised to another and there was no hope of having you. I have waited for you when there was no hope of you coming. Now that there is hope, how can I not wait?

She was reading his card when Damon arrived.

Actually, he interrupted her in the middle of the third reading. She put the card in her pocket as she greeted him, and Damon noticed this was the first time she had been warm to him since they were children. In fact, she was so warm that he took the liberty of kissing her on the cheek. Myrrah did not object.

They walked through the hundreds of roses he had sent her to the library in the south wing of the estate. The servants brought them tea and sweet biscuits while they discussed the works of the ancient writers of the past. His knowledge of English Literature and world history was astonishing, and it further endeared him to her. Myrrah was a lover of such knowledge, often referred to by those who were educated in the fields of mathematics, logic and absolutes as little more than trivia.

Damon abandoned his original plan of courtship. He had never been a ladies' man, and he was failing miserably in the impersonation. When he decided to pursue his love in his own dull and, as some would say, boring persona, he noticed a favorable response. Myrrah hung on his every word. He was so encouraged by her new attitude that he risked asking her to visit him in Argentina. He had no choice but to return home. The business with his brother, Grecian and the Grand Duke would have to be settled, and he dared not risk one of his brother's brash, hotheaded, ill-advised decisions. It might drag him into a war with the European Alliance over a woman. He had no fear of winning such a war, especially with Damien commanding the troops. However, a war would literally tear the alliance apart. Damon was, after all, the self-proclaimed defender of the Alliance. Never once did he think, when he was making the claim, that he might well have to live up to the responsibility that it carried. Here he was, ruler, diplomat, and statesman, and the only titles he wanted right then were husband and lover of Myrrah—not to mention potentially the second strongest leader in the Alliance when he and Myrrah united the South American continent. Damon's mind re-focussed upon her.

"Yes, I will join you in Argentina for a visit of state. I wish to meet the people. Will you arrange that?" she asked.

"Yes," he answered with great joy. It brought a smile to Myrrah's face to think a man could possibly love her that much. He regained his composure, and asked, "Can you be ready by morning?"

"I am packed. I will shop for clothes in Argentina," she said.

With that, he walked her to her quarters. Once there, she allowed him to kiss her, this time on the lips. He slept that night with a smile on his face, satisfied with a kiss. Premarital sex had never entered his mind.

Before returning to Argentina, Damon and Myrrah stopped to see Damien and Grecian at the pavilion. Damon openly discussed with her the matter of Grecian, the Grand Duke and Damien. He treated Myrrah as if she were his wife and they made all decisions together. Although she did not comment or give her opinion, she made it clear by her facial expressions that a war was out of the question. She did this whenever the subject reared its ugly head.

Damien said, on the subject of marriage, "We will marry when it pleases us."

"You can tell my daddy that he can't run my life anymore," Grecian chimed in. "If he does not mind his business, I may never marry Damien, just to spite him."

Damon could see she was no more than a child. He looked at his brother with disgust and said, "If I were you, I would wait until she is at least another year older before considering marriage. As for the threat of war, I will be able to delay the first shot until then. Are we all in full agreement then? I will tell Grand Duke Wilfred a marriage is in the near future. His daughter would like an engagement period of at least one year." Grecian gave Damien a puzzled look and said, "Did I say that? Yes I did say that. Is it all right with you Damien?"

Damien smiled at his brother's natural gift for mediating, and added, "We will wed one year from today. Tell the Grand Duke he is invited, unless, of course, we are at war." Damon winked at him. "I will tell him. We must be on our way. Incidentally, did I ever thank you for the tip? I love my life. I have not been this happy since I was a child. I'm in your debt."

"If you fix our problem with her father, consider the debt paid in full," Damien said. They talked to each other as if the women were not present.

Most of the conversation went over Grecian's head, but Myrrah understood and thanked Damien with a kiss on the cheek. "Thanks for the tip," she said. Then she embraced Grecian. "These are the best years of your life my child," she added, acting as if she were many years older than she was. "Guard them jealously and share them freely. Farewell Grecian."

When they parted, Grecian had tears in her eyes. She leaned against Damien and said, "Myrrah is a very wise woman. I wish I were as wise."

"You will be," he answered. "It comes with time, and you have time to spare." "Will Damon be able to fix it with Daddy?" she asked.

"It's as good as fixed already," he assured.

There was a parade waiting for Myrrah and Damon in Argentina. It seemed that everyone in the country had come out to catch a glimpse of Negrita. She was a legend on the continent, and they let her know that they loved her. The people's display of affection endeared Damon to Myrrah even more. In fact, she could honestly say she loved him. She took his arm and leaned on him for support. His strong arm held her up as the colors went by. The crowd chanted, "Negrita, Negrita, Negrita" over and over until her name was echoed by every voice on the continent. She was now their queen.

Myrrah agreed to marry Damon and unite the continent. The system of government was changed to allow them a king and queen, and the continent was renamed the South American Empire. After the coronation, which Grand Duke Wilfred III attended, Damon dispatched a secret coded message to the duke:

My friend and ally, all of your enemies are my enemies. All of my allies are your allies. Do nothing to change the balance, and you will never have to test the strength of that bond.

Signed, Damon and Myrrah, Monarchs of the South American Empire.

The next time they saw the grand duke was at the wedding of his daughter, one year from the date of the message.

> *"It is the duty of my wife and me to rule the alliance with absolute power. The success of this concept relies on our subjects, they must trust us absolutely."*
>
> Trojan

Chapter Forty-two

Trojan and Conzeula, Lords of the Alliance

And it came to pass, in the ninth month of the year 2100, that Rameses stepped down from the throne as Lord of the Alliance, in favor of his son Trojan. Trojan had married Conzeula, the daughter of Tyler Samuel and Brillosa Turner. Trojan had chosen to live with his bride among the stars on a weather satellite orbiting the earth to rule the Alliance from there.

Secretly, he had rearmed the weather satellites when he assisted lady Marion Matilda and Everett Jr. in arming the New World Beneath the Sea, eight years before. Now that Marion Matilda and Everett Jr. had reached the age of retirement and would soon turn the government of the New World over to their people, Trojan asked them to secretly disarm their lasers. Their power in the Alliance would remain unchallenged as long as he did not disclose the secret of their disarmament to the world. Lady Marion Matilda trusted Trojan's decision to disarm the weapons without argument. She believed he had the solution to world peace.

While he and Conzeula were Lords of the Alliance, Trojan ended the threat of war on the planet by threatening to annihilate any country making war against another country. Conzeula, unlike her predecessor Elizabeth Susan, ruled the Alliance alongside her husband as an equal. There were no decisions made without her input. This marked the first time in the history of the Alliance that a woman's influence openly shaped its policies. She was, without question, a lord of the Alliance, and holding all the rank and privilege that went with it. It was she who wrote the law disarming the planet, and appointed Damien the new Lord Protector of the Environment. His predecessor, Canyon Mesa Stone, had recommended Damien as his successor, suggesting his police powers be extended to give the lords of the Alliance the option of using the laser beams to enforce the law.

Trojan never visited the planet. Conzeula was his emissary and she traveled to and fro between the heavens and the earth, appearing without warning like the Almighty watching over mankind in the Garden of Eden. It was on such a visit to Earth that Conzeula landed her two-seated spacecraft high on a mountain range in Tibet, one of the countries in the Asian Alliance. She stopped there often, on her visits to Earth, to taste the pure melted snow water on its way to the streams below.

Crouched by a stream of ice water trickling down from a glacier, she heard a noise that sounded louder than thunder. The earth shook and split apart, leaving a canyon between her and the space craft. The canyon was about a mile across and seven miles deep. The heat from the molten lava created a foggy mist that hid the picturesque view of the glacier-covered mountain. Conzeula was lost in the heavy fog that surrounded her. Her only guide was her memory of the panoramic glacier and the taste of the ice water to recreate the scene. She closed her eyes so that she could clearly see the new divide in the earth in front of her and across the wide expanse to the space craft on the other side. She saw the edge of the canyon, a step in front of her, and began to back away to safer

ground. She envisioned the space craft and estimated it to be five feet from the edge. Then she
remembered the homing device built into her wrist
watch. She hit the switch on the side, activating
the tractor bean.

The spacecraft lit up and began to make musi-
cal sounds. Soon it began to move across the divide toward her. She couldn't see it, but she could
hear it coming. As the spacecraft came nearer, the
sound grew louder. She placed her homing device
on the ground and walked away from it so the craft
would not land on top of her. Conzeula watched it
as it came to earth, landing softly with a quiet thud
beside her. She ran her fingertips over the spacecraft as if she were looking for damage, and she
opened the door and got in. She launched the craft
in search of a safe landing field and called Trojan
to tell him of her close brush with death.

Trojan was not overly concerned for his wife's
safety. She was the best pilot in the Alliance. He
was at a disadvantage when it came to showing
sympathy for a pilot of her ability. He expected her
to exercise the skill she did to save her life. He did,
however, ask her to backtrack and go over the part
of the story about the earth splitting, and the resulting divide. He said to her, as he would have to
anyone who had survived such a potential disaster, "Would you consider it to have been an earthquake?" as he searched his instruments for any
indication of the disturbance in the atmosphere.
Conzeula was not upset by her husband's unsym-
pathetic quest for the truth. After all, she was unharmed. She waited until he said, "Connie, are you
there?" before she answered him. The reference to
his pet name for her indicated his love. For Trojan,
an indication was as good as a declaration.

She smiled and answered, "I don't believe it was
a quake. There was something unnatural about it,

something man-made, but unintentional."

"Give me the exact coordinates, and I will see that Damien investigates," he responded in his business as usual manner. After receiving the numbers he said, "A group of scientists from the European Alliance requested permission from the Asian Alliance to conduct an excavation in those mountains." Then inaudibly, almost as an afterthought he said, "But they were denied."

"What did you say Trojan?" she asked.

"Nothing important," he said. "I will take it up with Damien. See you when you return, Angel." Static ended their transmission. She was unable to say good bye to him. *Static, she thought to herself, was a problem solved seventy-five years ago. The only way we could have static is if we were near a nuclear reactor.* She dismissed the thought. *The Asians wouldn't dare since they are our cousins.* Then her thoughts returned to Trojan. He had called her "angel". He was so obvious. He only called her pet names when he missed her.

"Don't worry my love, you won't be lonely for long. I'm coming home," she said, talking to herself out loud. She had not made love to him before she left, and her menstrual cycle was due to start in two days. She charted her course and determined her E.T.A. at eighteen hours, three minutes and five seconds. That would give them exactly five hours, fifty-six minutes and fifty-five seconds. "Enough time to come at least once," she said laughing and lifted off.

Trojan was asleep when she arrived. Conzeula wanted to surprise him, so she had not given him a schedule of her flight plan. She was ready for landing instructions when the flight master asked her to identify the craft.

"The Star *Queen*," she answered.

"Your Majesty," he babbled, "your flight plan

was not recorded. I did not expect you." He engaged the craft onto the tractor beam as he began giving her landing instructions. It was imperative to shut the craft down at the exact second the tractor beam took control, or it would be torn apart by the thrust of the craft's engines and the pull of the tractor beam. The flight master was extremely nervous when he met her at the landing bay. She had flown in undetected by his instruments. Had she been the enemy, they would have all been dead. He knelt before her with his eyes cast down. He was expecting nothing less than a demotion in rank.

"Don't worry," she said, "no other pilot in the universe could have flown that close to us undetected. We will adjust the radar screen so that it can never happen again."

Relieved by what he heard, he lifted his eyes to meet her gaze, and said, "My Queen," with a reverence that she had not noticed until then. She thought about how he had said it for a few seconds, and then remembered her haste.

"Trojan," she said aloud, and off she went to their bed chamber.

She entered the room silently, not wanting to wake him up before she was ready to make love to him. She tiptoed into the bathroom and filled the tub with water, softened with bath oils and rose petals from the Asian Alliance. She felt like soaking in a bathtub, combing her hair and pampering herself. She wanted to be extra soft and feminine for him that night.

At the end of the pre-love ritual, Conzeula crawled nude into bed beside Trojan. She kissed him softly on the lips, then covered his face with as many kisses as possible without kissing the same spot twice. He never so much as stirred as she moved her kisses to his neck and onto his bare chest. She circled his nipples with the tip of her tongue. Then she moved down the middle of his chest with the flat of her tongue to his pubic line. His eyes were still closed, but his penis was erecting. She placed his testicles in one of her hands and lightly rubbed his penis with the other. When his penis was fully erect, she put it in her mouth. She sucked very gently, careful not to nip him with the sharp edges of her teeth. Trojan opened his eyes to see Conzeula's head bobbing up and down between his legs. He pulled her on top of him, kissing her with a passion never before displayed by him.

"God, I'm glad your back. Do you have any idea how I've missed you?" He asked between the kisses.

"No," she said in a throaty and sexy voice. "Show me."

He maneuvered her body so he could place his head between her legs. His tongue penetrated her vagina, and her legs tightened around his head. He held his tongue erect as she moved her body in a circular motion on his face while holding his head. She thrust her pelvis forward on his tongue, moving wildly. He cupped her buttocks in his hands, restraining her as he sucked the fluid from her until she lay motionless with her eyes closed. He outlined her lips with the tip of his tongue. Her eyes opened, her lips parted and she felt his tongue in her mouth. At the same time, his penis penetrated her vagina, sending a rush of pleasure to her brain. She was holding onto him for dear life. Moving with the speed of a mad man, his body tensed and became as hard as a rock. It then went limp, lifeless, exhausted and spent.

That night she received all any woman could ask from a man, sole proprietorship of his heart, body, mind and soul, the ultimate price of true love. Conzeula had used all five hours, fifty-six minutes and fifty-five seconds. In the morning they would talk more of her trip to earth, and the new canyon in the mountains of Tibet.

It was cold, and another snow had fallen on the mountain when Damien and six of his men investigated Conzeula's divide, as Damien referred to it. Trojan insisted it was not a quake. Of course, such a reference was never made to their faces, and no one in their right mind would ever repeat it. They walked around the divide. The lava at the bottom moved more slowly than Trojan had described, and Damien attributed that to the cooling process. It was turning to rock. Their instruments showed high radiation levels around the divide.

Conzeula may have been right, he thought as they continued their investigation. They followed the radiation readings to the edge of the glacier, where the readings ended as if a window had opened and then shut. They flew over the glacier, trying to pick up more radiation readings. Damien reported to Trojan by videophone while in flight over the glacier.

"Something is happening out here," he reported, "but what, I don't know."

Grand Duke Wilfred III, Grecian's father, was talking to his daughter by videophone from the European Alliance.

"Hello princess. How is my fair-haired baby? Are you happy?" he asked.

"Oh yes, Daddy. Damien has been named Lord Protector of the Environment. Isn't that wonderful?" she said in her naturally naive manner.

"Yes," he responded without enthusiasm. Old news.

His cold answer prompted her to ask, "Daddy, aren't you happy for us? I mean the appointment and all. Isn't it exciting?"

"Yes, of course it is, my dear. He would have

been my choice if the choice was mine to make,"
he said with strained approval. She could see he
was lying, but she didn't press the issue. If he really approved of Damien's appointment, he would
have called and congratulated him personally as
soon as it happened. She should have known there
was something unusual about the call. Her father
had not asked to speak to Damien. Grecian waited
for her father to go on with the conversation, trying to put her suspicions away and give him the
benefit of the doubt. Sensing that he had put her
on the defensive, he tried to smooth Grecian's ruffled feathers by pretending that he had called out
of parental concern for her welfare.

"Princess," he began, "you are so far away, and
I guess I just miss you."

"Daddy, it's not like I just left home. I was married to the baron for a year before his death. You
never claimed to miss me back then."

He thought for a second, and said, "I missed
you then too, but I didn't know how to tell you I
missed you. Understand, Baby?" He paused a second. "I'm much older now. With your mother gone,
I suppose I'm just lonely."

When he said that her heart went out to him.

"Daddy, I miss you too."

With that statement he knew she was ready to
be his talkative minister-of-information daughter.
"I don't want to bother you, I will talk to you again,
another day perhaps," he said.

Feeling exactly like he knew she would, Gre-
cian said, "Daddy, I want to. I want to talk to you.
How have you been? I want you to know I miss
Mommy too."

"I don't want to talk about me," he said. "I want
to talk about you and your marriage. By the way,
how is my son-in-law?" This was Grecian's cue—
she loved to talk about Damien. The grand duke

listened as she went on, and on.

Finally, he interrupted her, "Where is he? Let me speak to him."

"He is in the Asian Alliance on an investigation of some kind involving Conzeula. The Lord Protector of the Environment is a serious position, you know. Trojan himself called. He left early yesterday morning. As a matter of fact, Daddy," she added, "Damien is the second most important man in the Alliance next to Trojan, of course. They talk all the time, you know?"

The grand duke had to restrain himself from saying, "They are cousins, you know." Instead, he listened as his euphoric daughter continued to bombard him with her husband's attributes. Unable to take anymore, and finding the information he was looking for, he said, "Grecian I must be going. We will talk again soon, okay, Baby?" Before she realized the conversation was over, he was gone.

Damien talked to Grecian that same evening. He called to tell her that he would not be home for a while. He asked her what she had done all day while he was away. He knew Grecian loved to talk on the videophone. Any inquiry he made about her interests would spark a conversation. Damien had only to listen. Even if he did not make any comments, she would never notice she was doing all the talking.

The words, "Daddy called a while ago," caught his attention. Now, he was interested. His father-in-law never called. He listened attentively as she told him how much Daddy thought of him.

"Grecian, did you tell your father where I was?" he queried. "He did ask, didn't he?"

"Of course he asked. He called to talk to you, and yes, I told him where you were. He was really proud of you being named Lord Protector of the

Environment, you know." She then added, "Damien, he said you would have been his choice if it had been his choice to make." She was elated that her father really liked her choice for a husband.

Damien didn't have the heart to spoil the quintessential moment Grecian had shared with her father. He listened until she was tired of talking, then told her he loved her and said, "Goodnight, my love."

Damien's mind worked overtime that night, trying to put the pieces of the puzzle in place. He thought about what Trojan had told him of the scientists from the European Alliance and the excavation permits being denied. He thought about the static that had ended the transmission between Conzeula and Trojan. It might indicate a nuclear reactor. In his head he went over the high concentration of radiation levels he had found around the divide. Finally, his thoughts turned to the conversation that Grand Duke Wilfred III had with Grecian about his whereabouts. He knew that somewhere there was a connection, and he was determined to search until he found it.

The grand duke was visiting the Asian Alliance. He was there on behalf of a team of scientists from the European Alliance, the scientists who were denied excavation permits in the mountains of Tibet. He claimed he had been asked to intercede for them in the matter of the necessary permits. Since his daughter was married to Damien, he believed he would naturally be in a position to ask a favor of his son-in-law's cousins, Emanuel and Odessa. He had gone first to the Chinese Emperor with his request. He had once served as an ambassador to the Chinese Court when he was a young man, years before the Chinese came into the Alliance. The emperor gave him a letter of introduction, but made no recommendations as to the disposition of his request. In fact, he wrote, unbeknownst to the duke, that he had known him at court to be an ambitious man from an ambitious European family. "May your best judgment prevail," he added.

Grand Duke Wilfred was granted an audience with the king and queen of Oman, as well as the lords of the powerful and combined Eastern and Asian Alliance. His head bowed, and he was down on one knee as he said, "Your Oriental Majesties, Rulers of the East, near and far, I have come to beg a favor for a group of my countrymen." Emanuel motioned for him to rise. Odessa leaned over to her husband.

"He hands the Orient to us as if it were his to give," she said in a voice inaudible to the duke.

"He simply reminds us that we are the heirs apparent, should the others die," Emanuel whispered in a tone just as low.

"Oh," said Odessa as the Grand Duke approached the thrones. A guard signalled to him that he was as near as caution permitted. He stopped advancing, and Emanuel spoke.

"What wish can we grant our European ally," he asked, as if he didn't already know.

The duke knew it was a figure of speech. He did not get his hopes up that it would be that easy. He asked, "Do you by any chance remember a group of scientists from Germany who requested a permit to excavate in the mountains of Tibet?"

"Yes I do," said Emanuel, speaking for Odessa too. "We denied them the permit. Anything that is found within the borders of the Asian Alliance is a national asset. That is the law. However, if there is something that we can do within the law, please let us know."

The grand duke was about to argue his point when Emanuel interrupted. "Just the other day, a mining company executive offered us seventy percent of the profits if we would grant him the right to mine the same mountain. We mistook the business proposition for a bribe, and had him executed on the spot."

The grand duke swallowed and cleared his throat.

Emanuel said, "We know that was never your intention, as the father-in-law of our cousin Damien."

Odessa addressed the grand duke for the first time. Her choice of words put him at ease. "How is your daughter Grecian, my cousin's wife?" she asked.

Grand Duke Wilfred was happy the subject had changed from graft and death to the acknowledgment that his daughter was their cousin, at least by marriage. He answered with a sigh of relief, "My daughter Grecian is fine. I was just talking to her a few days ago, before my trip here. She is so happy with Damien," he added.

"I'm glad to hear that in light of Myrrah's recent divorce. On the other hand, if she is half as happy as Myrrah is with Damien's brother Damon, then she is in heavenly bliss," said Emanuel.

"Blissfully happy," said the grand duke. "It is as you say. They are in heavenly bliss."

High on a Tibetan mountain in the Asian Alliance, hidden deep in one of the many caverns, the team of scientists from Germany worked on a plan to build a laser beam. The grand duke had been unsuccessful in his endeavor to obtain a permit. They worked in the caverns without authorization, clandestinely, in an attempt to balance the power of Trojan with a weapon of their own.

The grand duke was greeted by the other conspirators with less than a welcome as he entered the make-shift laboratory in the cave.

"We must work to build the laser somewhere outside of the European Alliance," one of the scientists said, mocking the grand duke's words.

"And don't forget his influence in the Asian Alliance. He will even get us permission to build the laser right under their noses," another added.

"Yes, after all, he is practically related to them by marriage. The Lord Protector of the Environment, is his son-in-law," a third one remarked.

"I would love to see what kind of mongrel pups are produced from that litter," said a fourth.

By now the grand duke was enraged. "You, Sir, have the nerve to rebuke me? Your daughter is married to one of those people, if you can call them that, from the New Race in Southeast Asia, and I disowned the bitch," he replied in defense of himself.

Suddenly a voice from across the room intervened. "I don't care who your daughters fuck, I was promised a laser and so far, all I have are complaints and excuses." The voice was that of Lord Zeigfrid, the grandson of Franz Stolz, the Neo-Nazi leader killed during the exterminations in Germany in the year 2021. He had escaped the relentless door to door search for blood relatives of the slain, conducted by Cheyenne's Dakota Moon's Force of Five Thousand. Moon had believed that if just one were left alive, they would all live to regret it. At the time, he believed it would be the child, Tomorrow, and her sister Greta who would betray them. Thank God, he was wrong.

"I have tons of money invested in this project. I expect to be able to blast that hybrid bastard Trojan out of the sky by the end of next month. I hope I have made myself clear. Either he dies or you die, and right now none of you seem to serve a purpose," said Lord Zeigfrid. He was a clone of his grandfather, tall, blond, artificially tanned and handsome. His persona radiated power and wealth, a combination that caused him to be the foremost leader in the European Alliance despite his youth. He was a historian; he had majored in European history. He was the world's leading authority on German history, especially the exterminations of 2021. It was there that he had lost his grandfather and his father in the Holy War, and he had been obsessed with avenging their deaths since his childhood.

The grand duke had never been so nervous. His life has been threatened twice in the same week, by people he never had reason to fear. He decided to tell Lord Zeigfrid about his conversation with Grecian.

"So," said Lord Zeigfrid, "your son-in-law Damien, the Lord Protector of the Environment, is hot on our trail?"

"Mind you, I have not spoken to him, but I believe it to be true," said Grand Duke Wilfred.

"Nothing must jeopardize the laser," Lord Zeigfrid said. "Dismantle the laboratory here, and reassemble it in the countries of our homelands." He went on to say, "You will build the laser in four sections in four countries and reassemble the parts in Germany at the Castle Stolz. Even if we are discovered, they cannot prove a conspiracy without the complete weapon."

Once again, the conspirators agreed, united by the wisdom of Lord Zeigfrid, and they went about carrying out the new plan.

Damien and his men had flown over the mountain range a thousand times, but never at night. The pilot spotted a spark of light and Damien ordered him to fly down for a closer look. The inspection revealed the entrance to a cave. They went in. The cave was vacant, but it was easy for a trained eye to see that it had once been occupied. Their instruments picked up the high concentration of radiation, but little else was left behind. Damien knew someone had been here, but who it was and what they were doing was still a mystery.

These were the exact words he put into his report to Trojan and Conzeula:

My Lords, we have discovered traces of our enemies in a cave in the mountain range. They are gone. All that is left of their existence is a high level of radiation. Your servant, Damien, Lord Protector of the Environment

"Damien draws closer to solving the mystery," said Conzeula to Trojan after reading the report.

"How can you tell that from such a brief report?" he asked her.

"He tells his wife little," she said, "so there is little that she can repeat."

"You mean she is suspected of being a spy?" Trojan asked.

"Of course not," Conzeula replied. "It's just that when she starts talking, she goes on."

"Yes," he agreed, "she does go on, doesn't she?"

"And on," they said in unison, laughing about how they had always thought she talked too much, but never mentioned it before now.

From the safety of his castle, behind locked doors, the grand duke pondered his position in the European Alliance. It was clear to him that Lord Zeigfrid was a madman. The duke was a conspirator, but he had never agreed to use the laser to assassinate Trojan or his wife. He thought they would use it to negotiate a more even distribution of the power. He had been duped by Lord Zeigfrid. At first, Lord Zeigfrid had needed him to secure the excavation permits. Since he had returned unsuccessful, they had no further use for him.

Now he had barricaded himself in his castle, surrounded himself with guards and awaited an attempt on his life. Frightened to the point of paranoia, he talked to his daughter on the videophone. He believed his only hope for remaining alive was if she could talk Damien into allowing her to take her rightful place as a leader in the European Alliance. Damien would rule at her side. Under those conditions, the grand duke would abdicate his title. Even Lord Zeigfrid would not openly challenge Damien's claim to his wife's lands and title. With the Lord Protector of the Environment as a leader in the European Alliance, his own safety would be guaranteed.

Near the conclusion of the conversation, Grecian said, "Daddy, you have deceived me for the last time. How can I ever trust you anymore?"

"Grecian, please. You are my only hope. Try to understand I want to fight to save the Alliance, just like you," he pleaded with his daughter.

His fear of death and the tears in his eyes moved her to say, "Daddy, I can only ask. I am not making you any promises. I will abide by whatever decision my husband makes about you."

"Remember Grecian," he said in a last desperate act to sell his daughter on the idea, "he will become a Lord in the European Alliance. This is the only way his family will ever get in, short of bloodshed."

"Yes," she answered, "I know. The last refuge of Caucasian purity, the European Alliance," she said in disgust.

Momentarily returning to his old self, her father immediately seized the opportunity to agree with her on something. "The way foreigners pour into the Alliance everyday, soon Europe will fall into the melting pot and homogenize like the rest of the Alliance despite the violence with which they are greeted," he said.

Feeling herself falling prey to her emotions, Grecian ended the transmission with her father saying, "I will tell Damien everything you said Father. I'm sure he will get back to you. Goodbye Daddy," she said, choking back the tears.

"Goodbye Baby," he replied the way he used to when her mother was still alive. The transmission ended with both of them feeling their relationship was rekindled.

Damien, who had not been home in a fortnight, returned from Tibet. Although he was puzzled by the mystery of the divide and the high concentration of radiation in the mountains, he was weary from his trip. A hot meal, a warm bed and a good night's sleep ranked right up there with sex on his list of priorities. His priorities were determined when he looked out a window and sighted Grecian running toward the house. The smile on her face rejuvenated him, and suddenly he knew again why he loved to come home to her. As she reached the gate, he momentarily lost sight of her in the glare of the sunset. It was then when he made a promise to himself that the next time he left, she would go with him. He would never deprive himself of her love again. He walked to the door to meet her. She tripped on the top step, falling into his arms. He carried her to the bedroom, kissing her with an insatiable hunger only her lips could satisfy.

The next day, they ate breakfast and talked of her father and the European Alliance. Grecian spoke with a newfound maturity. She spoke of the significance of having a member of the family as a leader in the European Alliance. Then she said, like the little girl Damien had met before they were married, "Oh please, let's go Damien. Lets go take it. It is mine and I want it. She ended the conversation by saying, "Damien, I can give us that—Lords of the European Alliance."

Somehow, from this short conversation in which she did all the talking, Damien knew she could.

Damien made his report to Trojan by videophone. He told him of the grand duke's proposition to Grecian. They agreed that, whatever else was going on, Grand Duke Wilfred's proposal opened a window of opportunity for the family, just as Grecian had suggested. Such an opportunity could not be allowed to pass them by. Trojan made the decision for Damien and Grecian to visit the European Alliance. Once there, Damien would examine the situation and report his findings. As the Lord Protector of the Alliance, he was to continue his investigation in Tibet. However, the possibility of gaining a place in the European Alliance without bloodshed would be his first priority.

A heavy fog surrounded the castle, giving it an aura of impending doom. A guard lowered the draw bridge so they could cross the moat surrounding the castle. Damien could see the crocodiles fighting over scraps of food as the limousine rolled slowly over the creaky, old bridge. Damien had never liked the drafty, old castles of the European Alliance, but the joy on Grecian's face from being home again, made up for any discomfort he might have felt. She was so excited when the limousine came to a stop, and the chauffeur got out and opened the door, that she ran over and hugged the servant who came out to take the luggage. And he was so pleased the lady Grecian still remembered him, the servant bowed, kissed her hand and called the other servants out to greet her. They lined up on the steps as if for a military inspection. She remembered most of their names and made a point to speak to each of them individually.

Damien again noticed the newfound maturity in his wife as he watched her being greeted by the servants. The little girl he had married had become a woman. Even more than that, she was regal. On this day, at this time, there was not a woman in the Alliance who could equal her. Time had molded her individuality into a distinctiveness that singularly defined her. It had shaped her personality with the chisel of character that could only have been done by the Divine Sculptor. She caught Damien staring at her, beaming with pride. She returned a smile that illuminated the world around them, and she lightly squeezed his hand. They walked through the doors of the castle, arm in arm. The little girl had returned home a lady.

The servant brought lady Grecian and her husband Damien's luggage to the room in which she was raised as a child. She walked slowly into the room, leading Damien by the hand as if they were passing through a portal into another time. She seemed to be sharing with him the only virginity she had to offer—her past. It lay within those walls, unadulterated and unpenetrated, waiting for him to examine it. The room was exactly the way she had left it when she went away to marry the baron. It was the one place in her life that he was never allowed to enter.

From the entrance, she searched the room with her eyes, looking for the virtues she had left behind to give them to her true love. It was a small price to pay for safe passage from adolescence to adulthood. Sensing the intensity of her thoughts, Damien kissed her lips, bringing her back to his world. He was jealous of every unspoken thought she did not share with him. Grecian knew this, and purposely withheld just enough of her mystery to keep him searching for a truth she had not already revealed to him on the first night they made love. Unbeknownst to Damien, he owned Grecian, body and soul, a price for which he paid dearly. He loved her like a man possessed. It was a passion she returned with equal devotion.

She sat on the edge of the bed, watching him unpack and put away their clothes. When he was finished, he knelt down in front of her and put his head in her lap. She ran her fingers through his hair for a few seconds.

"Don't forget why we are here," she whispered in his ear. "Let's go see Daddy."

They found Grand Duke Wilfred in the library. He was much more relaxed since Grecian had arrived with Damien. The same officer that had accompanied him to see Damon sat outside the library door. He rose when they entered the hallway leading to the library and knocked on the door, announcing them to the grand duke. He stepped aside to allow them to enter, closed the door, and went back to his post. They stood with their backs to the closed door for a second. Then Grecian walked over to her father. His arms stretched out in anticipation of his daughter's greeting. She hugged him and kissed his cheek. She seemed to hold back the warmth she wanted to display.

She reached back to take Damien's hand saying, "See Daddy, he came," all the while thinking to herself, Oh Daddy, please don't let me down.

His grip was still firm despite his seventy years.

"Thank you for coming, Damien. You can't imagine what this means to me," he said.

The grand duke was still a handsome man. His tall, lean, muscular body proved that physical training was imperative for a long life span. Damien stared into the dull, steel gray eyes of the older man. The apathetic, lifeless gaze in them told Damien the grand duke's heart was not into what he knew he must do. The grand duke proceeded to tell Damien of his plan to abdicate his title in favor of Grecian, and of course, her husband.

Damien asked about his sudden concern for Grecian's future. Without giving him a chance to answer, he asked him point blank, "Who is trying to kill you and why?" If Damien was going to protect the grand duke, he would have to know who or what he feared. The grand duke asked Damien if he was going to accept the proposition. If not, he would not betray everything he believed in and had spent his life fighting to preserve. Damien sat with his back to his wife. She stood behind him with her hands on his shoulders. The grand duke could see Grecian was clearly in her husband's corner. Any decision he made would be for the both of them. He saw the increased level of maturity in her since she had been with Damien, and he was proud of her. She was no less the woman her mother had been. He envied Damien for that love. He had once shared such a love with her mother, and the grand duke knew what he was missing in his golden years.

"I want to know all that you know about the high concentration of radiation in the mountains of Tibet," he said to the grand duke, as if a place in the European Alliance was unimportant to him. If this had been a game of poker, then Damien would have just executed the perfect bluff.

The Grand Duke knew that Damien was holding the trump card. He looked at Grecian for a sign of support. but all he saw in her eyes was Damien staring back at him. Finally he said, "Zeigfrid, Lord Zeigfrid"

Damien's brain began to sort age-old information. He sat there for ten seconds as if he were in a trance, then he said, "The House of Stolz. Franz Stolz." His father had told him about the Neo-Nazi leader who had been killed during the Exterminations. "Tell me about Lord Zeigfrid,"

Damien said to the grand duke. "Tell me about the radiation. Tell me everything, and tell me now."

"We were going to build a laser beam," the grand duke said with tears in his eyes. The tears were for his betrayal of his countrymen. "It was not for war, at least that is what I thought at first. Then Lord Zeigfrid said he was going to blow Trojan out of the sky. I knew then he was a madman. I came here, locked myself in and called you."

"The laser," Damien said. "Get back to the laser. What happened to it? Where is it now?"

"They are completing it in separate stages and when they are finished, they will assemble it in Germany, at the castle of Lord Zeigfrid of the House of Stolz," the grand duke answered. When he finished speaking, the grand duke seemed relieved of a heavy burden.

Grecian left Damien's side and went over to her father. She hugged him and said, "Now Daddy, I know you are one of us."

As they stood there embracing, he said to her, "You know, Baby, all my life I have been one of them. They have done nothing that I can say I have not done. All that they are, I have been. And now I am, as you put it, one of you."

"You are too hard on yourself, Daddy," Grecian replied. "The only thing that you have become is humane, the way you were when mother was alive."

"Grecian, my child, your mother overlooked my faults—so much so, that I didn't believe I had any."

"Well," said Grecian, "that is all in the past. We are here to change things in the European Alliance. We are accepting your proposal. Right Damien?"

"Yes, we accept," Damien said, thinking to himself how happy this would make Trojan and Conzeula. It was more than either of them had hoped for. In his report to Trojan he wrote:

My Lords, we have identified the enemy. A laser beam is being developed in Germany. Beware of Lord Zeigfrid of the house of Stolz. He survives.

Your Servant, Damien, Lord Protector of the Environment

In a public will, Grand Duke Wilfred abdicated his seat in the European Alliance, leaving it to his daughter Grecian and her husband Damien, the Lord Protector of the Environment. The eyes of the world were upon them. It marked the first time a seat in the European Alliance was occupied by an outsider.

Lord Zeigfrid was in his castle. He was pondering the new situation in which the Europeans had been placed. The laser was not yet completed, and he dared not challenge Damien before Trojan and Conzeula were dead. He was counting heavily on the first days after their deaths, hoping that during the confusion, the lack of leadership would allow him to gain control of the Alliance. His greatest fear was that the grand duke had divulged his true identity. Time was not on his side as he sought to contact the grand duke by a secret messenger.

"The treacherous bastard," he said, talking to himself. He read the public will again for the fourth time. "We must work fast, before Damien brings in his forces to man the castle."

How much of the planet is still safe from the invaders? he wondered. *I knew that brat bitch of the duke was going to be trouble when she married the outsider. Not a drop of Aryan blood in his veins. Even if there was, he would still be unfit for a seat in our Alliance.*

"Calm down," he said aloud, "I must make contact with the duke. Only then I will know for sure." Then he recalled his deepest fear. If Damien already knew who he really was, Damien would be waiting for his troops to arrive before coming for him. "Insurance," he said, speaking out loud again. "I need some kind of insurance against being apprehended. What? What would guarantee my safety from the invaders? What?"

Still there was no word from the grand duke.

Receiving Damien's message, Conzeula decided to join Damien and Grecian in the European Alliance since it was she who had accidentally discovered the key clue that uncovered the plot to assassinate the Lords of the Alliance. She wanted to be there as the mystery unfolded, the guilty were exposed, and punishment was metered out. Not wanting to debate this decision with Trojan or Damien, Conzeula left without informing Trojan of her destination, and without an invitation from Damien.

She was en route to the European Alliance when her craft was intercepted by Lord Zeigfrid's men, and detained as his houseguest at the Castle Stolz. Conzeula was confined in one of the upper bedrooms, near the tower. Lord Zeigfrid assigned a lady-in-waiting to attend her needs. A guard was placed outside of her door as added security. Although she knew of the plot against her life, Conzeula had no fear for her immediate safety. She sensed that Lord Zeigfrid needed her alive as a hostage, or she would have already been dead. The Star Queen was equipped with a homing device that sent S.O.S. signals back to the satellite whenever she was away from it for more than an hour. The signals could then be traced back to the point of origin. As a result, she was confident in spite of the peril. Her situation was, unless escalated, a temporary condition.

Lord Zeigfrid visited Conzeula on the first day of captivity. He was impressed by her display of bravado. Looking in the face of danger, she had told him Trojan would leave no stone unturned until he found her. The pictures the lord had seen of her were beautiful, but they did her no justice. She was absolutely breathtaking. He decided that she was probably right, Trojan might love her that much. If so, he concluded, then she had just confirmed what he had always suspected. She was indeed the insurance policy he sorely needed.

The S.O.S. signals from the Star *Queen* had drawn the attention of a search party. They found the craft parked on the border of the European Alliance, intact without any sign of trouble. When Trojan read their report, he breathed a sigh of relief. Conzeula was alive.

Damien's men raided the laboratories of the conspirators simultaneously and found all but one part of the laser beam. Damien saved Lord Zeigfrid for last. Trojan wanted to deal with him personally, just as his father Rameses had dealt with the senior Stolz during the Exterminations. Interrogation of the prisoners confirmed the guilt of Lord Zeigfrid. The capture and confession of one of the men who had kidnapped Conzeula sealed Lord Zeigfrid's fate.

For the first time in twenty-two years, Trojan returned to earth. He and twenty members of his personal guard took charge of the rescue of Conzeula. The storming of the Castle Stolz, and all other aspects of Lord Zeigfrid's apprehension, had been left up to Damien. The castle was surrounded and Trojan was at the command post with Damien and the twenty officers, planning the siege.

"Lord Zeigfrid will kill Lady Conzeula as soon as the castle is stormed," Damien warned Trojan.

Zeigfrid had the first joint of Conzeula's pinky finger cut off and sent to them to prove his intent. It had been removed painlessly, with surgery, to prove his humanity. Nevertheless, she was without a part of her finger, and he promised the next part of her body would be a breast. Trojan was furious, but he called off the siege and withdrew all of the men except Damien and six of his best officers. They were at a stalemate. Trojan demanded to see his wife alive or he would storm the castle again. He warned Zeigfrid that if Conzeula was dead, he would move Heaven and Earth to get to him.

Damien carried the message, but his word alone would not be enough to alter this decision. Trojan would have to see her alive with his own eyes. Damien carried the message personally to Lord Zeigfrid, telling him to bring Conzeula to the top of the wall at twelve o'clock noon the following day. Trojan would see his wife, alive and well. Then they would negotiate the terms of peace.

Lord Zeigfrid had Damien taken into custody upon his arrival. He sent a message back to Trojan that Damien and Conzeula would be on the top of the wall along with him at noon the following day. Trojan ordered a crossbowman to position himself for a shot at Lord Zeigfrid when he appeared on the wall at noon. The crossbowman, a European by birth, was the best in the Alliance. His orders were to shoot only if he could get a clear shot without hitting Conzeula or Damien. Under the cover of night, the crossbowman took his position.

At noon the next day, two guards brought Damien and Conzeula to the top of the wall. The crossbowman waited patiently for Lord Zeigfrid to appear. Thirty seconds passed as Damien, Conzeula and the guards stood silently on the wall in anticipation of Lord Zeigfrid's arrival. Then he suddenly appeared.

"Well, they are here as you requested," he called out to Trojan. Just as he was saying, "and unharmed," the crossbowman let the arrow fly. It pierced the lord's throat, crushing his Adam's apple. The head of the arrow exited the back of his neck, and he clutched the shaft of the arrow with both hands, choking, coughing and spitting blood. He was still alive as he stared into Conzeula's eyes with a look of eternal hatred. He was dead with his eyes open when he toppled from the wall head first into the moat below. The awaiting alligators fought over his remains, ripping his dead body to shreds and digesting it.

Conzeula hid her face in Damien's chest as Zeigfrid fell off the wall, and the threat to their lives ended. The two guards threw down their weapons and knelt on one knee with their heads bowed to Conzeula and Damien. One of Damien's men crashed through the door with his sword ready to strike. He would have slain the guards had not Damien called him off saying, "They yield." Damien made it a point never to slay a faithful soldier under orders. He was known for this throughout the Alliance, and the guards depended on it for their lives. That, combined with the fact that the guards made no attempt to resist the assault, saved their lives.

Three more of Damien's men came through the door followed by Trojan. At the sight of Trojan, Conzeula ran to the safety of his outstretched arms. He kissed her lips, and her forehead, then he kissed her right cheek and then the other. He ran his hands up and down her arms as if checking for damage. Then he took the hand of the missing pinky finger and delicately kissed each of the remaining fingers on her hand. He put his arm around her waist, and they walked over to Damien. Trojan placed his free hand on Damien's shoulder. Without speaking, he said thank you.

Without responding, Damien bowed his head as if to say, My lords. The emotional, yet silent communication between the two men left tears in Conzeula's eyes. As they walked away, Trojan's hand slipped from Conzeula's waist. They left, walking hand in hand to their ship, escorted by two of Damien's men.

Damien had the conspirators put to death without a trial, as Trojan knew he would before he or Conzeula could protest the action. It was a game Trojan had learned to play from the powers before him: feign innocence when Absolute Power dares to supersede the Law.

Grand Duke Wilfred died in his sleep soon after the executions. He drank a potion prepared for him by Damien, and served by his daughter Grecian. It was his wish to die with the conspirators whom he had once called friends. The grand duke represented the last of the old leaders of the European Alliance. Unlike the others, he was given a funeral comparable to that of a king. Trojan ordered every leader in the Alliance to attend.

Conzeula arrived wearing a diamond pinky nail prosthesis. With the diamond finger nail, it was impossible to tell the difference. It became the fashion statement of the day. Every woman of discerning taste had the first point of their pinky finger surgically removed and replaced by a diamond fingernail prosthesis.

In the year 2093, the sun did not set on the Alliance. The children of the Ghost Shadows ruled the planet. My father Dakota Moon left me to finish telling our story in the year 2047. He went on to fulfill his destiny. He left me an eagle feather and then went to take his seat on the council of chiefs beside his father and the Great Chief Osceola.

The passings of the Ghost Shadows began with the death of Maxwell Mason Stone in the year 2043. He was followed by my father in 2047. The year 2048 brought us together at the death beds of

Everett Henry Jones, Calvin Coolidge Chipman and Samuel Nathaniel Turner. In April of 2049, we lost Ny Li Tu. Moses Cribb followed soon after. He no longer had a reason for living. Rameses built a pagoda in his mother's memory in the Southeast Asian Alliance. Even though it was a pagoda, it was more of a museum. A statue of her in her youth stood at the entrance, just as she was when Moses found her in the jungles of Laos. The nude portrait of her, that once hung in the mansion, hung there for all the world to see. To the New Race that lives there, her name is held sacred. It was in this little corner of the world that she was born. Before the year was out, George Lee Brown, Alexandro Jorge Valdez, and James Edward Magee passed on, one after the other. They had gone to meet their leaders, Stone, Cribb and Ny Li Tu on the other side of the passing where they were waiting to guide them to the place beyond.

Along with these people from the twentieth century, passed the threat of the Apocalypse: War, Famine, Pestilence and Death.

About The Author

Montana Spillman was born in Mount Vernon, New York in 1943. He enlisted in the United States Army after graduating High School in 1961. He was trained in chemical, Biological and Radiological Warfare by the U.S. Army and served in Southeast Asia during the war in Vietnam.

His ability to tell stories has motivated him to put into writing the many myths and legends of past civilizations and civilization yet to come. His stories are fiction, with a hint of truth to hold the reader's interest.

WATCH FOR THESE NEW COMMONWEALTH BOOKS

JUNE 1995	ISBN #	U.S.	Can.
❑ POWER DEFICIT, Frank Kelly	1-896329-09-8	$5.95	$7.95
❑ THE BLOODY RENEGADE OF A'RADI, Betty B. Simmons	1-896329-60-8	$6.95	$8.95
❑ THE LONG WAY HOME, Ray Davies	1-896329-20-9	$5.95	$7.95
❑ FINGERS OF THE BLACK HAND, F. Joseph Rosati	1-896329-46-2	$5.95	$7.95
❑ P.O.W., Gil Hash	1-896329-01-2	$4.95	$6.95

JULY 1995			
❑ THE WIRE FENCE, Henry A. Craig	1-896329-18-7	$4.95	$6.95
❑ BLACK ALERT, Julian Hudson	1-896329-03-9	$6.95	$8.95
❑ SEARCH FOR JUSTICE, Schlegel, N	1-896329-56-X	$6.95	$8.95
❑ SACRIFICING INDEPENDENCE, Adrian Golding	1-896329-36-6	$5.95	$7.95
❑ THE COUNTESS, Harry H. Sullivan	1-896329-68-3	$5.95	$7.95
❑ GOODBYE TOMORROW, Gryzelda Niziol-Lachocki	1-896329-36-6	$4.95	$6.95
❑ FIONA, Jacqueline Baity	1-896329-04-7	$4.95	$6.95
❑ MEDICAL DOMAIN, Michelle Burmeister	1-896329-14-4	$4.95	$6.95
❑ THE BLACK CHAMBER, William G. Hyland, Jr.	1-896329-07-1	$4.95	$6.95

Available at your local bookstore or use this page to order.

Send to: COMMONWEALTH PUBLICATIONS
9764 - 45th Avenue
Edmonton, Alberta, CANADA T6E 5C5

Please send me the items I have checked above. I am enclosing $_____ (please add $2.50 per book to cover postage and handling). Send check or money order, no cash or C.O.D.'s, please.

Mr./Mrs./Ms._____

Address_____

City/State_____ Zip_____

Please allow four to six weeks for delivery.
Prices and availability subject to change without notice.

WATCH FOR THESE NEW COMMONWEALTH BOOKS

JULY 1995

		ISBN #	U.S.	Can.
❏	THE RAINBOW, Herbert A. Gold	1-896329-34-9	$4.95	$6.95
❏	WOMEN OF OSSOSSANE, E. Shade	1-896329-58-8	$6.95	$8.95
❏	THE WORLD WEAVER, C. Etchison	1-896329-26-8	$4.95	$6.95
❏	THE DARKHILL MURDERS, R. Ziegler	1-896329-78-0	$4.95	$6.95
❏	JUST BECAUSE I'M BLACK, Rafael A. Alvarado	1-896329-02-0	$5.95	$7.95
❏	STORM TREASURE, J.E. Sanford, Jr.	1-896329-54-3	$4.95	$6.95
❏	WOODRUFF'S FIREBASE, D. Celley	1-896329-16-0	$6.95	$8.95
❏	FIX BAYONETS - CHARGE!, R. Gordon	1-896329-38-1	$5.95	$7.95
❏	THE SECRETS OF YASHIR, L. Carolle	1-896329-22-5	$4.95	$6.95
❏	DRAGONFLY, Herbert & Mary Wells	1-896329-72-1	$6.95	$8.95
❏	THE LAMARCK INHERITANCE, M. Reece	1-896329-41-1	$5.95	$7.95
❏	THE FOLLOWER, Gina Pfeffer	1-896329-39-X	$4.95	$6.95
❏	THE HANDS OF TRUST, J.A. Green	1-896329-40-3	$4.95	$6.95
❏	TUNNEL'S END, Marcia Whitley	1-896329-12-8	$4.95	$6.95

AUGUST 1995

		ISBN #	U.S.	Can.
❏	WALLENBERG'S DIARY, C.H. Martin	1-896329-15-2	$4.95	$6.95
❏	DANCING IN CIRCLES, D. Ouellete	1-896329-35-7	$6.95	$8.95
❏	A RIVER OF TIME, David L. Ruggeri	1-896329-48-9	$4.95	$6.95
❏	NO REPRODUCTION, Selma Genge	1-896329-30-6	$5.95	$7.95
❏	SECRETS IN LOVE, Anita J. Guest	1-896329-99-3	$4.95	$6.95
❏	THE BUDDHA'S SECRET, Tonie Rich	1-896329-45-4	$4.95	$6.95

Available at your local bookstore or use this page to order.

Send to: COMMONWEALTH PUBLICATIONS
9764 - 45th Avenue
Edmonton, Alberta, CANADA T6E 5C5

Please send me the items I have checked above. I am enclosing $_____ (please add $2.50 per book to cover postage and handling). Send check or money order, no cash or C.O.D.'s, please.

Mr./Mrs./Ms._____

Address_____

City/State_____ Zip_____

Please allow four to six weeks for delivery.
Prices and availability subject to change without notice.

WATCH FOR THESE NEW COMMONWEALTH BOOKS

SEPTEMBER 1995	ISBN #	U.S.	Can.
❑ COMRADES, AVENGE US, Stephen Esrati	1-896329-24-1	$5.95	$7.95
❑ MORGAN, A.M. Bjornstad	1-896329-10-1	$5.95	$7.95
❑ QUESTIONS OF COLOR, Sara Smith-Beattie	1-896329-64-0	$5.95	$7.95
❑ LUCK OF THE DRAW, Charles Young	1-896329-76-4	$5.95	$7.95
❑ THE WINSHIP FAMILY, Michael J. McCarthy	1-896329-25-X	$6.95	$8.95
❑ RETURN TO FALLING HEATH, D.A. O'Connor	1-896329-31-4	$5.95	$7.95
❑ P.S. I LOVE YOU, W.J. Brandon	1-896329-06-3	$4.95	$6.95
OCTOBER 1995			
❑ DETECTIVE FOR HIRE, Kenneth F. Mayo, Jr.	1-896329-18-7	$4.95	$6.95
❑ THE SEA MAIDEN, Doris J. Bayles	1-896329-08-X	$5.95	$7.95
❑ BECAUSE SHE CAME FROM ATLANTA, John O'Flaherty	1-896329-33-0	$4.95	$6.95
❑ THE TORRID LANDS, Keith Hallam	1-896329-44-6	$4.95	$6.95
❑ TO BE DAMNED, Kenneth Miller	1-896329-29-2	$6.95	$8.95
❑ REMINISCENCES OF WWII- THE LAST GOOD WAR, Irvin D. Magin	1-896329-13-6	$4.95	$6.95

Available at your local bookstore or use this page to order.

Send to: COMMONWEALTH PUBLICATIONS
9764 - 45th Avenue
Edmonton, Alberta, CANADA T6E 5C5

Please send me the items I have checked above. I am enclosing
$_____ (please add $2.50 per book to cover postage and
handling). Send check or money order, no cash or C.O.D.'s, please.

Mr./Mrs./Ms._____

Address_____

City/State_____ Zip_____

Please allow four to six weeks for delivery.
Prices and availability subject to change without notice.

WATCH FOR THESE NEW COMMONWEALTH BOOKS

OCTOBER 1995

	ISBN #	U.S.	Can.
❏ OF OTHER GODS, Bryan Millar	1-896329-27-6	$5.95	$7.95
❏ NIGHT OF POWER, Gregory R. Gillespie	1-896329-32-2	$4.95	$6.95
❏ RAVEN'S SONG, Lyn Huges-McDaniel	1-896329-05-5	$4.95	$6.95
❏ ABANDON DREAMS, Melva McCann	1-896329-70-5	$6.95	$8.95
❏ LOSS OF COOLANT ACCIDENT, Walker, Ian	1-896329-80-2	$4.95	$6.95
❏ MAUDLIN SCOURGE, Reidy, Mary Denis	1-896329-43-8	$4.95	$6.95
❏ OUT OF THE RED, George G. Siposs	1-896329-62-4	$5.95	$7.95
❏ HE'S MINE, Rhonda Ruzek	1-896329-50-0	$4.95	$6.95
❏ GO TO HELL AND MAKE A U-TURN, Marci Martin	1-896329-17-9	$4.95	$6.95

NOVEMBER 1995

	ISBN #	U.S.	Can.
❏ A SENSE OF HISTORY, Peter P. Passman	1-896329-37-3	$4.95	$6.95
❏ ANALYST SESSION, Terrence Gallaher	1-896329-28-4	$4.95	$6.95
❏ DECEIT'S SWEET VICTORY, Joyce H. Williams	1-896329-74-8	$4.95	$6.95
❏ BEYOND THE WALL, E.S. Dove	1-896329-82-9	$4.95	$6.95
❏ THE SEED OF CALAMITY, Ted Markey	1-896329-52-7	$4.95	$6.95

Available at your local bookstore or use this page to order.

Send to: COMMONWEALTH PUBLICATIONS
9764 - 45th Avenue
Edmonton, Alberta, CANADA T6E 5C5

Please send me the items I have checked above. I am enclosing $_____ (please add $2.50 per book to cover postage and handling). Send check or money order, no cash or C.O.D.'s, please.

Mr./Mrs./Ms._____

Address_____

City/State_____ Zip_____

Please allow four to six weeks for delivery.
Prices and availability subject to change without notice.

A chronicle of the life of Dakota Moon, a man known to an ancient civilization as the Messiah. The coming of Dakota Moon would fulfill the prophecy of a legendary American Indian...

A Choice Of Arms

by

Montana G. Spillman

Available at your local bookstore or use this page to order.

❑ 1-896329-66-7 – A CHOICE OF ARMS
   $4.95 U.S./$6.95 in Canada
Send to: COMMONWEALTH PUBLICATIONS
            9764 - 45th Avenue
            Edmonton, Alberta, CANADA T6E 5C5

Please send me the items I have checked above. I am enclosing $_____ (please add $2.50 per book to cover postage and handling). Send check or money order, no cash or C.O.D.'s, please.

Mr./Mrs./Ms._____

Address_____

City/State_____ Zip_____

Please allow four to six weeks for delivery.
Prices and availability subject to change without notice.